POWER PRIVILEGE & PLEASURE

QUEENS OF KINGS (BOOK 4)

LAQUETTE

POWER PRIVILEGE & PLEASURE

QUEENS OF KINGS (BOOK 4)

LAQUETTE

Power Privilege & Pleasure: Queens of Kings Book 4
Copyright © 2015 by LaQuette All Rights Reserved
Published by: Hot Ink Press

No part of this literary work may be replicated conveyed in any form, by any methods, electronic or mechanical, including photocopying, recording, or by any data storage and recovery system without expressed written permission by the Publisher except where permitted by law.

Cover Artist: Taria A. Reed

Edited by: Elizabeth A. Lance

Disclaimer:
This is a work of fiction, any similarity to actual persons living or dead, products, businesses and locations are purely coincidental or used in a fictional manner.
This work of fiction contains adult content: depictions of sexual acts, explicit language that may be objectionable by some readers. This work is intended for adult audiences of 18 and older. Reader discretion is advised.

DEDICATION

To Piper Kay, Lexie Craig, and Shyla Colt, thank you for helping this fangirl accomplish her writing dreams.

ACKNOWLEDGMENTS

To God, from whom all blessings flow, thank you for the gift, the desire, the support, and the opportunity. To Damon, this does not happen without you. Love you forever. To Sterling and Semaj, my heartbeats, the best parts of me. To my family and friends, thank you for putting up with my craziness. To Sarah and Hot Ink Press, thank you for the opportunity and the support. To Shyla Colt, thank you for treating me with such kindness and for always opening your door to my many crazy questions. To Piper Kay, I will never be able to thank you for making me, "Push the fucking button." To Elizabeth, thank you for making my crazy sound amazing. To Lexie Craig, thank you for supplying me with my new motto, "Hustle until you don't have to introduce yourself" (unknown). To all of my JMC and LIJ people, your love strengthens me. To Samantha, thank you for doing what you do. To my Loungers, you guys hold me down and keep me going. Thank you so much for the loyalty and encouragement. To the readers, you will never know how much I have loved writing the Queens of Kings series. Thank you for taking this journey with me.

Keep it sexy,
    LaQuette

Power Privilege & Pleasure
Queens of Kings (Book 4)

When truth isn't the best answer & duty must come before love...

Alexis-Jeovonni "A.J." Tenetti: attorney, CEO, master manipulator, must make what's oftentimes the unpopular choice. She is the most prolific legal mind of her time. Her mind sees what others' can't, bending people and circumstances to her will.

Elliot "Alan" Quillen, vice president of Searlington Realty, is running from his past, hiding from pain. Cast aside by his heartless family, he refuses to be manipulated by anyone ever again. All he wants is peace and solitude. His goal seems within reach until a fated meeting with A.J. Tenetti leaves him angry, frustrated, and burning with desire.

When danger cloaks her like the night and she refuses to let him in; Alan has to make a choice. If he's going to master the master he has to either follow her rules, or create his own.

She was born to conquer a nation; he was made to conquer her...

Will they continue to battle each other, join forces against A.J.'s enemies, or will

they realize that her power coupled with his privilege will equal the ultimate
pleasure?

CHAPTER 1

Five years earlier...

Alexis-Jeovonni stalked slowly down the stairs taking care of each silent step she made. She had a full schedule today in her office, but before any of that began she needed to make a stop to take care of a potential problem.

That's what she did, that's who she was...the problem solver. For her clients, for her family's business, she was the one charged with finding impossible ways out of unbelievable troubles. No one was better at it, no one was more dedicated to it, and even when those around her were unaware of all the chaos, she still worked to keep blessed calm and order.

Shoes in hand, she placed a stockinged foot on the last step and gingerly allowed it to bear her weight. Just a few more steps to the front door and she would be able to make a clean escape.

"I thought children were supposed to sneak into the house in the middle of the night, not out of it."

A cold tingle of shock moved its way down her spine. *Damn...I'm caught.* "Papà..."

"A.J.," Jeovonni Tenetti stood at the top of the stairs, arms crossed tightly against the expanse of his broad chest. His reddish brown locks streaked with glints of silver sparkled in the darkened hallway. The raised brow and tightly drawn lips were the only indicators A.J. needed to interpret her father's displeasure.

"I'm not sneaking, Papà. I was just trying not to disturb you."

Her father let a heavy sigh escape his lips. "It's not even five in the morning. Where are you going?"

A.J. rolled her eyes. How many other grown women had to deal with this kind of scrutiny from their fathers?

"Papà, it's been a long time since I've needed a curfew. I'm a big girl; I can take care of myself."

Jeovonni Tenetti shook his head and leaned carefully on the banister. "It's not your ability I doubt, daughter, it's your willingness that I question."

"Papà, I'm going to the office, I have a lot of work to do."

"Tenetti Enterprises business?"

She shook her head. Lying wasn't how she operated, at least not with her father. For him, there would always be truth. He might not like her answers, but they would always be truthful.

"Legal business. I have to head off a potential problem for one of my legal clients. I need to get it done before the start of work."

"You push yourself too hard, Alexis-Jeovonni."

Looking at her father, she could see why her mother had fallen so deeply in love with a man who was in every way her opposite. At sixty-five, Jeovonni Tenetti was a distinguished gentleman. He was six feet even with a golden Mediterranean tan with salt and rusty brown hair, and eyes the most vivid shade of green she'd ever seen.

But her mother swore it wasn't his devastating looks that made her fall so deeply in love with him, but his smooth, silky accent, a crazy mix of old-world Italian and Brooklyn that often kept people wondering about his origins.

"You confuse me so, *Cara*," Jeovonni shook his head, a wavy lock falling down just short of his eyebrows.

A.J.'s chest filled with warmth as the nickname her father kept just for her crossed his lips. She loved that word. *Cara*...Italian for the endearment, dear, always made her feel as if she were being physically surrounded by her father's love. There was no place safer in the world as far as she was concerned.

Her father worried for her. Once upon a time, she'd given him plenty of reason to. But that was all behind her now. Now...now her life was all about solving problems, not creating them. Her focus on her work alone would forever keep her out of the kind of trouble that nearly destroyed her seven years ago.

She closed her eyes to the shadowy memories threatening to climb out of the dark grave she'd buried them in all those years ago. She could feel the phantom pains of broken bones that long ago healed. Her chest tightened in response, her breath hitching as her senses relived each blow, every kick, every plea for help. A cold chill walked across her skin as she struggled to click the mental lock in place that kept her past exactly where she wanted it...dead and buried, but it wouldn't turn easily.

It's not real, it's not happening. You're fine now. They can't hurt you anymore.

She felt a strong touch on her shoulder draw her out of the mental fog she was twisting inside of. She blinked her eyes free of the thick clouds of past hurts and found shining green eyes so full of love and concern staring down at her.

"*Cara?*" Jeovonni's smooth baritone was filled with heaviness.

A.J. shook her head slightly, how much time had her past robbed her of this time? When had her father had time to reach the bottom of the stairs without her noticing? Not today, not ever again.

"*Cara*, work won't fix it." Her father's voice was burdened with the sadness only a parent could feel at a child's devastation.

"That's where you're wrong, Papà," she said as a weak smile slowly climbed her full lips. "My work fixes everything...that's what I do, I fix everything." She stood up on the tips of her toes and pulled her father's hulking form down closer to her lips. She popped a quick peck on the olive skin of his cheek and headed for the door with shoes in one hand and her briefcase in the other. Today would be a good day. There would be no other options.

CHAPTER 2

*E*lliot Alan Quillen, III, Alan to those that knew him closely, stepped out of the yellow taxi and instantly flipped the collar on his leather jacket up. It was early fall in New York, and the crisp nip in the air had his California tan shivering.

If this is the nice weather Kenneth was talking about, it'd been way too long since Kenneth experienced what truly nice weather was really like. The cabbie walked around from the back of the yellow crossover vehicle and handed Alan his suitcase. Alan shook his hand in thanks and simultaneously slid a bill large enough to cover the fare and tip in the man's hand.

The house he stood in front of was quaint. It looked like something hardworking people were happy to come home to every day. It was nothing like the castle-like monstrosity back in California that he'd lived in since his birth thirty-two years ago.

He rang the bell once and heard footsteps coming toward the door. In a rush, the door swung open and a statuesque sepia-brown beauty stood before him. The warm smile that graced the smooth skin of her face traveled from full pouting lips to kind smoldering brown eyes.

Her smile drew his own and just as Alan was about to introduce himself, the woman turned her head briefly over her shoulder.

"Kenneth, there's a pretty-ass white boy at the door for you."

The brashness of her sentence left him with his semi-offered hand in the air.

"Is he blond?" Kenneth's familiar voice traveled to the door.

"Yeah, with sexy blue eyes," the young woman answered.

Alan's mouth dropped open, still a little unsure of what he was supposed to say. Oh there were lots of things he wanted to say, but if this woman was who he thought she was—Kenneth's wife—then all of the things he wanted to say would likely get him punched in the mouth.

Just as he was able to regain a little of his composure, Alan heard Kenneth's voice moving closer to the doorway.

"Are they sexier than mine?" he asked the woman, eyes never leaving hers, hands wrapping around a trim waist and landing on full curvy hips.

"Oh, baby, no one's anything is sexier than yours," she said as she reached up and pulled Kenneth down for a hungry kiss.

Damn, that's what my friend is coming home to every night? Alan cleared his throat and waited for the couple to peel themselves off of one another.

Kenneth finally broke away from the sultry kiss and turned his still simmering blue gaze to Alan.

"Heart, meet my frat brother, Alan Quillen. Alan, my wife, Captain Heart Searlington."

The mocha beauty snuggled into Kenneth's chest and turned kind brown eyes to Alan, gracing him with a smile.

"Hi Alan," she said quickly, then tiptoed and placed a swift kiss on her husband's lips. "Babe, I gotta run. Messing with that damn Belt Parkway, I'm gonna have to hit my lights and sirens to make roll call on time. I'm gonna be stuck in captain school all damn day, so no telling what time I'll be home. Don't fuck up my kitchen; I spent all last night cleaning it."

She reached up to touch the long dark strands of Kenneth's hair, stretching the cotton material of her shirt across the lines of her body. Alan let his eyes walk the full, curvy outline of her body until his gaze tripped over the solid shape of a handgun holstered on the woman's hip.

"Be careful out there, Heart." Kenneth's voice pulled Alan's gaze back up to a more respectable level. "Love you," Kenneth said and touched a gentle, alabaster hand to the warm chocolate brown face of his wife.

Heart breezed past Alan and headed to the dark sedan parked in their driveway. Within moments she'd backed out and was disappearing down the block.

"Damn," Alan said.

Kenneth's face lit with laughter. "Yeah, that's usually the reaction most people have to meeting my lady." Kenneth waved Alan inside allowing him room to maneuver his suitcase. Once he'd set it down at the bottom of the stairs, Kenneth opened up wide arms and pulled Alan into a hard man-hug.

"Damn, Quillen," Kenneth slapped Alan's back with enthusiasm. "It's been too long, man. It's damn good to see you on my side of town again!"

Alan laughed. "Your side of town? More like your side of the country. The cold ass side of the country I might add."

Kenneth waved his hand in the air and ushered them toward the kitchen. "Man, it's barely nippy outside; this is like perfect fall weather in New York."

"Kiss my ass," Alan added as he sat down at the island in the middle of the roomy kitchen. He smelled the rich aroma of coffee filling the air and the chill wrapping around his bones was aching for a cup. "It's fucking cold outside; pour me a cup of coffee."

Kenneth laughed while he poured steaming liquid into a mug and handed it to Alan followed by cream and sugar.

"That's 'cause you're a bitch-ass Southern Californian that can't take anything lower than seventy degrees."

Alan sipped the light and sweet brew and let the welcome warmth permeate and uncoil his insides. Alan smiled and nodded his head. "Yeah, this is true."

Alan matched the bright smile on Kenneth's face. "You seem really happy. I suppose that's due to the captain?"

Kenneth nodded. "Yeah, man. My woman is amazing."

Alan chuckled at the dazed look clouding Kenneth's eyes. "Apparently," Alan said as he lifted the mug to his lips for another sip of coffee. "How did you of all people manage to convince a woman as beautiful as Heart to marry your whoring ass?"

"Heart and I didn't have what's considered a traditional courtship. She was the lead investigator on Merri's kidnapping case. We didn't really get along when we first met, but there was this crazy attraction between us."

"So you seduced her?"

Kenneth shook his head. "Not like you're thinking. Heart was against having anything to do with me."

"Sounds like a smart move on her part. How did you convince her to give you a chance?"

Some of the joy that brightened Kenneth's crystal blue eyes bled out and was replaced by an unmistakable cloud of sadness.

"She was shot protecting me and my family during Merri's recovery. The injury was life-threatening and she nearly died in my arms. She required a great deal of rehabilitative care and she was pretty much alone with no one to look after her."

"She has no family?' Alan asked.

"No, quite the opposite. She has this amazing extended family that adores her. When she was shot, man they came out in force. At the time her family included her grandmother, who passed right after we married, an uncle, and four cousins. Unfortunately, her cousins and uncle either lived out of state or were in the military, so their time wasn't their own, and her grandmother's health at the time didn't allow for it."

There was something in Alan's heart that twisted a little. He didn't know Heart at all, but anyone suffering like that without the benefit of a support system garnered his compassion. He understood what happened when a formerly abled adult could no longer care for themselves.

"So you stepped up?" Alan asked.

"Yes. I did. The truth is I've never regretted a moment of it. That time that she was rebuilding her life was horrible and dark for her. But in that darkness we found each other...connected in a way I've never connected with anyone else. We just...fit."

Alan watched as Kenneth looked down at the strong metal band on his marriage finger and began to stroke it gently with his thumb. Such a small gesture spoke volumes of how Kenneth valued the woman that put that ring there, and the union it represented.

"So how've you been, man? What's going on with you?" Kenneth asked cautiously as he sat across the counter from Alan.

Alan watched him. He'd known Kenneth since freshman year in college. They'd roomed together in their dorm, pledged the same fraternity, taken the same classes, and stayed in the same general circles for the last ten years of their lives.

His friend had always been serious. Kenneth knew how to have fun, he partied with the best of them in college, but there was always this stark seriousness that danced behind his eyes. It was always evident that he was always thinking about something.

But now, sitting across from Alan, the tenseness that always seemed to shroud Kenneth was gone. He was relaxed, his eyes were wide with laughter, and he was smiling. Kenneth...king of brooding, was actually sitting across from him smiling.

A knot began to form in Alan's stomach, a heaviness clawing at his chest. He wanted what Kenneth had, that serenity that seemed to be pouring off of him. That security and assurance that his life was headed in the direction he wanted. He remembered what that was like.

By sheer reflex he looked down at the watch on his left wrist and began the inevitable calculation that happened anytime he thought of those happier times.

Two years, nine months, three weeks, four days, sixteen hours, eleven minutes, and twenty-seven seconds since it all went to hell and my world exploded.

Shaking his head and pulling himself from the personal torture chamber that resided in his mind, Alan nodded his head, not quite sure if he wanted to answer Kenneth. The truth was a complicated thing with all sorts of peaks and valleys and winding roads that didn't seem to have a clear end in sight.

"I'm good, man," Alan said simply, dropping his eyes, hoping to hide the truth in his coffee cup.

When Alan lifted his gaze he saw blue eyes locked onto him and knew he was as good as caught.

"Really," Kenneth said with a lifted brow. "You didn't really sound all that good just now when you said it."

Alan nodded, took a sip of his coffee, and met his old friend's gaze.

"Honestly, Kenneth, I'm just tired. I just needed to get out of California and away from the Quillen clan."

Kenneth braced both hands on the countertop and waited a beat before speaking. Alan knew that was his way of calculating his plan of attack when it came to pulling out information that wasn't necessarily happily given.

"Elliot acting up again?" Kenneth asked.

Elliot Alan Quillen, I, was Alan's grandfather. He was an insufferable man who'd made a career out of bringing misery to Alan's life. Just the thought of him made the muscle in Alan's jaw tick.

"He's outdone himself this time."

"What did he do?"

Alan pressed a firm thumb against the slow throb that was beginning to build at his temple. That was a usual response to the thought of his grandfather—pain and discomfort. After thirty-two years he should really be used to it by now…but apparently, not so much.

"He pulled me into his office last week and sat me down. You know he's not giving the company to my dad because he doesn't approve of what my dad does for a living?"

Kenneth shrugged his shoulders. "He doesn't like the fact that your dad makes a ridiculous amount of money as the "it" television producer of like the last four decades? I'm not really seeing what the problem is."

"Kenneth, my dad makes a shitload of money producing the shows he creates. But he's not making his money the real way, the Quillen way."

Kenneth crossed his arms across his chest and raised his brow. Alan smiled. His friend was never fond of the evil old man that sat as the present head of the Quillen family.

"So how's he trying to manipulate you now, Alan?"

"He told me that I've done an amazing job with the work I've done at the company these last ten years, but he's still uneasy about stepping down and retiring and leaving the company in my hands."

Kenneth let out a sarcastic huff. "So the billions of dollars in new revenue that you've generated for his company over the years isn't enough? What else does the old coot want?"

Alan twiddled with the coffee cup in his hand, needing something to distract him from his rising anger.

"He wants me to marry Allison. Says it will settle me down, and once I'm settled, he'll feel more comfortable placing the family legacy in my hands. Can you believe that shit?"

Alan watched Kenneth's jaw tighten in frustration. "Is he fucking kidding me? It's only been…"

"I know exactly how long it's been," Alan said, cutting Kenneth off, trying desperately not to start the time calculation in his head over again.

Kenneth nodded his head. "Yeah, sounds like just another leash he's trying to put around your neck. But man, if you're even entertaining the idea, don't. EAQ is not worth signing over your life to that moneygrubbing barracuda, Allison. You'll never see peace again if you marry her."

"I know," Alan huffed. "You don't have to preach to this choir. There isn't enough money in the world to make me take on that weight around my neck. Dating her has been enough of a hardship. I just…I'm so done with kowtowing to the old man just to get my due. I'm tired of turning my head to his questionable business practices. I need a change so badly right now."

Kenneth placed a firm hand on Alan's shoulder. "If you really need a change, why won't you agree to fill this position I'm giving you at Searlington Realty permanently?" Kenneth asked.

"I'll think about it, but my head just isn't in a space to take on anything permanently. I'll stick around and help you run your company while you settle into married life. That's all I can promise right now," Alan said.

"That's all I can ask...for now," Kenneth offered. "Well, I gotta get to the office and get the place ready for you. We're already in the middle of the week, you can start on Monday. Take the next few days to get settled in and become acquainted with the city."

"Sounds like a plan. Before I do, is there anything you need me to prepare for on Monday? Any meetings I need to prepare for?"

Kenneth nodded. "I'll introduce you to everyone in the office, but we won't have any internal meetings scheduled. The only person I really need for you to sit down and meet with on Monday is my lawyer. A.J. will break down what your office role will be, beyond what HR has already told you. You'll probably need to sign off on some things as well. Mondays can be a little crazy for A.J., so you might have to take a trip to Tenetti Enterprises to take this meeting. Regardless of where it takes place, you'll need to take that meeting before you can start on any official work for the business."

Alan nodded. "Ok, tell him I'll be ready whenever, wherever he needs me to be."

Kenneth stopped for a moment and gave him a strange look. *"He?"*

"Yeah," Alan answered. "A.J."

Something sparked in Kenneth's eyes and a broad smile lifted his lips. He looked as if he wanted to say something, but decided against it. Instead he gave Alan a quick tilt of his head and headed out of the door leaving him alone with his thoughts again.

Shaking his head and dismissing his friend, Alan sat down. This move might have come out of something ugly, but being here now, all Alan could do was hope that it was enough to give him a reprieve from a life he wasn't so sure he wanted any longer.

CHAPTER 3

Another long-ass day.

Stepping outside of her office to Carole's empty desk, A.J. opened a file cabinet and instantly found what she was looking for. The file organized according to Carole's very detailed cataloguing system. "God, I love her," A.J. smiled, "if I could get her to organize my life the way she does my office, my world would be perfect."

The ding of the elevator brought A.J. out of her musings, her eyes lifting to the metal doors sliding slowly to their open position. She saw the square tipped shoes first. Then her eyes crept slowly up the sharply creased leg of his navy pants. As her sight climbed higher, she found a single button closing the lines of the suit jacket against a narrow waist, those lines expanding out as she met broad shoulders. An arm slightly flexed as the man placed a hand inside of his pocket, detailed a brief outline of the sculpted muscle beneath the perfectly tailored material of the jacket sleeve. When the host of the tasty eye display stopped in front of Carole's desk, A.J. finally lifted her eyes to a shockingly blue gaze that brought her examining scrutiny to a crashing halt.

Damn.

Blond hair cropped into short layers with tapered sides, was finger combed into a stylishly simple haircut. The sharp angles of his face blended into a strong jaw that was shaved clean. He smiled at her. Bottom lip fuller than the top, his pleasant smile curved his lips in to a perfect bow and displayed teeth too perfect and white not to be the result of a very skilled cosmetic dentist.

Perfect...too perfect. Damn.

"Hello." His smooth baritone crawled out of his mouth and in to the air, sliding over her skin like warm oil.

"My name is Alan Quillen. I'm here to see, A.J. Tenetti. Would you let him know I'm here please?"

Her pulse jumped slightly at the sound of her name on his lips.

My name has never sounded so good. It really should always sound just like he said it.

She stared at him for a brief moment, her mind still caught up in the musical sound that enveloped her name when those familiar syllables crossed his lips.

She replayed those sentences over in her head on a continuous loop until she stumbled over the last one. *"Would you let him know I'm here?" Is that what he asked me? Did he just call me a him?*

"Him...ah...A.J. Tenetti? Is that what you said?" *Real smooth A.J. You sound like a clueless idiot.*

"Yes." The lightly sun kissed skin of his face pulled into that kind smile again, doing strange things to her mind and pulse. At the moment both were slightly erratic and she wasn't exactly certain of when she'd lost control of them.

She blinked away the fog that was filling her head, and forced herself to focus on the task at hand.

You're supposed to interview this man, not fall under the spell of his sparkling teeth.

She blinked once more and grabbed on to her resolve.

Time to stop sexing this man with your eyes and get down to business.

She felt her spine snap iron straight. She was CEO of a global monster that crushed its competition, she didn't do dreamy-eyed, brainless chick. No, she ran shit, and the smooth and sexy picture of tasty man-flesh standing before her was not going to make her lose control of the way she ran shit. *Not now, not ever.*

She made her way around Carole's desk and walked past the man, catching a brief whiff of a clean scent mixed with a heady, woodsy aroma. Damn, she wanted to stop and stand as close to him as their bodies would allow and just breathe him and that intoxicating scent in.

Nope, not gonna happen today.

"Please follow me, Mr. Quillen," she said as she led him into her office, and motioned for him to take a seat at the long conference table.

"Can I get you something to drink? Coffee, water?"

He smiled that smile of his again, making her stomach muscles clench in an almost reflexive action.

"Coffee if you have it," he answered.

Once he was seated, she walked over to the coffee pot, poured a cup for him and placed a small cup of sugar and creamer on a tray beside it.

"Thank you, Miss…"

She turned to him, painting her "I gotcha now," smile on her face. "Tenetti…A.J. Tenetti."

Alan carefully swallowed the coffee in his mouth. The first sip was like heaven, this last mouthful, the one that accompanied this woman's introduction, that one was bitter as hell. Everything in him wanted to spit it out, but his practiced business veneer kept his face straight, and his smile impassive.

He blinked for a moment, and rewound the last few minutes of the conversation until she was back at the counter on the side of the room where she was preparing his coffee. Her back turned to him, Alan watched the petite woman carefully. *God, she was sexy, curvy, the firm muscles of her ass and thighs framed perfectly by the pencil skirt and the nude sheer stockings she was wearing. Not to mention the stiletto heels she was walking on.*

He let his eyes crawl up those platforms. He'd forgotten how much he loved a woman in platform high heels.

How did I ever forget that? I've always loved those things.

The red pair of shoes she was wearing were at least five to six inches high. Standing six feet tall himself, he'd wager without those tantalizing shoes she'd probably stand somewhere around the middle of his chest.

This all struck him as very odd. It had been a long time since he'd allowed himself to openly appreciate a beautiful woman's form. He wasn't quite sure what that meant, or why of all women, his traitorous body was choosing this one to react to after all this time. He discreetly pressed the heel of his palm to his crotch and readjusted himself.

Damn, am I actually sitting here getting hard at the sight of this woman? You're not a teenager, Quillen. Get a fucking grip.

Alan took one more sip of the steaming brew, and brought himself right back into the awkward moment his mind needed a second to escape from. Fortified, he put the coffee cup down and turned to A.J. with a meaningful smile.

"Please, forgive my faux pas," he said with a nod of his head. "It was completely tactless of me to assume the owner of this company was a man. I assure you, it was in no way a reflection of my views of women in positions of power in the business world."

She gave him a humorous smile. He could tell there was no fire behind it, just good old-fashioned amusement.

"It's all right, Mr. Quillen, you were correct in your assumption that a man owns this company. My father and I share the same name…well part of the same name. He's Jeovonni Tenetti I'm Alexis-Jeovonni. He still owns the company, but I took over as chief executive officer two years ago when he was battling illness."

"The problems that only someone with a generational name can understand," he said.

"I take it you know a little about that?"

"Yes," he nodded. "I share the same name as my grandfather and father. Elliot Alan is a mandatory name for the first-born males of every generation in my clan."

From across the conference room table, he watched a flicker of light sparkle in her seductive amber gaze. Hazel eyes with specks of green lit with understanding at the mention of his proper name.

"Elliot Alan Quillen? As in the EAQ Quillens?"

Damn she's quick. Since birth, Alan was always addressed by his middle name. It turned out to be a blessing as he attempted to carve out his own place in the world when his career began. Depending on the situation and the circumstances involved, being a direct descendent of the great and powerful Elliot Allan Quillen wasn't always a good thing.

"Yes, the very same."

She nodded as if she were mixing all of the information that passed between them in a mental mixing bowl.

"So, you're heir to one of the most powerful men in the business world, according to your résumé, you're number two in the company? I know from my research of you that you actually know what the hell you're doing when it comes to running a company like EAQ." She leaned back in her chair and crossed her legs. "So my question to you is…why the hell do you want to come to work for my client?"

Alan placed his borrowed key in the door of the Searlington household and was immediately enveloped by the seductive smells floating in the air. So good, they pulled him in the direction of the kitchen where he found Heart diligently mixing something on the stovetop.

"Dear Lord what is that and may I please have two helpings of it?"

She stirred the bubbling pot once more, placed its lid in place, then lowered the burner under it before she greeted him with a welcoming smile.

"Give it about another twenty minutes of simmering and you can have as much as you like."

She waved him to a seat at the table and brought him a beer from the fridge. He took the opened bottle, and chugged half its contents in one big swallow.

"That kind of a day?" Heart asked as she sat across the table from him.

"Not as bad as it appears, but a little crazy."

"You interviewed with A.J. Tenetti today? How'd it go?"

"Better than I assumed. Especially after I referred to A.J. Tenetti as a *he* in front of A.J. Tenetti."

"About that, I told Kenneth he was dead wrong for not telling you the truth."

"No worries, I'm used to Kenneth. He's a stickler for letting people find out just how stupid they are all on their own without any help from him. Don't worry though, payback is a mother."

Heart giggled with him, nodding her head in agreement. "Did you get the job?"

"I had the job before I walked in there. Kenneth offered it to me before I set foot in New York," he answered.

Heart shook her head. "My husband may have offered you the position, but trust, he wasn't signing off on shit until that predator in heels gave her okay. Kenneth trusts that woman implicitly."

There was something about the way Heart said, "*that* woman," that made the hair on his arms stand up.

"I take it you're not A.J.'s greatest fan?"

"Not even a little bit," she laughed. "Can't stand the ground she walks on. But, my husband trusts her, and for now, that's good enough for me."

Deciding to ease out of a subject that obviously didn't thrill Heart, he focused on the positive of the situation. "I officially start in about three weeks. Kenneth and I thought it could be sooner, but apparently there are some legal things that need to be worked out first. Until then, I have to go back to California and pack up my life and move it here to New York. Guess I ought to let that husband of yours find me some place to live."

"You could, or you could just stay here with us."

Alan lifted the glass longneck bottle to his lips and drained the remaining contents of it, the last of it tasting a little bitter in his mouth.

"He told you, didn't he?"

Heart shook her head and took a seat across from him at the table.

"Kenneth hasn't told me anything about you other than you became close friends in college and have continued that friendship for almost a decade. Let's just say that like recognizes like. I don't know what's chasing you, but as someone who's battled her own demons, still battling them in fact, I know that look very well. Being with Kenneth has taught me that fighting those demons by yourself isn't always the best thing. Sometimes having reinforcements means the difference between coming out the victor, and being conquered. Not to mention, you're going to be working closely with Kenneth, which means you'll be working closely with A.J. Tenetti. That chick is a piece of work. Trust me, when it comes to her, you're going to need all the help you can get."

Alan didn't doubt her; he held no misconceptions about how tough it would be taking on this new job with his new boss and his new boss' protector. Just the thought of Alexis-Jeovonni Tenetti was doing strange things to him, and right now he wasn't ready to explore exactly why that might be.

"I think you may be right. I'm going to need all the help I can get with my new boss. But I think for now, I'll focus on getting to know my new friend the police captain."

Heart closed her eyes and laughed, long, dark lashes resting on the mounds of her high cheekbones.

"That really is an honorarium at this point. I'm not actually captain of anything right now. I've passed the test, I've attended the graduation, and received the promotion and bump in my salary. But I won't receive my command until I complete this department-mandated training."

"Why's that?" Alan asked.

"I'm going to be the youngest captain ever in NYPD history. There's a lot resting on my success, so the department is doing all it can to make sure I'm ready for the job. For the last three months I've been shadowing my current captain, learning the day-to-day. In another three months they will evaluate my progress and decide exactly when I should take over command or if I need another six months of training."

Alan watched the woman sitting across from him. Sharp eyes that reflected an acute intelligence coupled with warmth that he rarely found present in the world. He watched her wrap his friend up in that warmth every night that he walked through the door. As soon as she heard the click of the door she was moving to greet Kenneth with a smile, helping him ditch the worries of his day. That was a priceless trait in a significant other, not only the ability to help a man forget, but to also possess the desire to do so. Kenneth was wealthy beyond reason, and it had nothing to do with dollars and cents.

"You're really good for him. You know that don't you?"

"Kenneth?" she asked. "Why do you say that?"

"Kenneth was always a loner. He pretty much did things by himself all the time. But even though he was a loner, I always sensed that he hated not being anchored to something. Out of all the women in his past, I've never seen him this centered and balanced. You do that for him."

Alan watched Heart stand up and walk back to the stovetop range.

He could see she was slightly uncomfortable, stirring the pot rather rigorously.

"I'm glad I do that for him, because he certainly does that for me," she said while still stirring the pot.

His friend Kenneth was a lucky man to have such a devoted partner. Sitting there watching the statuesque beauty prepare their evening meal, Alan couldn't help but wonder if fate would ever allow him to be that lucky.

He shook the passing thought out of his head and focused on this new opportunity Kenneth placed in front of him. He'd chalk up Heart's warning about A.J. to hyperbole and eagerly await this new experience. After all, his friend wouldn't have opened this door for him if there wasn't a positive to be gained from this experience. And of course, A.J. was probably all bark and no bite. Considering she was only Kenneth's attorney, and she wasn't stationed inside of the Searlington Realty office building, how much could she actually interfere in Alan's work life? How bad could this woman—who was barely over five feet without the "fuck me" heels she wore—really be?

CHAPTER 4

*P*resent...

"*J*ust who the hell do you think you are?" Alan yelled as he barged into A.J.'s office. He could hear the hurried footsteps of her bulldog, Carole closing in quick behind him. He didn't care; there was nothing that was going to keep him from having it out with that meddlesome witch sitting behind the sleek desk in the corner of the room.

"Ms. Tenetti, I tried to stop him—" A.J. stopped Carole from warming up to fully panicked tirade by simply raising a single manicured fingernail.

"It's all right, Carole," she soothed, her voice quiet and unbothered by the frenzied interruption. "I was expecting Mr. Quillen would show up soon enough."

Carole simply nodded and backed out of the room, leaving Alan alone with his intended target.

"Can I help you, Quillen?"

Her voice was dripping in smug condescension, and the unfettered smile pasted on her face was bringing his already present anger to a fiery boil.

"You know damn well why I'm here, A.J. You fucked me over yet again, sabotaging a deal I had in place. I'm tired of this bullshit. I'm the fucking VP and I can't make a single business decision without your approval. That shit stops today."

"Quillen, we both know that's a safety clause put in place to keep you from going rogue in Kenneth's company. It's never been a problem over the last five years," she spoke casually. "I don't understand why it warrants all of this ire today."

He slammed his hand down on her desk hoping to knock off that smirk painted across her ruby-colored lips.

"You know damn well why it's a problem now. Kenneth's in the fucking hospital recovering from a gunshot wound. When he was around I could simply have him sign off on the damn paperwork and never had to worry about involving your cagey ass, but with him out of commission, I can't run the company unless I go through you. This is bullshit and you know it. I've done nothing but work my ass off for Kenneth over the last five years. This fucking leash you have on me is only going to drive his business away."

She stood up from her desk and walked across to the bar. She was wearing a black fitted pencil dress. He didn't know what it was with this woman and that particular cut of dresses and skirts. But it never failed, every single time he'd seen her she was wearing a pencil skirt or a dress. Whatever she wore, it always fit every curve she possessed from her tight waist, to her firm round ass that almost danced as she walked from one end of the room to the next, to her full thighs that made his fingers itch with the desire to touch them.

She filled one glass and then another with water. She motioned him to the conference table and brought the two glasses to him as she sauntered across the room on the skinniest designer heels he'd ever seen.

Shit, why'd I look down at those fucking heels? Just the sight of that perfect arch in her foot, coupled with the definition of her muscular calves, and his dick decided that was the perfect moment to wake up and say hello. Refusing her offer of a seat at her table was out of the question now. It was either sit down and conceal the hard on building behind his zipper, or stand there and risk the cocky lawyer finding out just how much she really got under his skin.

"Alan, this really isn't a personal slight against you," she offered. "This is business, nothing more."

"This is a lack of trust, A.J. I don't know what I've done to warrant it, but this is strictly because you don't trust me."

"I don't trust anyone," she responded. "Not when it comes to my clients' best interests. Kenneth and I instituted this policy long before you came to Searlington Realty."

"A.J., I'm trying to run a business. I can't drop everything I'm in the middle of to track you down for an okay every time I need to get something accomplished."

"Unfortunately, that's the only way you're going to be able to get anything done until Kenneth returns to work," she answered while a bold streak of arrogance and amusement sparkled in her hazel eyes.

"You think this shit is funny?" he asked. "I was ready to close a deal that was going to bring millions into the company," he rumbled, the room shaking with the unexpected boom of his voice.

She tilted her head slightly, staring at him, appearing to really see him and his anger for the first time since he'd come barging into her office. She backed her chair away from the table and stood up. Her face settling in to a canvas of hard tight lines accompanied by the ticking of her jaw.

Was that anger?

In all the years they'd been fighting, in all the years they'd kept this seemingly ongoing professional tug of war between the two of them, she'd never seemed bothered or concerned with his anger. If he was honest, that was the thing that pissed him off the most about her. While he was ready to punch something, she was always the picture of calm, never concerned with the fact that he was ready to break things after being in her presence for more than five minutes.

Finally, after five years of her passive-aggressive bullshit, we're really going to have an honest argument.

Almost giddy with the fact that he'd seen a glimpse of actual emotion from the woman standing in front of him, he decided to keep pushing for more. He couldn't really say why it was so important to him, but there was just something about the knowledge that he'd finally been able to make her lose her shit even in the slightest way, that made him feel like this was a win in his column.

"You made me look like a fucking fool," he bellowed. He inched closer to her, stepping into her personal space. He pressed and pressed until she was backed up against the table. But even though he had her cornered, her shoulders were pulled back in defiance and holding her head up in that stubborn confidence that she kept in place no matter the circumstance.

"If you felt like a fool, it's probably because you are. You've worked for Kenneth for five years now. This is not news to you, Quillen. You know damn well you can't make a move without Kenneth or my say so. You were foolish for not setting things in proper order before you ever sat down to close that deal and you know it. Don't try to blame the shit your arrogance got you into on me."

She was standing there, hands on her hips, chest heaving, eyes wild looking like the perfect mix of anger and sensuality he'd ever seen. Before he could stop himself he looked down at that luscious mouth of hers and his dick jumped with excitement again, filling and thickening and pulling all of the blood flow from his brain.

That's the only explanation he could think of for the words that fell out of his mouth next.

"You have the sexiest fucking mouth I've ever seen," he growled. "It would look so much prettier stretched around my cock than spewing the venom you insist on spitting."

He waited for the slap that he knew was coming. If he'd been on the receiving end of a statement like that he'd certainly have been looking to hit someone. But she didn't hit him, even though she had every right to. Instead, she stepped closer into his space and spread those fuckable lips into the most alluring smile.

"If you think you're man enough to get me to put my mouth to use like that, Quillen, then make me. Or are you just all talk?"

Finally! After all these fucking years he's finally catching on.

A.J. pressed herself into Alan's personal space. She hoped she didn't have to give him much more of a clue. Shouldn't her body pressed against his be enough of an obvious statement that he'd get the hint? Well if it wasn't, for damn sure she was only two seconds away from spelling her desires out frankly and clearly.

Five years ago this sexy ass blond man stepped into her office and she hadn't been able to stop wanting him since. For the life of her she wasn't exactly certain what made her crave Alan Quillen so much. He was generally a really nice guy. He possessed this fresh-faced look about him, bright blue eyes, wheat colored hair. He was always polite, and his disposition—even when she did things to purposely piss him off—was usually mild-mannered and sweet.

It annoyed the shit out of her quite frankly, made her try to push him to his limits every time they came in contact with one another. Was she just that much of a bitch that she wanted to provoke him? Yeah. But there was more to this than just fucking with the man for kicks. A.J. read people. Honestly, her ability to do so was one of her strongest attributes. Her ability to see beyond the bullshit and get a glimpse of the real person behind the representatives that most people displayed in public always kept her several steps ahead of the opposition.

There was something unique about Quillen, something she hadn't been able to name in all the years they'd known each other. Beneath that wholesome and polite image he projected lived something hot and fiery.

She saw it briefly in their business dealings whenever he became passionate about something. A quick spark in his eyes or a brief tick of his jaw, whatever it was, it never lasted long enough for most people to catch on. Good thing she wasn't most people. She recognized obedience school training when she saw it. Like A.J., Quillen came from money. If his background was anything like hers, he'd probably learned from an early age to never act out in public. Never let others know they could anger you, never be anything but polite when in the presence of others.

Yeah, she'd been taught those same rules of social and business etiquette. She'd adopted most of that into her persona, all except that one about being polite. That was utter bullshit right there. She said what she meant. If folks fell all in their feelings about it, then that was on them.

But there was something powerful that rumbled beneath the surface of Alan Quillen that she was instantly drawn to. It'd taken her five years to push it to the surface, but hard work was never something she ran from.

Her tongue darted out of her upturned lips and instinctively traced the full bloom of her smile.

"What're you gonna do, Quillen?"

She waited a beat, watched his eyes dance back and forth as he warred with himself. Her smile spread even wider. You only fought when you wanted something badly. Even if she couldn't goad him in to action at this moment, the battle behind those artic eyes already told her everything she needed to know to win this particular game. Elliot Alan Quillen, III wanted her, and since she wanted him too, she was going to get everything she'd set out to get when she'd first met the man five years ago.

She felt a strong hand slide up against the curve of her hip while its mate locked around the back of her neck, pulling her closer into his space. Excitement sparked in the center of her chest and spread out through her body. Her nipples pebbled up into diamond hard peaks the moment they met the hard muscle of his chest. He gave her another hard tug pulling her quite literally on top of him.

The bulge between his legs pressed into that strange space

between her belly button and her mound. She'd always cherished being petite, never envied the tall girls, but right now, what she wouldn't give to have that impressive firm length, and by the feel of it girth, pressed between her pussy lips instead of just above them.

He secured his grip at her neck and pulled her closer to him as he lowered his mouth. Her heartrate inched up a few beats beyond her usual sixty-five per minute. Her skin prickled with anticipation and dampness slid down her walls saturating the sheer material of her panties.

His mouth was just above hers, another millimeter and she would have exactly what she'd been asking for. She stretched her neck, trying to close that tiny bit of distance between their lips when the slow, sexy drawl of his voice filled the air between them.

"You'd like that wouldn't you?" he asked. "Me forcing you, taking the blame off of your shoulders, absolving you of your responsibility in this, is that what you want?"

She swallowed, trying to get her tongue to move, but for some reason it wasn't following her command. Instead, she felt herself falling deeper into the lull of his voice.

"There's one thing you need to learn about me. I don't play other people's games, A.J. If you want me—and everything about the way that you're damn near humping my leg tells me that you do—you're going to have to ask me, tell me what it is you want."

Wait. What? Huh? Did he just...?

She was trying to pull her thoughts together when an insistent buzz began crowding inside her head.

Alan walked her back toward the table, his hands still keeping her pressed against him. The fresh scent of him intoxicating her, adding to her confusion. She felt a slight bump and realized she was pressed against the conference table. He dropped the hand resting on her hip and leaned forward. He reached slightly behind her and picked the phone up from its cradle.

"Yes, Carole...Ms. Tenetti is indisposed at the moment...in her bathroom...as soon as she returns."

The click of the phone returning to its cradle cleared her thoughts long enough for her to push against the solid wall of chest pressed against her.

"Where the hell do you get off answering my damn phone?"

"You didn't really seem capable of it at the time," he answered. He raised a single finger to quiet her attempted interruption. "Your father is on his way up here. Unless you want him to see you all flushed and hungry for me, I'd suggest you go in the bathroom and do whatever it is you need to do to make yourself look a little less…needy."

He stepped away from her, granting her freedom from the imprisonment of his body. Fire poured down the length of her spine and made her take a step toward him. Just as her mouth opened, she could hear her father's laughter mingled with Carole's outside her door.

Her eyes pulled into hard squints. She was out of time. She turned expertly on the designer heels on her feet, the click of the bathroom door falling firmly into place as she heard Quillen's laughter seeping through the spaces of the door frame.

"This ain't over, Quillen."

CHAPTER 5

"Is he still working for Kenneth?"

A.J. continued absently scrolling through the report on her screen as she fought to stomp down her anger into the floor beneath her sharp heels. If her father wasn't sitting on the opposite side of her desk she'd be throwing things to rid herself of this rage Alan Quillen started.

"*Cara, va tutta bene?*" Jeovonni questioned.

The familiar sound of her father's voice in their native tongue pulled her full attention to him.

"*Tutto va bene, Papà,*" she replied. "Everything's fine. I just had a great deal of work on my plate before Quillen interrupted me."

"Does he still work for Kenneth?"

"Yeah, he does, for now," she offered.

"Is it not a good fit, him working for Kenneth?"

She shook her head. "Quite the opposite, Papà. He's actually really good at what he does for Kenneth. He's not a realtor, but he knows business, and he knows how to make deals. He's made Kenneth a ridiculous amount of money. Kenneth keeps trying to get him to sign on as a permanent fixture, but he always turns it down. Only ever renews for the annual contract terms."

Her father nodded his head, the copper waves of his hair shifting slightly with each movement.

"What is his educational and business background?" he asked.

"He has undergrad and graduate degrees in business, specializing in ethical business practices. I think he intended to be a compliance officer for his grandfather's company. He served as CEO of EAQ for approximately five years before he came to work for Kenneth five years ago."

Her father continued to nod as if the up and down motion of his head helped him process the information better.

"Why do you ask, looking to replace me as CEO already?"

"CEO, no," he answered. "I rather like semi-retirement. Getting to spend time with your mother and our grandchildren is too precious to give up for this. I like being able to pop in from time to time, dabble when I want to, then go right home to my lovely wife. But I'm always interested in new talent. You never know when it may come in handy."

She watched him cautiously. Her father long ago mastered the art of double speak. She excelled at it so much because she learned from the master. Still flipping his words around in her mind, she decided to push them in the "return to later" pile.

"So what brings you down here?" she asked.

"Can't a man check on his daughter and his business at the same time?"

She let questioning eyes scan his face, looking for anything that would clue her into her father's thoughts.

"You afraid I can't handle things here?"

"No, I'm afraid you'll do whatever you have to in order to make things work here."

"Then I'm a little lost. Why are you here?"

He stood up and walked over to where she sat. Slumped shoulders mixed with a slacked mouth and dull eyes painted with pain.

"Cara..."

The broken sound of his voice felt like a tight vice around her heart. She turned her face away staring blindly at nothing just beyond the corner of her desk.

"It's been nearly twelve years," he whispered.

She picked up the pen resting on her desk and began twirling it between two of her fingers. It was mindless, but it forced her to focus on something other than the fine fissures beginning to pull at the seams of the scab holding her together.

"I don't need to be reminded of how long ago it was, Papà. It happened to me, I was there."

"And your mother and I have watched you bury yourself in your work. First the D.A.'s office, then your private practice, now your practice and my business…it's too much."

She pulled in a deep, slow breath hoping to prepare for this familiar argument. She should be used to it by now. This conversation used to happen almost daily. Over the last decade and a half it'd come to a slow crawl of about one per year.

"Papà, I know you and Mamà love me. I know you only want the best for me."

"We want you happy and healthy, A.J. No matter how you try to fake that, you can't. Pretending is only going to make it worse."

She felt herself sinking, felt her control slipping away, felt the fear that always ushered in the panic that would consume her. She stood up, quick steps taking her to the mini-fridge in the corner. The outside seemed to be closing in on her; the brightness of the present being swallowed whole by the darkness of the past. She could feel the tremors beginning to take hold. She closed her eyes attempting to chase away the murky clouds swimming behind her lids, if she didn't get a handle on it soon the pain would trigger the angry visuals that always followed. Those images, the anger and rage being directed at her, those were the most terrifying parts of her ugly past.

The anxiety was latching on, doing its best to pull her down beneath the surface. She could feel cold tendrils wrapping around her flesh, she could hear the echoes of screams trying to break free from the depths of her subconscious and shove their way into her present.

She shoved a shaking hand inside the fridge, grabbing the first bottle her trembling fingers made contact with.

The biting cold forced her eyes open, helping her shake free of the chains of her past. She twisted the cap off of the bottle letting it fall wherever it landed and turned the bottle up to her lips quickly. She didn't even taste the liquid pouring in, only cared that the cold doused the burn of painful memories. When her lungs began to burn from lack of air, she pulled the bottle away from her lips. Her chest heaved and her lungs swallowed the air in greedy relief.

Her breaths were fast and fierce at first, but slowly gentled into a soft murmur as each one brought her closer to normalcy. She'd won, again...she'd won. She'd kept it from happening again, kept herself from letting it control her, letting it take her power away.

"I'm fine, Papà," she uttered with her back to him, too afraid of what laying eyes on him might do to her flimsy restraint. "If the only thing you came here to do was lecture me about my work schedule, then I really can't spare a whole lot of time. You hired me to do a job. If you'd just get out of my way and let me do it, we'd all be better off for it."

"*Cara...*"

She took one final breath, squaring her shoulders, pulling her fallen armor back into place. A.J. turned toward her father, finally able to lock gazes with him. "If you've nothing further to discuss, I've got a great deal of work left for me, and not enough hours in the day."

Jeovonni's lips flattened into a thin line. He lifted a hand in objection, then let it drop back down to his side. He pushed his hands into his pants pockets and widened his stance. "How's Kenneth?"

A slight moan left her lips, a mix of relief that her father changed the subject and concern for her longtime friend.

She moved back to her desk and slid into her seat with ease motioning for her father to do the same.

"He's getting better. He's been home for a few days now. He actually called to set up a meeting tonight, but I declined. We've rescheduled for a few days from now."

"Have the police figured out who's behind the shooting?"

She shook her head. Heart MacKenzie Searlington was a bloodhound on the police force, but she and her officers still hadn't figured out who and why someone would try to kill Kenneth.

"Don't worry, Heart has the entire NYPD at her fingertips. She'll keep him safe, or die trying."

He nodded. The few times Captain Searlington granted them an audience, she'd made it very clear she'd protect her husband and their infant son from all threats.

"Do we need to contact Teague?"

A.J. opened a draw in her desk and pinched a tiny antacid pill from her ever pleasant supply. She popped it on her tongue and waited for it to diminish the nausea the sound of that name always brought up.

"No," she answered. "At the moment, it has nothing to do with us."

"You certain?" he questioned.

"Yes, this was all about that damn center Kenneth is insistent on opening in East New York. The resident thugs and hustlers seem to be taking exception to a brand new drug treatment and counseling center being opened within their borders."

"Are you sure?"

Quiet swelled in the room as she let the question dangle in the air. She understood her father's concern. In their situation it was always necessary to carry a healthy dose of suspicion when things fell to pieces. Was it just a coincidence, the universe toppling over on itself for some unknown reason? Or worse, was it the shadow that had been chasing you for nearly more than thirty years?

She knew the monsters lurking in the shadows were very real, but for the moment, she'd chuck this one into the tragic coincidence bin and wait for further information before she involved her less than favorite federal agent, Teague Maher. For now, she'd leave this to Heart.

Trust the devil you know...

On most days A.J.'s tolerance of Heart slid from mildly annoying to aggravating and vile. Not one for adding unnecessary headaches to her already full life, A.J. definitely only saw the woman when she was obligated to. Those times usually occurred when Kenneth somehow forced the issue. But when it came to Kenneth's safety, she didn't think there was anyone better to protect her friend.

"We don't need Teague, at least not yet. If something happens to make me think otherwise, I'll let you know."

He nodded his head and stood. He gave her one more nod and walked quietly to the door.

Her stomach began to bubble again as she thought of what could happen if her assessment of this situation was wrong. She reached down into the drawer again pulling two more antacid pills from the case, frowning when the taste of chalk and mint attacked her taste buds.

In the span of a few moments she'd quashed the start of a panic attack followed by a threat assessment meeting. *Could this fucking day get any worse?*

"Oh," she heard her father's voice fill the room again. "Since you've no pressing plans this evening, make sure you're home for dinner. Your mother is determined to make a meal worthy of a king. If you value your life, I'd suggest you be there at seven."

"Why on Earth is she going through all this trouble? We're a small family; we can't eat all that food."

"True, but you know how your mother is. No worries though, I invited Alan to help us with the bounty. As a single man, I'm sure he'll be more than happy to take home leftovers."

Before she could register what he'd said, he'd waved off and closed the door. Discussion ended, mandate issued. In that moment she realized two things. The first, yes this day could very well descend even further into the fiery pits of hell. The second, the man who'd humiliated her, made her pant like an animal against a table in her office, was going to be sitting with her and her family at the dinner table.

"Fuck me."

A.J. heard the heavy buzz of the security door being opened before her hand touched the bell. She took quick steps inside the old building that faced the police precinct across the street. This house blended in with all the other houses on Essex between Dumont and Sutter Avenues. She'd purposely had Kenneth design them that way. Short, two-story, red-bricked houses that each possessed the same small patch of grass next to a short concrete walkway that led to each door. She'd wanted all of the houses to look the same. Blending in was the first rule of remaining hidden from your enemies, and every occupant of every attached house on this block needed to stay hidden.

The Steal Away Project was something she'd poured countless hours and money into over the last ten years. She herself had suffered much like the people behind these doors, the only difference between them being A.J.'s money, access to resources, and her loving family that kept and protected her until she could stand on her own feet again.

The women and their children in these houses weren't as fortunate, many of them were reliant on the very people who abused them for their basic survival needs. A.J.'s money and connections at the very least gave them a brief haven for respite while they worked toward a new life.

"Hey Ms. Tenetti, you're just in time for dinner." A.J. smiled at the twenty-one-year-old Carla who was standing in the kitchen pulling plates down from the cabinet above her head. Carla was a thin Puerto Rican woman with sable-colored hair and ebony eyes against creamy skin. Six months ago when Carla arrived at Steal Away, she'd been bruised and nearly broken. After her boyfriend slash pimp beat her mercilessly for daring to take some of the money she'd earned on the stroll to put a glazed donut and a small cup of coffee in her belly, the young woman made the very difficult decision to seek help getting off the streets.

In the time she'd been a participant in the Steal Away program she'd worked hard to turn her life around and take control of her own destiny again. Continuing education courses, mandatory counseling sessions at Kenneth's new center, a warm bed and hot food, and Carla was more than well on her way to obtaining her goals, taking her life back.

"No Carla, I'm actually just stopping in to drop off some papers for you. The foundation just approved your request for the tuition grant. You're all set to start LaGuardia in the fall."

"Are you for real, Ms. A.J.?"

The woman's face beamed with a mix of caution and excitement. When life threw the kind of curves at you that Carla dodged, it was easy to be suspicious of anything positive.

"Yes Carla, it's true. In the six months you've been here you've worked the program, earned your GED, reached out to help the other ladies in the program that've come after you. You're a model applicant."

She reached into her bag and retrieved an envelope. "Take these, read them, and if you have any questions, call me. Other than that, sign them and you're on your way to college."

Carla grabbed A.J. into a fierce hug, crushing the very expensive material of her business suit and A.J. couldn't have been happier. Another one of her ladies had dared to fight back and she'd won.

CHAPTER 6

A.J. stood at the computer desk peeking at the security camera that monitored the front door of the family's duplex apartment. This was the fifth time in as many minutes that she'd checked for Alan's arrival. When her search turned up empty, she looked down at her watch to check the time.

"You know dinner doesn't start for another fifteen minutes, don't you?"

She rolled her eyes, a consistent reaction to the shit that often spilled out of her brother's mouth. She loved John to pieces, and despite his ability to wear on her last fucking nerve like a scouring brush, the two siblings were very close. Her love for her brother notwithstanding, his ability to focus in on the things she wanted hidden was a character trait she often cursed him for. Just like that poster slogan, if he saw something, his ass felt compelled to say something about it. Unfortunately, Alan was a topic she really didn't want to share with her family right now, especially not her overbearing big brother.

She waved John off; she'd figured out a long time ago that ignoring him was the quickest way to get him to move on. She drew her gaze back to the monitor and sure enough, her brother left her standing there alone to return to the rest of the family while she continued her musings about the self-assured executive.

She felt a chill pass through her; she always did when she thought of Alan. His cool blue eyes, his golden hair, his built fucking body, they were all individually and collectively responsible for this ever-present shiver that would strike her at the most inopportune times. Like when she was in the middle of a business meeting and she locked eyes with him across the table. Or when she was researching a legal matter and her mind would wonder off thinking about how the fuck he made those damn suits he wore look so damn good.

This man was turning into a problem and she couldn't for the life of her figure out why. He was a man, a ridiculously attractive man, but still just a man. There'd never been anything this intriguing about the male of the species that ever knocked her off her game. But with Alan, just a look from him and her focus was compromised.

Let's face it, she was brilliant. So even when her brain wasn't functioning on all cylinders, she was still twelve steps ahead of everyone else. But it just irked her that with the slightest look he could pull her out of her zone.

Alan was quiet, confident, and intelligent. These were qualities that she valued. And yeah, it was a complete turn on that he possessed those three qualities in spades. Just thinking about the way he owned the fucking boardroom when he conducted Searlington Realty business was more than enough to make her body hum with anticipation that had shit to do with quarterly reports or legal motions.

If she'd only met him before the day he'd walked into her office and she'd hired him. She would have fucked him, enjoyed what she knew would have been a fantastic ride, and kept it moving. That's what she always did with the sexy powerful men she'd come in contact with over the years.

But plainly put, Alan wasn't them. He was the second-in-command to a dear friend and legal client, a man she'd spent the last five years working closely with. She couldn't let sex fuck that up. Not when Kenneth and his business had so much riding on them working well together.

The heated exchange they shared earlier in her office was the closest she'd ever come to letting him see what she'd been aching for all this time. She'd known from day one she couldn't have him, so she'd set out to make him as miserable as his sex appeal made her. She'd decided that the quiet calm he always seemed to be cloaked in was the one pressure point she could attack until he finally exploded. There was no way she was going to be the only one frustrated in this scenario. If she couldn't get the dick she wanted so terribly, then he couldn't keep that blessed peace he walked around with every day.

She took a deep breath trying to quiet the prickly sensation dancing across her skin. She knew she couldn't have him, but damn if the tight lines of that man's body didn't make her want to snatch a taste of him.

A dinging sound coming from the hall pulled her attention back to the monitor. She watched Alan step out of the elevator with a large brown shopping bag in his hand, taking one sure footstep after another until he was standing directly in front of their apartment door.

She stepped away from the monitor and headed the few steps toward the door. She was in mid-step when she felt a drum-like pounding in her chest. *What the fuck is that? Nerves? I don't do nerves. Why is my ass so happy that this man is here? It's just Alan, he's just Kenneth's employee...he's just...*

Alan wasn't *just* anything, and that right there was the problem. He wasn't just some anonymous trick she was jonesin' for. If he was, she'd have scratched that particular itch already. Sexual attraction she could deal with, this however, was something else. Her brain knocked it around for a moment and came to the conclusion that now wasn't the time to analyze this situation. Right now she needed to pull herself together and answer the door before John saw her fumbling over opening the door for their guest.

"There a reason you're standing in the hall not answering the ringing doorbell?"

Too late, she was busted. She gave the angriest glare she could manage to her teenage-brained, man-child of a brother and twisted the knob to the door. She swung the door open and nearly toppled over on her socked feet when she finally met his gaze.

Dammit A.J., she screamed in her own head. *Get a fucking grip.* Two perfectly pink lips curled into a wide grin showing what had to be every tooth in his beautiful blond head. Bright white teeth sparkled back at her just like they did on the actors in chewing gum commercials. There was a flash that twinkled and she could have sworn she heard the customary ding that went along with it.

This has to stop now.

"Is it alright if I come in?" he asked, lips still curved in to that welcoming smile that just made you want to wrap yourself up in its radiating warmth.

She shook her head briefly, shaking free of the trance that smile was trying to place her under.

"Ah...sure," she said quickly. "My mother and sister-in-law were about to set the table. You're right on time."

*A*lan looked down at the petite woman before him. She was wearing a fitted red t-shirt that hugged her high-sitting breasts at just the right angle to make a man's mind wonder. A pair of dark wash jeans held the curves of her thighs and legs flawlessly. If there was a god in heaven she was going to turn around and let him follow her down the hall so he could get a view of what he already knew was a perfectly symmetrical ass.

His eyes kept moving on their downward journey until they fell on small feet covered by red long slouchy socks that reached the bottom of her calf. He pointed down to her feet. "Should I take my shoes off?" he asked.

"Not mandatory, but spending hours at a time in stilettos at work means I wear nothing but socks when I'm home." She smiled as she wiggled her toes.

He tilted his head slight to side taking in the sight of this woman. At work, she was all sharp angles, dangerous, something to be wary of for fear of the harm she'd bring. Here, standing in the hall, she was soft curves, with welcoming warmth radiating from her.

He was about to comment on her appearance when a mixture of savory and sweet aromas wafted through the air and forced his attention toward the back of the hall.

"What is that amazing smell?" he asked.

Her smile brightened a little, amusement shaking her shoulders. "That's Gracelyn Tenetti's kitchen. One never knows what's coming out of it, but you can be certain it will be delicious."

He closed his eyes and scented the air, pulling in a deliberate, full breath of those delectable smells. When he released the breath, it spilled past his lips in a soul-deep moan.

A bright bubble of laughter interrupted the moment and he opened his eyes to find A.J. leaning against the wall, watching him, enjoying the strange spectacle he must be making standing in her hall with his nose in the air, sniffing and moaning.

"Do I look like a complete weirdo right now?"

"No, wait until you've tasted the food. The only way I can describe it is foodgasm. Come on; let's get the introductions out of the way so we can eat."

They walked down the hall and around a corner where her father stood waiting for them. "Alan, glad you could make it," Jeovonni beamed. He extended his hand to Alan and gave it a firm shake. "I'm glad you could spend an evening with us, can't believe it's taken all this time to make that happen."

"Being Kenneth's second keeps me pretty busy. But by the wonderful scents filling the air I'd say I've been missing out."

"You have no idea," he answered. "I've been married nearly four decades and I must say I've never won an argument, not because I wasn't right, but for fear of being cut off from my wife's cooking."

"Is my husband in here telling lies again?"

Alan turned to follow the sweet but full voice entering the room and found a woman of striking beauty gliding across the floor. The petite height and the strong presence that commanded the room weren't the only attributes that clued him in to the fact that this was A.J.'s mother, Gracelyn. It was the remarkable resemblance between the two women. Gracelyn was the originator of the high cheeks and full lips that A.J. possessed. Save for a few lines near the crease of her eyes, the onyx hair and eyes, and the hickory tones of her skin, he was staring at Alexis-Jeovonni.

Unable to stop himself, he turned his eyes to A.J. to make certain his eyes weren't playing tricks on him. Once he confirmed his initial assessment he nodded his head. Yes, there were in fact two women who shared the almost exact face and they weren't twins.

Alan returned his eyes to the beautiful woman who looked anything but matronly. Much like her daughter, the casual nature of her clothes did nothing to hide a firm physique. If it were true that women turned into their mothers, then Alexis-Jeovonni had nothing to fear from time.

"Mr. Quillen, don't believe anything this slick-talking man says," she added. "He's never been right in almost four decades of marriage. I just take pity on him and keep feeding him to stop him from running his mouth."

In what looked like a practiced move, she leaned into the open space her husband created for her between his arm and his chest and raised her cheek in expectation for the light peck Jeovonni happily supplied. After all those years of marriage the two seemed to have a synchrony about them that could only have come with a careful mixture of love, time, and understanding.

Alan extended his hand and she moved it aside with a quick wave of her hand and stepped into his personal space. She wrapped slender, but strong arms around his waist and gave him a hearty squeeze.

"Handshakes are for strangers. If I'm going to let you sit at my table, then you're family; hugs are for family."

Slightly unsettled, and a little uncertain of what he should do, he looked to both the husband and the daughter that certainly knew her better than he for guidance. They each just shrugged their shoulders and shook their heads.

Understanding who the true boss in this family was, Alan leaned into the hug and mirrored her embrace. Unfamiliar warmth ran just beneath the surface of his skin. He tried to think back to the last time one of his family members greeted him like this. As if he were treasured, his absence palpable and significant to those left behind. If only that were true, these last five years of his life might have been much different.

Refusing to allow his family to encroach upon this rare moment, he held Gracelyn a little tighter and placed a soft kiss atop her head.

"Thank you so much for welcoming me into your home," he stated. "I wasn't certain what we were eating, so I brought a white and a red bottle of wine. I hope that's all right."

She gently took the shopping bag he offered and peeked inside of it. "A man that brings something to add to the meal?" she queried. "Boy, your mama raised you right. Come on and follow me into the dining room. We'd better get in there before my son eats everything except the wooden legs of the table."

Alan followed her into a large dining room. It was filled with the usually trappings one would find in a dining room. Large pieces of elegant furniture, a curio of some sort lining one of the walls. A chest that held silver and china for a service of eight to twelve was right there next to the butler's entrance where it was supposed to be. But there was something different about this room, something that made this a family's dinner table instead of a place where strangers ate.

The walls were covered with large portraits of their family. The painted images were moments in time throughout their history together. A wedding portrait of the Tenetti's, a painting of A.J. and John when they were children climbing on some sort of playground structure, a portrait of John carrying his wife over the threshold on their wedding day, another of twin babies he assumed were John's daughters, and one of the entire family, all of them surrounding A.J. as she stood in a cap and gown holding her law degree in front of her chest.

That twinge of warmth rolled through him again. He could feel the connection that bound these people together by more than blood.

"John, Maxine, you all know Kenneth's friend, Alan?" Gracelyn inquired.

Alan walked over to John and gave him a friendly man-hug with the requisite back slap included. The two men knew each other in passing through Kenneth over the years. They weren't terribly close, but they were down for whatever when it came down to their mutual friend.

"Hey man," John called to him. "How you been?" John was slightly shorter than him, probably somewhere just under six feet. He possessed the same sable colored hair as their mother, and the same large obsidian eyes with broad shoulders, and chiseled chest that narrowed down into a tapered waist. John was a recording artist, one that danced as well as he sang. Although Alan was certain some of his physique could be lent to his moves on stage, he was certain there was a talented personal trainer somewhere in his arsenal coupled with a nutritionist too.

"Busy, but good," Alan replied before turning to Maxine and giving her a brief peck on her cheek. "Max, you look beautiful as always."

And she really did. Her hair was twisted into thin dreadlocks that cascaded down to her waist. Every time he saw her she wore them stacked and positioned on her head in a different and seemingly complicated design that always left him in awe of her ethnic beauty. The deep wine color enhanced the rich carob of her skin. Of average height with the slender build of a runner, she was the perfect opposite to her husband in almost every way.

"Where are those adorable angels of yours?"

"Angels?" she asked. "That's 'cause you've never spent any real time with them. More like the spawns of Satan. They're at my parent's house for the weekend," she answered. "John and I get to pretend we don't have kids for forty-eight hours."

"Yeah," John added. "So if you don't mind, let's hit this grub so me and mine can be up outta here in a few."

The Tenettis sat in what Alan assumed was their usual formation around the table. The parents sitting at both ends, John at their father's left, Maxine sitting next to John, and A.J. sitting at their father's right. There was only one remaining seat next to A.J, so Alan sat and placed the cloth napkin across his lap.

The conversation was as plentiful as the food. He couldn't really say he recognized much of the Southern cuisine on the table, but everything Gracelyn placed before him delighted his taste buds. He'd have to spend extra time in the gym for the next week, but the rich decadence was worth every mile he'd have to run and every rep he'd have to perform.

"So, Alan," Jeovonni called. "My daughter tells me you have a background in ethical business?"

Alan stopped chewing long enough to realize A.J.'s father was speaking to him. He wiped his mouth with his napkin and sipped a bit of wine before answering.

"Ahh, yes," Alan answered.

"What prompted that specific field of study?"

"I'm sure A.J. told you my grandfather owns EAQ."

"Yes, she has. T.E. has been in competition on occasion with your grandfather over the years," Jeovonni answered.

"Then you probably know better than most that my grandfather doesn't always have the most forthright solutions to his business problems. I didn't think we needed to fight dirty to win big. When I went to school, I met up with a professor who shared my ideology. He created a curriculum to center around it, and I decided I needed to learn the knowledge he possessed. I thought I could take what I'd acquired and use it to help better my grandfather's standard business practices."

"Did that not happen?" Jeovonni inquired.

"Not exactly," Alan offered. "My grandfather wanted to use my skills to attempt to dance around compliance issues. He didn't really want to do right, just appear to be doing right."

"Is that why you gave up being the head of his company to be second in Kenneth's?" Jeovonni asked.

The room became still. All of the clacking of cutlery against flatware ceased as everyone pulled their gazes from their plates and locked them onto Alan.

"Jeo," Gracelyn called. There was a sharp hint of reprimand in the tone of her voice. "Where are your manners? We invited him to eat with us, not be interrogated."

Jeovonni showed no sign that he was at all fazed by his wife's words. His gaze never wavered from Alan's, instead it became more focused, the expectation of an answer evident as he felt it bare down on him.

Alan gently placed his knife down on is plate and met Jeovonni's eyes. He probably should be a little irritated by the nature and tone of the question being lobbed at him. Instead, there was an overwhelming sense of revitalization. This man wanted to know something, and he didn't beat around the bush in seeking answers to his question. No games, no manipulation, just a straightforwardness that Alan rarely found in people of Jeovonni Tenetti's stature.

With the exception of Kenneth, Alan's experience with people in the business industry was they said and did whatever they needed to in order to get what they wanted, always seeking to get one over on the next person in order to best him.

"That was a very large part of why I left EAQ. I knew in order to run the company; I was going to eventually have to become what my grandfather wanted,"

Alan could feel the cold fingers of his past tickling the soles of his feet, trying to break free of the earth beneath him. He glanced down at his watch, a habit he couldn't help but succumb to whenever thoughts of his past life invaded his present.

Seven years, four months, one week, two days, twelve hours, six minutes, and thirteen seconds.

The mental calculation happened without fail. His mind automatically knew exactly how long it'd been since he'd known happiness, since he'd allowed the exploitations of his family, his grandfather, his own ignorance to destroy him.

"Alan?" A.J. called.

The unspoken—Are you all right?—lingering in the air. He felt the light touch of her hand on his wrist, blocking the face of his watch, snatching him from the waiting clutches of past pain. He blinked away the fog to see clear hazel eyes searching his face, bathing him in concern.

Their locked gazes still intact, Alan continued his previous thought. "I've seen firsthand what kind of consequences that type of behavior can have on people and I didn't want to be a part of it any longer."

"My daughter tells me your contract with Searlington Realty is currently up for renewal." Jeovonni's voice wedged its way in the middle of their silent side conversation.

Alan cleared his throat and turned to face her father.

"Yes, Mr. Tenetti. With Kenneth just returning back to work full-time since the shooting, we haven't really had the time to address it. I'm sure A.J. will have papers for me soon enough addressing the issue."

"Are you happy at Searlington?" Jeovonni asked.

Alan's eyes carefully assessed the elder man's face. The father was just as skilled as the daughter it would seem in keeping his face and body language impassive. Alan couldn't truly decipher what he was up to, but he held a sneaking suspicion that everything wasn't as sweet as the pie they were eating.

"I am. It's been good working with Kenneth. I admire him, and he's been a great friend to me."

"You'll get no arguments from anyone at this table. We all love Kenneth. But I wonder with your background in ethical business practices if your talents are really being used to their full potential. Real estate isn't really your chosen field, is it?"

"No, it's not," Alan answered. "Although I work with Kenneth, I'm not really the one selling property. I simply negotiate the terms of the sale, and always try to teach the people who do actually sell the properties to be ethical in their sales and to help clients make ethical choices."

"If you're able to do such things for a business like real estate that can often be fraught with fraudulent practices, then imagine how much more of an impact you could have in a position that was specifically designed for your talents and skillset."

Alan wasn't exactly certain how he should respond to Jeovonni's statement. He decided to sit back and give the man an opportunity to provide more details.

"Alan, my daughter is an amazing CEO. The things she's been able to do with my company since she's taken control of the helm have far exceeded my vision. But as the owner, I have to make certain that my company is structured in a way that will ensure its longevity. With A.J. leading, and with someone like you working beside her, I think T.E. would be unstoppable. How would you feel about coming to work for me as the new COO for Tenetti Enterprises? A.J. would run the ship, and you would make certain that the day to day operations fell in line with the ethical business practices you set in place."

Alan turned to A.J., silently asking if she knew anything about this. When she shrugged her shoulders, he returned his attention to Jeovonni.

"Sir, with all due respect, you don't need a COO for that. A compliance officer would work just as well, and it would save you a large sum in financial compensation."

"Yes, it would. But if the person who is in charge of how the company operates is specially trained in ethical business practices, then I'm assured that my company will maintain the course I've set when I created it in the first place. Things will be done right from the start, minimizing the need to repair them in the end. So what do you say, Alan, you want to work for me?"

Alan watched each set of eyes on him at that table. If he was gauging them correctly, they each held varying levels of the same shock that was dancing around in his head. "Wow, came for dinner, ended up with a job offer. It seems this is the table that just keeps on giving."

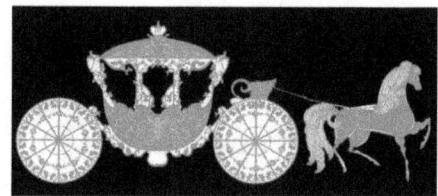

A.J. watched from the kitchen as her brother, father, and mother laughed with her...her what precisely? Alan wasn't exactly what she would call a friend. He was definitely the friend of a friend, but she wasn't perfectly clear on how their association was defined. Well, other than the fact that she wanted to lick him clean every time she laid eyes on him.

As much as she ached for him to satisfy the sexual tension that settled between them, it was eerily strange how well he fit into the domesticated scene with her family only a few feet away. In A.J.'s life men usually fell into three categories. Men she worked with, men she brought home to the family, and men she fucked.

Although men sometimes were able to move from the work to the family categories back and forth with little turbulence, once a man made it into her potential fuck category, they never transitioned to the others. She wasn't exactly certain how Alan managed to fit in all three categories so well, but he did. It truly shouldn't have worked.

A.J. didn't do relationships, she did one offs, and usually with no repeat in between so there was little to no chance of a man she'd slept with having anything to do with the rest of the compartments in her life. Yet Alan was sitting with her family, blending in as if he belonged, looking like sex on a fucking plate. *I am so fucked.*

She decided not to worry about figuring out the answer to this conundrum and just enjoy watching the scene unfolding before her.

"What has you smiling so hard?"

A.J. turned her attention to the voice interrupting her thoughts. Her sister-in-law, Maxine was standing next to her with an amused grin on her face. Together for fifteen years, married for thirteen, they met when Maxine was hired as the lead dancer in one of John's videos. They played the part of lovers on the screen and that somehow spilled into real life. It was very cliché, the singer and the dancer falling in love.

Maxine often joked with her that her job as his principal dancer is what made it possible for their marriage to thrive despite John's work schedule. It also helped keep the trifling chicks looking for an in at arm's length. Max told her on several occasions, "I trust your brother implicitly. Those bitches, not so much."

A.J. often shook her head when Max said things like that. Her brother took one look at the hickory-toned beauty with the neatly twisted waist-length dread locks and fell deeply in love. She imagined it was the no-nonsense personality of the Trinidadian-born beauty that managed to capture her brother's heart. Max took no shit from anyone. Making that clear from day one, John understood that if he wanted her love, he'd have to give her everything in return.

"Nothing," A.J. answered quickly as she sliced up the second of her mother's sweet potato pies and settled the generous pieces into dessert plates.

"Tell that shit to someone who doesn't know you," Max said with her lips twisted up in disbelief. "Alan seems pretty cool. Your brother speaks highly of him."

"He is cool, we work well together."

"Work? That's all that's between you?"

A.J. lifted her head and met Maxine's suspicious gaze. "We work together, Max. That's the only relationship we can have."

She attempted to go back to dishing out the pie slices when she felt a gentle hand touch her shoulders.

"It's been twelve years, A.J. When are you going to give yourself permission to live again?"

A.J. swallowed down the rising ball of darkness that was pushing up from her stomach, trying to make its way into her throat.

"It's been twelve years and I'm still broken. That's never going to change. Someone like Alan, who's perfect and good, he doesn't deserve to be saddled with someone as broken as me. I could never willingly do that to someone like him."

"Maybe that's a decision you should let Alan make? Does he know what happened? Have you told him about any of the family history?"

A.J. shook her head. "We just work together, Max. There's no need for him to know."

"Then why is he sitting at Mama's table eating her food?"

"Because my father invited him," A.J. answered.

Maxine leaned against the counter, arms crossed over her chest with an, "I call bullshit," look plastered across her face. "That might be the reason he's sitting in there, but watching you watch him, tells me way more about why he's actually here.

"Max," A.J.'s exasperation became evident in the elongated pronunciation of Maxine's name, "let it go, it's a non-issue."

"Until it isn't," Max answered before taking a tray of plates and walking back to the dinner table.

A.J. shook her head, and walked inside to the dining room, settling the second platter of dessert plates on the table and serving Alan his slice of pie last. She gathered the empty platter from Maxine, and placed them both atop the serving station against the wall.

She sat next to Alan at her family's table, an occurrence she still was having difficulty wrapping her mind around.

"Mrs. Tenetti, where did you learn to cook like this?" Alan hummed as he allowed the first bite of his second slice of pie to dance across his tongue.

"At my mother's side," she answered. "Cooking Southern comfort food is a tradition passed down from mother to daughter in my family. My daughter wasn't raised in the South, but I still made sure to instill as much of my heritage in her as I possibly could."

"You can make this?" Alan inquired just before shoving another heaping forkful of pie in his mouth.

"Yes, I can," she laughed as she watched him close his eyes and savor the sweet, spicy confection. "I don't get to spend as much time cooking as I'd like. The hours I put in for Searlington and T.E. don't really allow for it."

"I think I'm going to start asking for food cooked by you as a negotiation point for all upcoming meetings at Searlington." He smiled at A.J.

"I don't know about those terms, you may have to add something to the pot to make the deal worth my while."

She was laughing internally as she realized just where her mind slipped off to. Alan obviously caught on; there was a spark of electricity that brightened the subtle blue of his eyes when he looked at her.

The connection she possessed with this man crackled to life. When simple conversations across the dinner table turned into fodder for the explicit thoughts running through her head, she realized something. Whether she wanted to admit it or not, Maxine was correct, her attraction to Alan wasn't as innocent as she'd hoped. This thing between them was becoming an issue all too quickly.

When dinner was over, Alan helped Gracelyn clear the table. He would have gladly helped her clean up, but she ushered him out of her kitchen and said her husband would help her.

He walked back into the family room and found the room empty. He saw a slight sway of the floor-length curtain covering the balcony. He walked over to find A.J. standing there, curls released from the severe buns or rolls she usually wore at work. They lifted with each tuft of air, dancing around her slight shoulders, spilling down her back with the Brooklyn Bridge as a backdrop in the night sky.

"Beautiful," he whispered.

She turned her head, full lips turned up into a wide grin. Usually when he saw her smile it was always laced with a stroke of wickedness. A smile from A.J. Tenetti usually meant she was celebrating someone's demise. But standing here tonight, watching her in front of this incredible view, the smile held no malice. This was genuine, pure A.J., the full-blown version of the woman who'd touched him so caringly with such concern at her parents' dinner table.

"I know," her smile brightened. "...this view is killer, isn't it?" she asked.

"I wasn't talking about the view," he replied.

She turned around, her arms now spread wide across the balcony's edge, her back to the night, her hazel eyes sparkling, pulling him further out onto the structure until he was standing directly before her.

"Quillen, a girl might think you're trying to pay her a compliment."

"Simply stating the truth."

"Truth?" she asked. "I think it was earlier today that you essentially called me the reincarnation of the evil queen. Now you're ready to fuck me on my balcony."

And just like that they were back to their dueling corners. He shook his head and stepped even closer, removing any space between them. He said nothing; he knew words weren't what they needed. She was a master of words, she used them as weapons to protect and attack. Anything he said she'd use against him, and they'd end up in the middle of another argument.

He placed his hands in his pockets and leaned down slightly allowing his lips to briefly pass over hers. He looked down into her face, moments ago there was war in her eyes, now...now they sparked with heat. He pressed his mouth to hers again, removing his hands from his pockets and burying them inside the mass of curls framing her face.

He deepened the kiss, pressing for more, insisting until her resistance finally broke on the sweetest moan pouring from her hungry mouth. He pressed even more, licking inside her mouth, tasting the hint of spices from their shared meal.

He pushed his thigh between hers and cupped a handful of her ass, forcing her to drag her mound against the hard plane of his leg. Her breath hitched and he felt sharp nails raking down his back signaling her growing need. He broke away from the fevered kiss, dragging his lips down the soft contour of her jaw to the exposed flesh of her neck.

When her skin was caught between his teeth he felt her entire body shake. He bore down on that same tender spot again and her body yielded the same all-over tremor. He wanted to spend hours learning what other things made her body vibrate like that. Licking, biting, twisting, and pinching. Whatever it was, he wanted to know every sultry detail to make her body quiver until it broke apart for him.

His cock was rigid, throbbing behind his zipper, begging for a piece of this woman humping his leg on her balcony. If he let this continue any further he risked hurting himself, or embarrassing himself by blowing his load in his pants like a teenager.

Nope, not in front of this woman.

He pulled his lips from her neck and straightened to his full height. Taking the brief moment that stood between the separation of their bodies, and her realization that he was no longer touching her, he took in the image of wanton lust heating her skin.

She wanted him, but just like before, she'd baited him into touching her. He knew it; he'd known it the moment that comment about fucking her on her balcony fell from her lips. Well if she wanted to play, he was going to play, and more importantly, he was going to win. He would have this woman every which way he wanted her, but only on his terms. Only when she could admit to herself and him that she needed this as badly as he did.

When the wind sailed against her cooling flesh, her eyes opened. Her pupils widening until only a faint glimpse of her cognac irises could be detected.

"To answer your question, no, I'm not going to fuck you on your balcony. Not because I don't want to, but because when I finally have you, it's not going to be some quick hump against a wall. I want you spread open on my bed, legs wide, cunt split and dripping, begging for my cock. But as much as I want that, and as much as I know you want that, I'll never allow it to happen until you cut the shit and just be honest about what you want."

He could see the orange flame of her anger searing her skin, changing her honey-gold complexion to a richer amber tone. He could see her full lips pulling into a flat line across the tense angles of her face.

"Fuck you, Quillen," she spat. "I don't beg any man; I don't chase any man. If you're not man enough to come for what you want, fuck you. I'll just find someone else."

"No you won't, because we both know that you are most excited by a challenge, and that's what I am for you. I'm the one thing your rich daddy can't give you, princess, and we both know that means you'll eventually do whatever you have to in order to get what you want. You can have me, A.J.; you just gotta stop the games. Until then, seems we'll both be frustrated."

He took another step back, increasing the distance between them even more. "Mr. and Mrs. Tenetti," he called out into the apartment. When he heard their collective response he turned around and re-entered the apartment and greeted them goodnight. He turned back again, taking in the final glimpse of the fire consuming A.J. This wasn't going to be an easy task, breaking her, but damn if he wasn't going to try.

"You'll have to come over again, Alan," Jeovonni stated. "And please, make certain to think about my offer. Give me an answer as soon as you feel ready. In the meantime, I'd love to hear some of your ideas on ethical business practices regarding some of TE's business procedures. I'd be more than willing to compensate you for your consultancy. That won't violate your contract with Kenneth, will it?"

Alan shook his head. "No, I'm pretty much a free agent as long as I don't assist companies that are in direct competition with Kenneth's company. As long as TE doesn't fall into that category, I can help you out."

"Good then, I look forward to seeing more of you."

Alan nodded his head and broadened his smile as his eyes met with A.J.'s. "Yes, I can guarantee you'll be seeing much more of me around."

CHAPTER 7

A.J. stepped out of her low-riding sports car and onto the unleveled parking lot floor. She looked down as she stepped, afraid a misstep would cause her to injure herself or worse, break a designer heel.

Why did I let Kenneth talk me into coming to this damn mall? I hate malls.

They were filled with people milling around. The clothes were subpar, and the service was lacking. She gave herself a quick mental shake as she opened the door and entered the large expansive marketplace.

She was here for more important things, for Kenneth, and his son Amare. Just the thought of that sepia cherub and his blazing blue eyes and she couldn't help the smile that climbed onto her lips.

That little boy was a perfect mix of his mother and father. Kenneth's looks, Heart's complexion and assertiveness, he was something special. He was her something special or at least she wanted him to be.

She'd asked Kenneth for the coveted spot of godmother. She'd used every trick in her arsenal to get Kenneth to agree to her request, pleading, bargaining, hell, she'd even resorted to guilt. Unfortunately it wasn't solely Kenneth's decision. He had a wife, and his wife hated her.

So here she was, her C.L. Redbottom heels clicking away on the hard tile beneath her feet, as she maneuvered her way through the weekend crowd and made her way up to the food court.

A.J. spotted them easily once she stepped off the escalator. Kenneth was sitting back in his chair, his eyes fixed on his wife. Heart was seated across from Kenneth, her body stiff, her hand moving back and forth in front of Kenneth with sharp, cutting movements.

"This should be good," A.J. whispered. She stepped next to a kiosk sitting near their table to get a better view of the show that was unfolding in front of her. "The only thing missing is a bucket of popcorn."

"Heart, you know what this means to me. I don't understand why you just can't be nice to A.J."

"You don't understand?" Heart questioned. "Is this not the same chick that tried to get me to sign some shady pre-nuptial agreement without you even asking her to draw one up in the first place?"

Kenneth shrugged his shoulders. "Heart, she is my attorney, and I am ridiculously wealthy. We'd only known each other six months when we got married. A two-week engagement didn't lend a great deal of confidence to our being together out of love. She was just doing her job."

"Kenneth, you believe that bullshit if you want to. Doing her job would have been sending a messenger to deliver the papers, or making an appointment with me and encouraging me to bring my own attorney with me. That bitch showed up at my precinct unannounced and used her past connections with the district attorney's office to push past my desk sergeant and ambush me in my office. She slapped papers on my desk and tried to get me to sign them without reading them. That shit was sneaky, and it was personal."

A.J. laughed at that one. Heart wasn't a police captain for nothing. For damn sure it was personal. Kenneth meant too much to the Tenettis for A.J. to allow anyone to take advantage of him. It hadn't mattered who she offended when A.J. slapped Heart with those papers, the end result was that Kenneth was reasonably protected against any threat Heart could pose if their marriage ended.

"I haven't figured out what her angle is yet, maybe it's 'cause she always wanted her big brother's best friend," Heart pondered.

A.J. rolled her eyes. *Come on Captain Searlington. How do you ever solve any cases if you always jump to the obvious shit?*

"Or maybe it's because she really looks at you like a brother she needs to protect," Heart continued.

At least you're moving on to more plausible ideas now, Captain. A.J. shrugged her shoulders and continued to watch Heart's musings.

"That bitch is too personally involved where you're concerned. Not to mention, I don't trust her sneaky ass. Something ain't right with them Tenettis and I don't want you and Amare around them."

A.J.'s head snapped backward at that last comment, as if it were Heart's hand instead of her words that struck her.

Ok, shows over.

"Aww, Captain. You wound me, really you do," A.J. sang with feigned hurt as she moved closer to their table.

She watched as Heart rolled her eyes. A.J. waited to see a little shame resting somewhere on the young Captain's face. *It couldn't be too often that the subject of your bashing catches you in full rant. Something like that had to garner some level of embarrassment, even for the seasoned detective.*

A.J. let her eyes canvas Heart's face once more and she smiled. *Damn, this chick is a piece of work, not a drop of remorse anywhere in her body.*

"You really don't like me, huh?" A.J. asked with a playful smile.

"I don't trust you," Heart responded.

"You don't know me. Whenever I come around you all of a sudden become scarce."

"That's because I'm trying to keep from ringing your neck. What I do know of you rubs me the wrong way, why would I invest more time in you?"

"What do you know about me?" A.J. asked knowing the answer to that particular answer. *Nothing, not one single thing.*

A.J. watched Heart's eyes take the short walk down her petite body. Standing at just about five and a half feet without her shoes, A.J. was certain Heart's assessment shouldn't take all that long.

A.J. never wavered under the scrutiny. Why should she? Everything about her screamed in control business professional. She wore a sleeveless slate gray wrap dress that was belted at her tiny waist with a pewter belt to match the expensive handbag and six inch stilettos of the same color. A.J. sat down directly across from Heart, dangling one dainty leg over the other easing her shoulders back as she awaited the next jab Heart would throw at her.

"A.J. we're at a mall, everyone else in this mug is dressed in jeans, t-shirts, sweats, what us commoners call casual wear. It's comfortable, it's utilitarian, and it allows us to run into all of the stores in the mall with speed and ease. You just stepped in this piece wearing a designer dress, and shoes that cost more than the living expenses of most of the shoppers here.

"Every time I see you, you're either talking about the latest and greatest, or modeling it for our pleasure. Doesn't matter whether is cars, clothes, or housing, you always have to show folks that money is your god. I don't really want to be around someone like you, because if money is the only thing you respect, you'll sell anyone out just to get more of it."

The quiet at the table seemed to drown out the surrounding mall sounds. If the ticking muscle of Kenneth's jaw was any indication, he wasn't too thrilled with his wife right now.

This wasn't the first time Heart and A.J. came to blows, and considering that Kenneth insisted on being married to her, A.J. doubted it would be the last. In some strange way she occasionally looked forward to these debates. It was a chance for them to let all the bad blood out on the table without spilling any actual blood. This enabled them to continue on for however long it took before the next, "This is why I don't like you session," occurred.

A.J. sat back, clothes smooth, mind unfazed. Debating, arguing, that's what she did for a living. There was no one better at it, so if the captain wanted to come for her, A.J. saw no problem with taking the time to knock the lady cop off her perch.

"Assume much?" A.J. asked. A tiny quirk of the corner of her mouth let that, "smart as sin and sly as the devil," expression she wore in the courtroom flourish. "Yes, I like very nice things, mostly because I can afford them. I can afford them, because I work eighty or more hours a week getting shit done for my clients that no other attorney can do. I'm a fixer, when shit explodes, I'm the one that not only calls the cleanup crew, I manage those motherfuckers so that the mess is discarded in such a way that you'd never have known how fucked up things were before I stepped my pretty ass shoes on the scene. People like your husband pay me unimaginable amounts of money because I do the unimaginable. Money is not the god in this situation, Captain. *I* am."

I am a beast, fuck with me if you can, Captain.

Heart sat with her mouth shut, tight lines pulling across the woman's face. If A.J. could read Heart correctly she was either trying to decide on a witty comeback, or she was calculating if jumping across the table and wringing A.J.'s neck would be worth the bid she'd do in prison for assaulting an officer of the court.

A.J. smiled again, the same smile she put on for her competitors in the boardroom and the courtroom. The one that said, "You know I run this." And she did in fact run this. Otherwise Heart wouldn't be sitting across from her at this moment with her face flushed with a purplish color that was probably signaling some sort of pending internal explosion.

"Now, quit stalling and tell me why you really don't like me."

"My reasons are the same as I stated," Heart answered. "You're just superficial and I can't entrust my kid to someone like that. I want my child to know that money is cool, but that it doesn't define who he is or make him better than the next human being. I want him to embrace qualities that can't be bought, like integrity and compassion."

"There you go assuming again," A.J. answered. "I don't know why you think I'm some cold hearted princess who doesn't care for anything other than the amount of zeros in her bank account."

"You really do want to do this?" Heart asked. "Don't you?" Heart crossed her arms over her chest and leaned her head to one side as she continued to watch A.J.

For a moment a slight shiver danced across A.J.'s insides. It was as if she could feel that bronze glare slicing into her, opening her up to be placed on display. There were questions in that steady gaze; questions A.J. knew were better left unanswered.

"Alright counselor, you want the chance to stand up for our son, here's how you earn it. Kenneth and I are going to wait three months to Christen Amare; it's the only time I can get all of my family in the same place at the same time. So you've got until then to prove me wrong about you."

"And just how am I supposed to do that?" A.J. replied.

"By volunteering at Mac's Place."

"What?" The word was dipped in heavy sarcasm. "You want me to provide free legal service for the little criminal-children you babysit?"

"Remarks like that aren't going to win you any points with me. Kenneth tells me you spent many years studying classical forms of dance. I want you to pick two Saturdays a month for the next three months and create dance workshops for my kids. Show them how to do something other than make it clap on the dancefloor."

A.J. gave the proposition consideration. *Do I really have time in my schedule to do something like this? No.* She was stretched thin as it was. But when her eyes met Kenneth's she could see need and anticipation living in them. Her friend wanted this. He saw his wife extending an olive branch, and he wanted his friend to take it.

You're so lucky I love your ass, Searlington.

"I'll volunteer my dance services, but only under one condition, you take my class too," A.J. countered. "And if I were you, I'd hit the gym and work off the rest of that baby weight because Mistress Tenetti does not allow jiggling body parts on her dancefloor."

Check and mate.

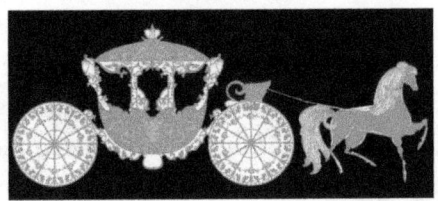

A.J. walked beside Kenneth as the three of them meandered through the mall. She smiled as she watched Kenneth pushing their son's stroller. He was this big, muscular man who wore the silliest look of happiness painted across his face as he looked down at the sleeping child. She looked over on the other side of Kenneth expecting to see Heart sharing the same giddy expression, but the captain's face was devoid of any emotion. *Maybe I pissed her off with that jiggling body parts comment.*

Her eyes were drawn to a couple of the display windows. She saw a couple of knockoff styles that intrigued her and made a mental note to have her personal stylist and shopper to pick up a few new pieces for her.

"Hey guys, let's head in here for a minute," Heart said. A.J. followed Kenneth, who followed Heart as she stopped near a makeup counter and turned to them. "When I say what I'm about to say, I don't want you to react. No matter what I say to you, you're going to stand here and smile and you're not going to look around. Got me?"

A.J. felt her fingers wrap tightly around the clutch purse in her hand. Heart may have been smiling, but the sound of her voice held no laughter, only fear. She fought the instinct to look behind her and turned her gaze toward Kenneth instead. They both looked at one another then returned concerned eyes toward Heart.

She greeted them with a toothy grin and soon Kenneth and A. J. followed with their own wide smiles plastered on their faces and nodded. A. J. felt Heart's gaze pass quickly over her shoulder. She couldn't see exactly what Heart was looking at, not without drawing attention to herself anyway.

She watched instead, still standing there with a fake smile plastered on her lips, as Heart pulled out her phone. "Kenneth," she whispered while still looking down at her phone as if she were just checking her notifications. "There are two armed men that have been following us all through the mall. I need you to unstrap Amare and pick him up in your arms. Do it slowly, no sudden moves. When I tell you, you're both going to head out the door and get into the car."

"And what are you going to do?" Kenneth asked her.

"I'm gonna do what I do."

"Heart, I'm not going to just leave you here. I'm not some weak—"

"It's not about that, Kenneth," she pleaded. "Please…let me do what I'm trained to do."

She picked up her phone, tapped a few numbers and placed the phone next to her ear. "This is Captain Heart Searlington of the seven-four precinct in the NYPD. I'm in Matties Department store in the Valley Stream Mall. I've got two unknown white males approximately six feet in height. One dark haired, one blond. They've been following me and my family inside of the last few stores we've entered and exited. They're each armed with at least one holstered handgun. We are currently at the C.A.M. makeup counter. I'm attempting to exit to the east parking lot through the side entrance. I'd be real grateful if some of my Nassau County brethren could give a Brooklyn girl a little assist."

A.J. placed a terse hand on Kenneth's forearm, hoping to God he would listen to his wife and get the baby to safety. Heart smiled again. Either she was playing it up for the men following them, or whatever she heard on the other end of her phone made her happy as hell. A.J. hoped it meant the dispatcher was sending an Emergency Service Unit armed with riot gear, very large guns, and tear gas. She knew Heart was damn good at her job, but A.J. was concerned that the two-against-one odds might leave the captain at a disadvantage.

Heart held her phone up and pretended to take pictures of A.J., Kenneth, and the baby. A.J. figured Heart was trying to get a shot of the men following them. She glanced down at the phone as if she were admiring photos she'd taken and whispered, "Get out now."

Kenneth held the baby tightly to his chest and the two of them left on Heart's word quickly walking toward the exit. They'd just pushed through the door when Amare let out a sharp wail and drew all eyes to their port of egress.

One of the men pointed to the other and they each headed for the door after Kenneth and A.J. Kenneth took one last look at his wife, then pushed A.J. through the door.

The last thing she saw was one of them reaching under his jacket for something. She heard Heart yell, "Don't do it! Don't be stupid, I will put you down! Put the guns on the floor and kick them over to me!"

Kenneth pushed her through the second set of doors and out into the parking lot just as two sharp and loud popping sounds rent the air.

Within minutes, the mall entrance was filled with police cars skidding to a hard stop. Kenneth told one of the officers his wife was a cop and she was still inside. The cops forced them back toward the parking lot where they stayed until moments later they saw Heart being escorted through the doors in handcuffs and pushed down into the backseat of a patrol car.

"Shit," A.J. whispered. "I knew coming to this fucking mall was a mistake."

CHAPTER 8

Alan walked inside of the gym with one goal in mind, run, jump, and lift until he burned the need for A.J. Tenetti out of his system. His entire day was one long headache because he couldn't seem to focus on anything but his growing desire for the woman.

He headed for the cardio section and quickly laid claim to the last of the empty treadmills. Setting a quick pace with the intention of punishing his body until it fell under his command again, Alan fell in step with the speeding belt under his feet.

He was still a little more than upset with himself that he hadn't realized A.J.'s game before that blowup in her office a few days prior. How had he not noticed this? How had he spent the last five years fighting with this woman from everything from business proposals to choices of restaurants for business lunches, and not recognized the fact that she was baiting him? It'd taken him all this time to recognize it, and once he did, he'd allowed her to do it again on her balcony.

He shouldn't have kissed her, shouldn't have come close enough to touch her. He should have kept things cordial and platonic and let sleeping dogs lie. The list of should haves was too long to count, but in the end, he'd still given in to his need to know what her fucking mouth tasted like and even worse, he was frustrated because he'd like that taste, and was now craving it.

An hour later, his hair was plastered against his skull, his lungs burned from the exertion, and his leg muscles blazed and quivered under the demand to keep such a hurried pace for such a prolonged distance. It was only when he questioned his ability not to face plant on the machine that he smacked the emergency stop button sitting in the middle of the console.

Trying to regulate his racing heart, he bent over in a tripod position, hands braced tightly on his knees as he struggled for large gulps of air. When he was reasonably certain dizziness wouldn't take over, he walked toward the weight area.

He could feel the irritation he'd spent the last hour trying to run out of his system clawing its way back in, spreading like a wicked virus. He turned sharply and headed for the weight room. The sight of the bench press stopped him in his tracks. There was no doubt pressing against heavy weights would give him the escape he need, but he knew he was too distracted to offer the attention necessary to keep himself from possible injury without anyone to spot him. A slight step to the right landed him in front of the punching bag instead. This was safe; he couldn't do too much damage to himself by punching out his rage. The poor bag might not survive, but he should be fine.

He taped his hands tightly then pulled on a pair of mixed martial arts training gloves. When he was satisfied with their fit, he settled into a boxer's stance before laying into the heavy bag. He gave the bag quick taps at first, swaying slightly from foot to foot as he worked out quick speed drills.

His mind replayed the scene in A.J.'s office through the steady rhythm his fists whapped out over the bag. The memory of her body pressed against him, the fire in those gold flecks in her hazel eyes, and the tightening in his cock when he realized her desire was a real thing, hitched his pulse up more than the exercise. His speed drills seamlessly turned into power drills as he tried to process all the thoughts in his head.

It wasn't A.J.'s desire for him that kept him so unsettled. Well, it wasn't the only thing. Yes, he definitely wanted her, he entertained passing thoughts of bedding her—in his head anyway. He'd known a long time ago that A.J. wasn't the type of woman he needed to involve himself with beyond a one-time fuck. She was smart, she was beautiful, and that ass made a man forget his own name at times, but she was also lethal when it came to her dealings with people.

He'd watched her cut people down with very little concern one too many times. He'd seen her plot an opponent's demise just for the fun it seemed to bring her. She'd no qualms about bending people to her will to get what she wanted; it appeared she possessed no care for the terror she could bring to someone's door in the name of personal triumph.

That type of woman was not the kind of woman he could venture to entangle himself with. Venomous vipers like A.J. who took pleasure in toying with their prey just to tickle themselves were deadly in his experience. He'd known women like her all his life. He'd allowed one to enter his life and when she was done, Alan was left with a dead wife, a broken soul, and no family to speak of. No, A.J. wasn't someone he'd give more than a nut and a thank you. Anything more and he was certain he'd find himself right back where he was five years ago…destroyed.

Alan wasn't about to be played again. Now that he knew she'd been playing with him all this time, or attempting to anyway, he'd deal with her on his terms and his terms only. If she wanted him, she'd have to admit it, and agree to what he wanted—a few good orgasms and a thanks on the way out of the door. Other than that, A.J. Tenetti could move on to some other fool who was willing to play her games. Alan was done.

He finished up his workout and walked the few blocks to his Williamsburg apartment. The mild breeze felt good against his abused body. A hot shower and he should have no problems finding sleep tonight.

Once inside he stripped, and headed for his shower. As soon as the stinging spray of water met skin, a relieved sigh escaped his lips. He stood there allowing the water to slide down the hard planes of his body, unknotting all of the kinks his workout hadn't been able to loosen.

He reached for the shower gel and began a slow lather up his arm and across his chest. His nail scraped against his nipple and instantly his mind conjured up an image of A.J.'s sharp tongue lancing across it.

"Shit."

He couldn't shake the image free before his dick responded, filling and thickening between his legs until it was jutting out proud and strong in front of him.

"Fuck it."

He wrapped his hand around his length to apply the perfect amount of pressure. One slow stroke, followed by two rapid ones and he was biting the edge of his lip to quell his instinct to give into his need to release.

He let his thumb trace the sensitive head, smearing the clear drops of pre-cum across his glans. A strong shudder nearly costing him his balance on the wet tiled floor forced him to plant a foot on the bench, and a hand against the wall for purchase. He placed the fingers of his free hand between his legs and gave a gentle tug to full balls that begged for relief. He knew this nut would be so sweet if he could prolong it. Unfortunately, images of a feisty lawyer with her tight pencil skirt around her waist, teetering on skinny heels, while she was bent over her desk with him slamming into her from behind, eliminated any possibility of him delaying gratification.

Without much input from him, his hips began to match the thrusting rhythm in his vision. He tightened his fist around his pulsing cock, giving it the friction it demanded. Within seconds he could feel his balls pulling up, his muscles tightening and releasing in preparation for his release. He felt the fire of his release from the bottom of his spine, coiling around each vertebra, zipping from the base of his cock, rushing up his length, then finally erupting from his tip.

He rode out the involuntary spasms that took command of his muscles as each spurt of cum dripped over his fingers and onto the shower floor. The last ripple barely leaving his ability to keep himself balanced and upright.

He finished cleaning himself, wrapped a large towel around his waist, and padded into the kitchen for something to drink. Pulling a bottle of water from the fridge, he leaned against the counter's edge as he turned the open bottle up to his mouth and emptied its contents in a few swallows.

Content with the current sense of relaxation coursing through his languid limbs, he headed for his bedroom with a brief smile. This was him; calm, relaxed, unfazed by the A.J.'s of the world.

"Not even you and all your glory can force me to be anything other than me, A.J. Not a thing you can do to fuck with my zen."

He picked his strewn clothes off of the floor and rummaged his cellphone out of his pockets. He gave it one last glance before tossing it on his bedside table and swinging his legs into his queen-sized bed. He closed his eyes and began his journey to sleep when the shrill of his cellphone intruded upon the silence.

He let it ring once more before he snatched it up, holding it over his face to see A.J.'s name lighting up the screen. He was tempted to let it go to voice mail. His thumb hovered over that reject button, but at the last moment he swiped accept and placed the phone to his ear.

"Yes?"

There was a pause; he knew she was there because he heard the quick pulls of her breath across the line.

"A.J., you there?"

"Alan?"

There was something missing in her voice, in the way she called his name. Usually her voice was bathed in the arrogant superiority that wafted off of her like cloying perfume. Usually he could hear pleasure filling her voice when she knew she was about to unleash some new form of corporate hell into his life. But tonight those natural elements were gone. Tonight they were gone and in their absence he could hear something else, uncertainty.

He pulled himself up against the headboard and turned on the bedside lamp. "A.J., what's wrong?"

"Alan…are you…could you…" her words stumbled off into air.

"A.J., what the hell? It's late and I'm really not up for any of your bullshit."

"It's not…"

"A.J., if you're calling just to fuck with me, I promise you, I'm really not in the mood."

"Alan?" she whimpered.

His attention sharply focused on her voice again. It sounded small, confused. A few seconds passed before the piece clicked into place, something was wrong. A.J. Tenetti was never without words. She was never tongue-tied. Her words were always eloquent and flowed with the ease of water from a jar. Alarm pulled him up and out of his bed, pulling the dresser drawers open in search of fresh clothes.

"Where are you? Is it Kenneth?"

"Yes…no…I…"

"A.J., you're not making sense, tell me where you are?"

"The Promenade by the Brooklyn Bridge," she answered. "Near Pierrepont Street."

"Don't move, I'm on my way."

A moment ago he was relaxed, enjoying the mellow that only a good, strong nut could bring—even if it did come from his own hand. Now he was grabbing his wallet and keys and rushing out the door thanks to Alexis-Jeovonni Tenetti.

"So much for not letting her fuck with my zen."

In the span of a few moments, her world was tilted on its axis. She'd sat next to Heart in an interrogation room while they cleared up the chaos of a shooting in a local mall. It was annoying, but nothing she wasn't really used to. She'd spent the first five years of her law career in the District Attorney's office. She'd known almost to the letter what would occur in that room. The cops pressed and asked the same questions repeatedly, making certain all bases were covered and all details checked out.

Heart answered the questions A.J. gave her leave to and allowed A.J. to intervene on her behalf on the ones A.J. shut down. It was too perfect; the entire situation just ran too damn smoothly. A.J. should have expected the devil himself to be waiting around the corner.

And he was, waiting and lurking not around the corner, but between the tabs of a manila folder on the desk in front of them. Morgue photographs, pictures of the man who'd attempted to pull a gun on Heart in the mall and earned two bullets to the chest as a reward. A.J. flipped through the photos, some from different angles, others of varying body parts, each more morbid and uninteresting than the last. Then with one last flip of her wrist, the last photo came in to view. It was a picture of an ink colored tattoo that covered the decedent's left wrist.

A diadem with a sword piercing through its middle, small and unassuming, simple in its design, the tattoo rested inconspicuously on the dead man's wrist. Most people probably wouldn't give the image a second thought. Unfortunately for her, a past encounter meant she couldn't just ignore what she'd seen. She'd witnessed it before, on the wrists of two people who'd come for her, the people who were sent by her uncle, Reign.

One simple image and the pieces began to all click into place. Kenneth's shooting was no longer some random crazy person, or some drug dealer looking to prevent him from opening his drug rehabilitation center. Just like that, she realized this wasn't about her friend at all; it was about her family and the monarchy, and protecting them no matter the cost.

She'd left Heart and Kenneth at the precinct to drop their son off at home. Once she'd delivered the infant safely to his nanny, she pointed her car in the direction of Brooklyn. When she was making her way through an empty Belt Parkway West, she uttered the words,

"Call Teague," and waited for the Bluetooth equipped car to connect her call.

"Long time no hear, A.J."

She rolled her eyes at the friendly greeting. Agent Teague Maher was anything but friendly. Standing more than six feet of burly muscle, he rarely allowed a smile to break the stoic glare he'd perfected over the years.

"He's back, Teague."

"I know," he answered.

That last kernel of hope that was buried deep inside her stomach was slowly disintegrated into nothingness by the bubbling bile she was fighting to keep down.

"We're locking everything down, Princess. Get your royal butt home so we can make plans."

Her eyes instinctively glanced up to the rearview mirror. It really didn't make sense for her to try and spot Teague or his men, if he had someone following her, she wouldn't know it until he was ready for her to know it.

She couldn't do this again. After more than twelve years of living in peace in this country, of being able to lead the life she'd worked so hard to create, she was going to have to give it all up.

Not if I have anything to say about it.

"See you soon, Teague," she answered quickly and disconnected the call. "If I'm going to give up my life again, I may as well have a taste for the road."

Without even thinking, she headed toward home, circled around longer than she wanted to find a parking spot, and headed on foot to the promenade. She sat on a bench that placed her in perfect view of the Brooklyn Bridge and took a moment to take in the scene.

The bridge with its intricate structure, built for strength and longevity, loomed like a dedicated protector, vigilant in its quest to protect the city. It was lit up with its twinkling lights, a jeweled crown in the sky, breaking through the dark of the lonely night. The majesty of it never seemed to wane in her eyes.

She pulled her cellphone from her purse and turned it over in her hand a few times. She pulled up Alan's number, not certain what she was going to say, but confident her oratory skills would fashion something slick and confident to tilt things back in her favor. The last two times she'd encountered Alan, he'd left with the last word and the win in his pocket. Perhaps turning things right side up would make this growing mass of nervousness sitting in the middle of her chest go away and she'd be able to recoup some much needed control.

Desperate to feel good and questioning why she would call Alan to do that, she slid her thumb across the screen and practiced her lines in her head while the call connected.

"Yes?" he answered.

The annoyance in his voice halted her for a second. Perhaps she should have thought this through a little more, weighed more of the possible outcomes. Alan wasn't someone she could trust with her secrets, he couldn't stand her on most days, there was no way he'd offer her a shoulder to cry on.

"Alan?" she responded. Her voice was shaky and small, so unlike the natural boom of confidence and finesse that usually sculpted her words.

She attempted to speak again, and was more than grateful when Alan took pity on her fumbling attempt to talk him and agreed to meet her, relief moved through her veins. She disconnected the call with trembling hands and pulled her arms around her as she sat on the bench.

Why was she so out of her element? Why had tonight shaken her so terribly?

Because you know it only gets worse from here.

The last time Reign entered their lives, he'd nearly ended her life. She was left with permanent injuries she'd never completely overcome. If she were to be completely honest with herself, she wasn't certain if she could withstand another battle with Reign.

"If the end is near, I may as well enjoy something I've always wanted. No time like the present to live for today and forget about tomorrow."

She caught a glimpse of Alan walking down the promenade. Even at this time of night his blond tresses illuminated the night. He wore a fitted t-shirt with sweatpants and sneakers on his feet. The chiseled cut of his chest and thighs were pronounced, making the casual wear fall as if they'd been created for him specifically.

When he spotted her, he broke into a light jog, muscles rolling under skin, making her mouth water. He wasn't even attempting to look sexy and yet his appearance, his movements, everything about him just oozed sex appeal.

"A.J.," he called. "Are you all right?"

He knelt down in front of her and took her hand before raising deep blue eyes to her face, asking questions that had yet to cross his lips. It was there, so evident, as bright as the lighting on the dark bridge that looked as if it was just a finger's width away in the backdrop. Concern, he cared.

She didn't fool herself into believing Alan possessed some deep affection for her, but he was a decent human being who didn't wish harm on anyone. Not even the woman who'd spent the last five years treating him like shit, pulling every trick in the book to get a reaction out of him. Despite all of that, he'd been concerned enough by her nonsensical call that he'd left his home and come to her.

She might not be able to trust him with her secrets, but by the look of the concern in his eyes, she could certainly trust him with her fear.

"Remember when you said you wouldn't have me unless I came to you like a woman, and admitted I wanted you?"

His eyes traveled across her face again, seeking more answers that she couldn't give. He nodded slowly, and bid her to continue.

"Well this is me owning my shit. I want you Alan. I have since the first moment I saw you. I've had a freakishly hellish day where I was nearly caught in a shootout between Heart and two men attempting to kill Kenneth."

"Is Kenneth...?"

"He's fine," she offered. "He and Heart are both all right," she whispered. "If Heart hadn't been there, if she hadn't been able to..."

The sound of the shiver in her voice made it sound foreign to her own ears. If Reign's thugs were able to complete their task, all of them could have been dead.

"A.J., I don't think now is a good time for you to make a decision like this."

She nodded her head, he was more than correct. She was scared, and shaken by the events of the day. Under normal circumstances she'd take the time to process all of it, but she didn't have time. There was no telling how long it would be before another attempt was made on her life. No telling if her assailants would one day succeed.

"You're right, but I still don't want to wait. Give me tonight, tomorrow will take care of itself."

A strange moment passed between them. He was still kneeling in front of her, still searching for answers that seemed to be eluding him. He wasn't the only one confused by her behavior. Common sense would have kept her holed up at home, waiting for Teague and his team to either secret the Tenettis away, or creating a brick wall between her family and those that would benefit from their deaths.

But instead of being secluded in safety, she was sitting here out in the open where anyone could get to her, asking a man to do what? Spend a few sweaty hours together; get her off a few times? If it were as simple as that, she would have given herself to Alan Quillen years ago. No, tonight she was looking for something else, something her life in recent years hadn't offered very much of, simplicity, honesty.

The simple truth was that she wanted Alan. She'd known making that desire a reality wasn't a possibility in the past. But now, now she might not have to worry about the consequences to her actions. There would be no fallout, no messy entanglements, because the dawning of tomorrow's sun would more than likely bring an end to this very-carefully orchestrated charade.

"Tonight…I just need…"

He stood up slowly and extended his hand to her. "Come with me," he murmured. "I promise I'll give you exactly what you need."

CHAPTER 9

Alan stood in his kitchen sipping what should have been his usual morning cup of coffee. If it were the start to any typical day, he'd be drinking his coffee and scrolling through the headlines on his tablet before he walked out the door to his office.

But it wasn't a typical day, not in the least. Not with Alexis-Jeovonni Tenetti curled up in his bed.

The buzz of a cellphone vibrating pulled his attention away from his musings. He looked down at the screen to see the word, "Papà," flashing across its face. His hand automatically reached for the phone, but just before he could touch it, he paused. There was no question he'd be overstepping all kinds of boundaries by answering this woman's phone, but the fact that this was the fourth time her father called in the last forty minutes made Alan question whether he should answer the call or not.

He thought back to last night, to the mess he'd found A.J. in. For most people, her state wouldn't have caused him so much concern. But there was something terribly off about his encounter with A.J. that led him to believe she needed someone to take care of her last night.

He swiped the call to voicemail and picked up the phone on his way to his bedroom. No sense in avoiding the inevitable, time to face the awkward moment that he knew was awaiting him on the opposite side of his bedroom door.

He tapped the door, hoping to give her a chance to prepare for his entrance. After pausing, he twisted the knob and walked in. Nothing could have prepared him for the vision of A.J. standing in front of the window, wearing one of his A-line t-shirts. The crisp white cotton material clinging to the curves of her body, stopping just below the curve of her ass halted his breath and his movements.

She turned to him, her face hidden in the curtain of honey and brown curls falling just below the swell of her breasts. Everything about her appearance this morning was so warm and inviting, so tempting. All it would take on his part were a few steps and she'd be in his arms, a few more steps and she'd be back in his bed, stripped of that tiny slip of material that stood between him and ecstasy.

His eyes walked back up the length of her body and settled on the soft angles of her face. When his eyes caught hers she dropped her gaze, a slight rose tint rendering her cheeks a deeper shade of brown than the golden tones she usually possessed.

Confident and self-assured, Alexis-Jeovonni was the epitome of assertiveness. Over the years her aggressiveness became a source of both enticement and foreboding. Look, but don't touch, always his motto where she was concerned. But standing here, watching what could only be described as bashfulness consume her, he'd never been more intrigued by her.

"I...I can come back and let you get dressed," he offered. He attempted to turn toward the door, but was stopped by the small sound of her voice.

"No, it's all right. After last night, I don't think there's any reason to be shy."

"Nothing happened last night, A.J."

She fiddled with her fingers for a moment and then walked toward the bed, crawling to the center and folding her legs underneath her.

"Nothing sexual happened last night, but something did happen." She patted the empty space next to her, asking him to join her. "You went out of your way to take care of me last night, and I don't really know why."

"All I did was meet you at the Promenade and let you crash at my place. You had a rough day; anyone would have done the same."

She shook her head. "No, I offered you sex, and you turned me down. Instead you brought me back to your place, let me take a shower, and then held me as I slept in your bed. Not even a saint would have let that happen without getting a little reward."

He leaned across her and rested his cup of coffee on the nightstand before meeting her gaze again. She was right; there were men out there that would have taken everything she offered and then some without thinking twice about it. He wasn't a saint. He was certainly tempted within an inch of his life when he felt the heat of her body pressed against him, her full curves fitting so perfectly into his flat planes. But as much as he'd wanted to run his fingers up and down the expanse of her supple skin, he'd known it was the wrong thing to do.

"Don't make me out to be some paragon of virtue, A.J. I was very tempted by your offer. I don't think I've made any secret about being attracted to you."

"Yeah, but you keep refusing to do so."

"I don't like the fact that you use your power and position to orchestrate a reaction out of me. Instead of just coming to me and telling me you'd like to spend some time in my bed, you use work. You create situations that you intend to piss me off, like the only way you can accept my attention is if it's given out of anger. I'm not looking to play those sorts of games with someone I'm sleeping with. I'm also not willing to let shit like that go down at work. I won't be controlled by anyone."

She nodded her head and began playing absently with some imaginary thread on his bedcovers.

"I don't get you," she whispered as her eyes skimmed down his face. "You come from wealth; you should be able to maneuver these games as well as I do. Why are you so against them? They're fun, yeah, but they also protect people like us from unsavory characters too."

"Truer words have never been spoken," Alan replied. "My grandfather is the master of manipulative games, and I studied at his feet."

"Then why?"

Alan watched her carefully, looking for any sign that this was just another plan in motion for her. Her eyes were open, free of the calculating glare they usually possessed.

Could he trust that openness? Something was different. In his opinion, the fact that they'd been in each other's presence for more than a handful of hours and there wasn't any bloodshed, was proof something significant had shifted.

But was it enough?

"My grandfather has never been a kind man. He doesn't consider how his actions impact others. He only cares about what he wants, nothing else."

"I've never actually met your grandfather. I've attended some of the same business functions over the years, and trust me, even that was too much for me. I've swept some of my clients out of his clutches a time or two. He isn't what I'd call a nice man."

"He's not. Three years before I arrived in New York, I met this woman on the beach. Most mornings I'd get to the beach in time to watch the sunrise, then I'd take my surfboard out on the water and just forget about everything my grandfather put me through the day before. That time of morning, the beach was practically empty, except this day; there was another surfer in the water.

"We surfed, and when we made it back to the beach we talked. We talked a lot, so much so I wound up shucking my work duties and playing hooky with her. Beth just made me see the important things in life, sunrises, love, not business."

His mind rolled back to that day a decade ago. He'd been young, just leaving college, still under his grandfather's thumb, but Beth's love took hold of his senses and made him focus on those life-affirming things that a man should grab hold to.

She didn't care about his money; she didn't give a damn about who his family was. She made him act like a real person, getting rid of the superficial shit that he and his family wore as proud accessories.

It was the thing he'd loved most about Beth, her ability to see through the manipulations and into the true person. It was also the one quality that set their fate in motion.

"I married her," he blurted out. "I loved her, and I knew if I allowed her to slip through my fingers, I'd regret it for the rest of my life. Unfortunately my family couldn't see the value in her. She wasn't like us, didn't come from generations of money and status. She wasn't prepared for all the backbiting. She didn't know how to play the game. She grew up in a normal family where shit like that doesn't happen."

He watched A.J. nod her head. After five years of watching her maneuver successfully in the business world he suspected she'd been given a first class education in manipulative mind games before she cut her first tooth. Although from what he knew of the Tenetti family, they didn't necessarily seem to play those games on one another, it was still obvious that A.J. understood how to play outsiders.

"She wasn't the right type of woman; my family didn't accept the marriage."

"And they gave the two of you hell as a result?"

Alan shook his head. If only it was that simple, if only they'd directed their fire at him, maybe things would be very different today.

"No, they directed their vitriol at her. If they'd have come for me, I could have defended her, us. But they pretended as if everything was fine in my face, and attacked her when I wasn't around. After nearly a year of their constant bullying and undermining, Beth just couldn't take it anymore. She feared them, feared for us. I didn't understand why she was so anxious, and when we talked about it, she would never tell me the truth."

"Why not? You were her husband."

"Yes, but they were my family, she was afraid I wouldn't believe her, that I would turn on her for accusing them of intentionally trying to rip us apart."

She was quiet, still watching him with interest and concern, but quiet nonetheless.

"One night she and I got into a major argument. She wanted me to leave my grandfather's company, start new somewhere else. I refused. I was a twenty-something CEO of a major corporation. No way in hell was I going to walk away from all that because my wife wanted to pick up and move. She begged me over and over again that night and I shut her down every single time. She decided she couldn't take it any longer, packed a bag and walked out the door. Before she left I told her if she left to never come back. And she never did."

"She divorced you?"

He shook his head. The familiar chill that always filled him when he thought of that dark moment from his past began to spread through him. He knew he was about to get lost in it when he felt unexpected warmth stem the chill. He looked down at his hand where A.J.'s was now laying gently over his. It was grounding him, giving him an anchor to the present when the past sought to drown him.

"It was late, she was upset, she jumped in her car to go only God knows where. According to the police reports, she was driving too fast on a cliffside road. She lost control of the car and went through the guardrail. She died on impact.

"About two years after Beth's funeral, I ran into her sister. She was kind of cold to me, and when I asked why, she chewed into my ass for not being there for Beth, for allowing my family to put her through all the shit she'd been living with during our marriage. I'd no idea what she was talking about until she filled me in.

"Even without any tangible proof, I knew that it was true. It started off as snide comments when I wasn't around. It escalated to my grandfather somehow fucking with the bank that owned her parents' mortgage; they were going to lose everything, all because my grandfather was trying to force her out of my life. I didn't know. I didn't see it, because I was too busy trying to gain my grandfather's approval so he'd name me heir. He snatched the one person I loved more than anything away from me. He bullied and tortured her because she wasn't our kind, and I sat back and allowed it to happen. All because of my greed and need for success."

Delicate hands touched both sides of his face and drew him closer to her. She placed tender lips on his and let her forehead rest against his.

"It wasn't your fault, Alan. It was an accident, nothing you did or didn't do contributed to it."

He closed his eyes, treasuring the feel of her warmth, wanting so desperately to believe in the words she was saying.

"She wouldn't have been on that road if I'd protected her from my family, or at least taught her how to defend herself from them. After I found out, I was kind of lost for a minute. Not feeling anything, just going on about my day without much thought or feeling for that matter. Then one day my grandfather called me into his office and told me he wouldn't put the family business in my hands unless I was settled down and married to a suitable woman from a proper family, specifically a woman named Allison who was the daughter of one of his business cronies. He actually said I'd mourned that woman long enough and it was high time I got on with life with Allison."

"He didn't even use her name?" A.J. asked.

"Why would he? Beth wasn't significant enough in his eyes that he would care about addressing her by her proper name. After that, I just couldn't do it any longer. I told him to take his company and shove it. I walked out with almost nothing. Most of my assets were tied up with the company. When I landed on Kenneth and Heart's door, I had a small amount of petty cash saved in an account that wasn't linked to the company and that was it."

"So all this is why transparency is so important to you?"

"What you see as standard operating procedure cost me everything. The life of the woman I loved, the job of my dreams, my wealth, everything."

"Alan, yes, I do know how to play manipulative games. I have to in order to do my job as both a lawyer and a CEO. I hold people's lives in my hand. If I don't do what I have to, people suffer. That aside, I'm not your grandfather. I would never so blatantly and carelessly play with someone's life like he did Beth's and yours. I'm a beast, Alan, there's no doubt about it, but I'm a beast at protecting those I love and defend. I stop threats, I don't bring them."

She tucked an errant curl around her ear, the action drawing his gaze to the sensual curve of her neck. He reached out a finger to glide down it, just needing to connect with her body in some way, no matter how small.

She smiled, the small shiver that passed under the pad of his finger causing her to close her eyes for a moment.

"So is that why you turned me down last night? Because you thought I was manipulating you again?"

He shook his head. If he hadn't seen her for himself, he probably would have thought the vulnerable state he'd found her in was a ploy to bend him to her will. "Last night you shouldn't have been making a decision about sleeping with me or not. You experienced something traumatizing. It rattled you. It would have been wrong to take advantage in that situation."

"But I agreed to it," she answered.

"Yes, you did, but I didn't think you were in the right frame of mind to really give consent. When I have you underneath me, I want it to be because you want to be there, not because you're running from something."

"When?" she questioned with her perfectly arched eyebrow rising for emphasis.

He nodded his head. "Yes, when," he answered. "…if you're willing to put the games behind us, and start fresh."

He extended an offered hand to her and waited for her to slide hers inside of his grasp. "Hello, my name is Elliot Alan Quillen, III, but most of my friends call me Alan. I find you exceptionally attractive and I'd like to spend some time in your company getting to know you. No games, no manipulations, just fun. Yes, I'd like to have sex with you, but even if I don't, I think spending time getting to know you will be worth it. How about you?" he asked.

He watched her roll her eyes, but the rise of high appled cheeks revealed she wasn't as annoyed as she pretended.

"Hello, my name is Alexis-Jeovonni Tenetti. I'm very much used to playing with my food before I eat it, but in your case I will make an exception. In your case I'd like to see what the real deal looks like upfront. I promise no games, no manipulations, just candor, for however long this lasts."

He nodded and lifted her hand to his lips before placing a gentle kiss there. "Counselor, I think we've just come to terms," he added.

"Not just yet," she added with a lifted finger. "I'd like to keep this private."

"As in you're ashamed to let people know you're keeping time with me?"

She laughed. It wasn't that cynical laugh he always heard when she was unleashing hell on someone. No, this was a genuine laugh filled with real amusement. The sight of her shoulders shaking and her lips pulling into a full bow drew a smile on his lips.

"Keeping time?" she asked through her laughter. "What are you, sixty?"

"Just tell me what's up. Are you seeing someone else? Is that why you need the secrecy?"

She shook her head. "No, if that were the case I would have been upfront about it. I don't think I've heard either of us mention we were looking for forever. I know I'm not. But the truth is I don't have enough time in my day to juggle something like that. I just...we share a good deal of people in common. You are best friends with my brother's best friend. Kenneth is a man who happens to be very close to me as well. I don't want either of them going all protective and getting in either of our faces about this. Not to mention, if this doesn't work out, I don't want to play who gets the friends in the breakup."

He considered her statement. She was correct; Kenneth did have a blind spot where this woman was concerned. Heart complained about it all the time. He wasn't quite certain involving their friends in this would turn out pleasantly.

"All right, I agree, with the added caveat that we reevaluate that stipulation should one of us feel the need to in the future."

She tilted her head to the side, her eyes considering him and his proposal. "Agreed. I think you could have been a very good attorney. Your negotiating skills are impressive."

"Believe me, my negotiating skills aren't the only things impressive about me."

She leaned in close, placing soft lips on his, slightly deepening the kiss as she let the tip of her tongue sweep across the tingling flesh of his bottom lip. "Believe me, Quillen, I plan to find out."

CHAPTER 10

Alexis-Jeovonni straightened her shoulders as she stepped out of the cab. A few moments ago she'd been at peace sitting and talking with Alan Quillen. He was smart, and funny, and his openness was a refreshing experience that she was still getting used to.

She dealt in stealth and intrigue, never letting anyone else become privy to her true thoughts until she was absolutely ready to. This being open thing and trying to be as transparent as she could in her position, was going to take some practice on her behalf.

No matter the difficulty, no matter the effort, she was still willing to try it. There was no question she needed Alan in her life, especially now that she was in the process of waging war against her enemies.

She'd spent her entire life running and hiding from the enemy, but now she was tired of that. She needed to go on offense for a change, set the tone of the battle, choose the place where the scrimmage would begin.

She'd always been reactive to Reign, but she was done with hiding and allowing Reign and his underhanded plots to dictate how she lived her life. Well, to hell with that. Spending time with Alan, knowing he would stand with her just made her realize she was going to have to end this campaign sooner rather than later. If last night taught her nothing else, it was that she wanted more tomorrows with Alan, she wanted the freedom to live out in the open in both her homeland of Azuria, and her borrowed land in America.

Alan demanded honesty from her, insisted she allow him to stand by her side, to help her during this crisis, and she'd agreed. The truth was she hadn't given him much of a fight; she hadn't wanted to fight him. After spending the night in his bed, after the care he'd offered her, she wanted more.

She'd never experienced anything like that. Everyone around her wanted something. In her experience, she recalled few interactions with people that didn't involve them attempting to acquire some sort of an advantage over her. But Alan didn't asked for a thing.

He'd held her as fear racked her body with shivers, holding her until she calmed beneath his soothing touch. He'd showered her with concern and given her a safe place to forget what was waiting for her in the real world, what was waiting for her upstairs in that grand apartment she shared with her family.

As soon as she placed a foot on the curb, she felt eyes on her. She couldn't see whom they belonged to, but she felt them nonetheless.

She stepped inside of the lobby and headed for the private elevator that opened on her floor. When it opened, two men dressed in dark suits with matching sunglasses were standing in front of the door.

"Morning, agents. Would you mind stepping aside so I can exit the elevator?"

They each looked at each other, as if neither were capable of making that decision on their own. Coming to some silent agreement, they both nodded to each other, then stepped apart allowing her exit. She went to punch in the security code to the door, but it opened from the other side.

She stepped inside, finding Teague Maher filling the limited space in the hall. His green eyes were nearly closed into angry slits and the red hair on his head and goatee seemed to get brighter with each passing moment.

"Morning, Teague," serving him the greeting with a bright smile. "Fancy finding you here."

"Are you fucking kidding me? Do you even realize how much manpower I wasted looking for your ass, and you walk up in here as if nothing has happened?"

"Teague, did I ask you to come looking for me, or give you any indication I needed your manpower?"

"Don't fuck with me, Princess. Last night Reign would have had your ass in a sling if the Captain hadn't been there. You should have come straight home instead of running to the surferboy's place in Williamsburg."

She narrowed her eyes, letting her cool gaze run down Teague's face. She wasn't surprised Teague knew about her whereabouts last night. He always had eyes on her, always knew what was going on in her life, even when she didn't want him to. Privacy was an illusion, one she foolishly still tried to hold on to considering people like Teague Maher existed in her life.

"Keep him out of this, Teague," she warned. Teague had meddled in her life since he'd taken over her case twelve years ago, the last time Reign was able to get close enough to her to strike.

"You're the one that brought him into this, A.J."

"He's not involved, Teague," she snarled.

"Don't play stupid, A.J., or at the very least, don't play *me* for stupid. The moment you started fucking that preppy you've been messing up. Did you really think I wouldn't notice? And if I noticed, don't you think *others* might notice too?"

He was right. Sooner or later Reign would discover Alan's significance in her life and undoubtedly attempt to use him to break her.

"I know he will."

"Then why would you bring him into the middle of this?"

She walked down the hall heading for her home office. She placed her briefcase on her desk, and seated herself. With practiced memory, she removed her slender rectangular shaped glasses and placed them smoothly on the tip of her nose with one hand. She looked up at Teague above their rim and smiled.

"Teague, I know Reign better than anyone, and I know damn well, he'll pick up on the fact that Alan and I are seeing one another. I'm planning on it."

"What's running through that brain of yours, Princess?"

"I'm tired of hiding from this maniac, Teague. I'm not going to let him scare me out of living or enjoying another moment in my life. It's time we neutralize that son of a bitch. And the best way to make your enemies mad enough to do something stupid is to live your life splendidly. That's what I plan to do, live my life with my family, my friends, and Alan if he'll have me. I'm not letting this opportunity with him fall away."

"So how exactly is that supposed to stop Reign?" he asked.

"It's not." She smiled. "It's supposed to draw him out so you can finally catch him. The only thing is, you're going to need some new blood on your team if you're going to successfully keep Reign from killing me and my family. Got anyone in your arsenal who you think is smart enough to outthink this crazy bastard and badass enough to protect us at the same time?"

An easy smile grew on his face and made his usually strong features brighten for just a moment.

"As a matter of fact, Princess, I think I do."

CHAPTER 11

"A.J.?"

The semi-loud bark of her name pulled her out of her drifting thoughts. She gave herself a mental shake and focused on her brother's face.

"Are you all right?"

She was still stepping out of the mental fog when her brother stopped in front of her desk.

"I'm...I'm fine," she answered.

John raised a questioning brow as he sat down at her desk. "I don't know that I believe that. You looked kind of out of it."

"Well, not all of us can be famous singers. Some of us have to actually work for a living," she quipped.

John picked up a paperclip from her desk and plucked it in her direction. She moved slightly to the side as it sailed past her head. Well into his mid-thirties and he was still behaving like a teenager. It was safe to say John would never grow up, a fact she secretly envied him for.

"So tell me, what has my baby sister so deep in thought that she doesn't hear her only brother calling her name?"

"A case I'm working on," she answered as she rooted around on the desk until she found another paperclip and tossed it back at her brother.

"You work too much, *sorellina*."

She laughed at that, she was thirty-two years old and he was still referring to her as his "little sister," in Italian.

"I'm fine, John, just a lot of work here in the office."

"You should spend more time having fun and living your life. You need to get away from this office sometimes, go do something to amuse yourself, get laid, just get from behind that damn desk."

She rolled her eyes. Only her brother would think it's appropriate to say something so crude. He really possessed the brain of a horny teenager.

"Thank you, but I don't think I really need my big brother arranging my sex life. It's just a busy time right now."

"And a lot of worry over Reign?"

The smile dripped from her face at the mention of their uncle's name. "I try not to give any thought at all to Reign, if I can help it," she stated.

"Neither do I, but according to Papà and Teague, he's back, and even worse, he's made two attempts on your life."

She knew John would be made aware of all this soon enough. It wasn't like he didn't have a vested interest in all of this craziness surrounding her safety. If one of them were in trouble, then all of the Tenetti's were in trouble.

"Teague is handling it, you've nothing to worry about," she stated in a matter-of-fact fashion.

"Don't do that," he uttered. His face was free of the amusement he usually wore. John was born to entertain. Even when he wasn't trying, he always seemed to bring delight to those he encountered with something as simple as his smile. Sitting here watching worry carve lines into his face bore heavily on her heart.

"John, we will handle it. Don't let this mess with Reign affect you."

"How can it not? I may not be in the family business, but Reign is targeting my family again, I'm not just going to sit by—"

"You have to," she interrupted. "You have to, John. If Reign ever found out about you, that you're one of us," she swallowed the words that were choking her, the thought of her brother or his family being placed in danger because of this political mess she lived in made her throat feel small. "Think of Max and the girls."

He sobered; he knew just as she that Reign would have no qualms about using John's twin daughters as a means to extort the throne from their father. They'd been able to hide his connection to them this long; they needed to keep up the subterfuge to keep those girls safe.

"What is Teague doing to keep this maniac from killing my family?"

"Teague is doing what he does, working behind the scenes to make sure we stay safe. He only lets Papà and I know bits and pieces as we need to know them."

"I'm just worried, A.J. I'm about to start this world tour. I'll be on the road for the next eighteen months. I'll only be able to pop in and out of the States on a handful of occasions while I'm touring. I want to be here, I need to be with my family."

"You need to live your life, John. This is not your lot."

He nodded his head as he stood and walked over to where she sat. She stood and allowed him to fold her into his tight embrace. He was worried. She could feel it by how firmly he held her, as if he was offering the only protection he could in that moment, praying it would be enough to cover her.

"I'm leaving Monday morning, Papà and Mamà are coming to spend the weekend at my place. I want you there too."

"I'd love to, but I have a bunch of Searlington Realty contracts to deal with this weekend. I'm actually going to be held up at Searlington with Kenneth's VP on both days."

"Bring him with you."

"Excuse me?" she queried.

"You're talking about Alan, right?"

She nodded.

"Then bring him with you. He and Ken are boys, and he's been nothing but cool to me, bring him with you. He can stay for the weekend, partake in the activities. My dancers are coming over so we can have a final rehearsal here in my studio. He can sit in, see how I make the magic happen, and when you guys need to focus on work, you can go out to the carriage house to get away from all the family noise. Do this for me, *sorellina*. I just need to know that I have all my family around me before I leave."

She heard the silent, *one last time*, lingering behind the depth of his onyx eyes. A sadness resided there he was attempting to hide, but failing to conceal.

"I'll call Alan in a few and make the arrangements. See you this weekend."

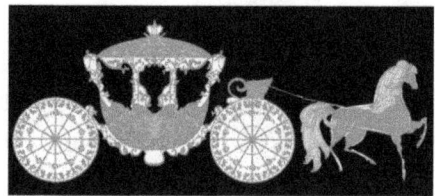

"And this is where you'll be staying," A.J. swept her hand across the room like a practiced display model.

Alan stepped inside of the carriage house and let a low whistle pass his lips. "This is really impressive. Who knew Long Island boasted of houses like this?"

"Kenneth built this house to my brother's specifications. He needed a place where he could be home, but still work from home. There are recording and dance studios downstairs. He soundproofed the entire house to keep from disturbing the neighbors while he works. Most of the music and the elaborate dance routines he creates happen somewhere in this house."

He walked around looking through each room filled with modern, yet comfortable décor. This was definitely a nice place. Not as large as the main house, but roomy enough to not feel like you were being closed in by the walls around you.

"Thank you for agreeing to come out here to work this weekend," she said. "My brother is going to be gone for a long time on this tour.

You schlepping out here helps me stay on track of my work, and see my brother off at the same time."

He walked closer to her, pressing his body against hers and lifted her mouth to his. The press of her lips against his, the sweet taste of her mouth on his made his dick plump up. When they'd agreed to get to know one another, the idea that their respective schedules would cause them to spend the last couple of weeks missing opportunities to spend time with each other didn't cross his mind. She could have asked him to spend the weekend in a desert for all he cared; time spent with this woman was always going to be a plus.

"You don't have to thank me. This is a win-win situation. I get to spend the weekend hanging out with one of my favorite recording artists, and get paid to do it. The fact that a good chunk of that time is going to be spent hiding away with you in this awesome bachelor pad, well that's just a bonus."

She dipped her head as if she wanted to avoid his gaze.

"Hey," he whispered as he forced her eyes back to his. "I didn't mean to imply anything. I wasn't suggesting that our time together needed to be spent doing anything more than working and hanging out."

She licked her lips and pulled the bottom one in between her teeth, catching it at its corner. "I'm really sorry to hear that," she said, a coy smile blossoming on that full mouth. "I was really hoping we'd be able to put the privacy, and my brother's soundproofed walls to better use than just hanging out and working."

Something akin to a growl crawled out of his chest, up his throat and out his mouth as he pulled her closer.

"Be very careful what you ask for, A.J. I do believe you might just get it."

He kissed her again, savoring her taste, aching to see if the rest of her body tasted as sweetly as her mouth did.

"Do we have any family appearances; that require our attention right now?" he asked between kisses.

"Well, I asked you to arrive early for a reason. My mamà is out shopping for dinner ingredients. I'm not expected to help her for another two hours. If you make good use of your time, I think we could each get off at least twice before then."

He pulled her away long enough to squint his eyes at her. "You wound me, woman. I promise I can do better than giving you only two measly orgasms in two hours. Who the hell have you been sleeping with?"

"Are we really going to discuss something like that now?"

"Agreed, where's the bedroom?"

She pulled him upstairs to the second level. The master bedroom was at the top of the stairs. She opened the door, and pulled him inside. Once he'd closed the door, she backed away from him, pulling her shirt from her jeans. She was about to reach for the button on her jeans when he grabbed her hand and stilled it.

This was moving way too quickly, yes, they were on a time limit, but he wouldn't rush this either.

"Hey, wait a sec. Come sit down here with me," he spoke softly, directing her to the queen-sized bed in the middle of the room.

"Is something wrong?" she asked.

He shook his head. "No," he answered. "I just want to make sure you understand that you don't have to do this, that I didn't come out here with any expectations."

"Are you having second thoughts about this, Quillen?"

"No, I just don't want you to think this is all about the sex to me. I hoped when we finally arrived at this point I'd have time to wine and dine you before we ended up screwing like bunnies. Not to mention, this is your brother's house. You sure he's not going to come for me if he finds out I'm screwing his baby sister?"

She crawled over to him, straddling his hips, planting the seat of her jean-clad cunt over his hardening dick. *Damn*, he hadn't even gotten her completely naked and he could feel his balls inching up.

She pushed against his chest, and he leaned back, taking her with him, until his back was flat against the bed. She placed her hands on either side of his head and braced the weight of her slim build on her locked arms.

"Funny enough, just before my brother told me to bring you over here, he insisted that I get laid."

"Your brother told you to bring me here to have sex with me?" He didn't care how cool John was, there wasn't a man alive who cared about his sister that would invite some shit like that to go on in his house.

She laughed a bit and shook her head. "No, John doesn't know that you and I have been seeing each other. He is concerned that I'm working too hard and not spending enough time enjoying the important things in life like fun, food, and fucking."

Alan nodded his head, he could definitely picture her gruff brother saying *those* words.

"You took care of me, Alan. You didn't have to, and even when I threw myself at you, you didn't take advantage of me. I've never met another man who'd do those things and didn't expect anything in return. I'm not sleeping with you because I feel as if I owe you something. I'm sleeping with you because I've wanted to fuck your brains out since you first walked into my office five years ago. The fact that you did all that nice shit for me beforehand, well, that just makes me want to get naked with you even more."

"God woman, that mouth," he chuckled against her lips.

"If my memory serves me, you said, 'You have the sexiest fucking mouth I've ever seen. It would look so much prettier stretched around my cock than spewing the venom you insist on spitting.' Did I get that right, Quillen?"

"Every fucking word," he growled.

"Then let us make better use of our time and my mouth," she suggested.

Her eyes never leaving his, she slid down his body until she was standing between his legs. She unbuttoned his pants and beckoned him to lift his hips up. When he complied, she removed his pants and his boxer-briefs, pausing only to remove both his shoes and socks before she slipped the garments completely from his body.

He leaned up quickly to remove his t-shirt, and in moments he was splayed before her naked, wanting, cock heavy against his abdomen, leaking in anticipation of whatever she planned for him. He wasn't concerned with what that was at this moment, all he knew was the moment she touched him, five years of secretly aching for one another was going to come to a blessed end in an explosive way.

That first lick of her tongue ran from the bottom of his sack, up the throbbing vein that ran the length of his cock, until it cupped the sensitive tip of his cockhead, made him grit his teeth in an attempt to maintain control over his body.

She swallowed him whole in one smooth motion, velvet heat, sliding down his length, making every part of his body bleed with bliss. He struggled to keep his eyes open, the tide of pleasure winding around him so strong, ready to drag him under.

The up and down slide of her mouth coupled with her cupped hand around his balls ensured he was ready to explode.

"Either I'm losing my touch, or you're just that skilled," he wheezed. "Whichever it is, if you keep this up, we're going to have to wait a few moments for the, 'me fucking you into the mattress,' portion of this movie that's rolling around in my head."

She took one last slide down on his cock and swallowed around the small portion of his crown lodged at the top of her throat.

"Fuck, woman!" he cried as her hot mouth moved up. She collapsed her cheeks and slowly moved back to the top, swirling her tongue around the crown, licking up the fat pebble of pre-cum sitting in his slit. "A.J.," he called out, halting her play. Her coy smile telling him she knew exactly what she was doing to him.

"I think we both know you're about to lose your shit because I'm just that talented."

Oh, she wants to play? Then let's. He watched her with half-lidded eyes and she stood at the side of the bed and peeled her jeans off. He was certain the seductive dips and twists of her full hips were purposely exaggerated to make him lose his fucking mind. It was working. If she didn't get her ass on this bed soon, he might be spilling his seed with his hand wrapped around his aching cock, instead of buried in her.

She made quick work of removing the few scraps of lace that

served as her underwear and then she proceeded to climb him like he was a fucking mountain and planted herself right on top of him. Her hot flesh touching his, creating painful sparks of lust where cock met cunt. If she rolled her ass just the right way, he'd slip inside with no effort at all.

Condom, his brain yelled. He gripped her hips, stopping that delicious rocking motion that was damn near hypnotizing him. He grabbed the underside of both her thighs and stood with her. Considering how petite she was, it hadn't taken much effort at all. But laying her on the bed in front of him, and stepping away from her for the moment it took to find his pants on the floor and pull a condom from his wallet felt like a Herculean task.

He climbed back on the bed and moved on top of her. He wasted no time getting straight to work. He ran his hands up the length of her body, hands stopping to worship the swell of her breasts. Large caramel nipples called to him. He fastened his lips around the pert peaks and reveled in the shiver she gave when his teeth grazed against them.

While he nipped against the tender flesh, he let his hand trail down her side onto her lower abdomen, then down to the smooth skin of her shaven pussy lips. He parted those lips with a single finger, allowing it to swirl at the mouth of her sex.

When he allowed it to sink inside, a slow moan crossed her lips while her legs fell open, making more room for him. His lips followed his fingers and soon he spread her wide while his tongue and lips pulled more of those hungry sounds from her mouth. His fingers and mouth alternating in their assault on the firm button of her clit, before long her hips were moving in rhythmic sway that kept begging for Alan to bring her to completion. He buried his face in her dripping cunt, while his fingers played with the spongy knot inside her walls. She sucked in a harsh, ragged breath, and then splintered into a sequence of quivering muscles and disjointed spasms while she grabbed onto the bedcovers and flailed beneath him.

"That's one, and we haven't been going twenty minutes yet," he crooned as he wiped his face free of her sex juices. He captured her mouth again, loving the fact that he finally learned the answer to his question. *Yes, A.J. was in fact sweet all over.* He rolled slightly to the side, and ran his hand over the bedspread until his fingers felt the small foil packet he was looking for.

He pulled away from her just long enough to open the condom and quickly sheath himself. He spread her legs a little wider and slowly slid inside her waiting warmth. He inched inside slowly, he was thick, and long, and hurting her wasn't his intention. When his balls finally rested against her ass they both groaned their satisfaction. The sensation of being balls-deep inside this woman made electric shards of light dance behind his eyes, and zip through his brain down the length of his spine.

The need to move overpowered him. He snapped his hips in a hard snap, much harder than he'd intended. He looked down to see if he'd hurt her; instead he found blissed-out features on her face. Eyes closed, mouth open, jaw slack, breath seemingly frozen.

He should have known tender wouldn't do for her, not this woman, with her sharp wit and course nature, she would want more than soft kisses and tender touches. So he gave it to her, hard, fast, deep, until she was writhing beneath him, clamoring for an anchor somewhere in the bedsheets or the headboard, until his muscles burned with fatigue.

She was on the brink again. He could see it in her dilated pupils, in the hungry breaths she took. He crushed his mouth to hers; pulling the soft flesh between his lips he applied just enough pressure to straddle the line between pleasure and pain.

"You want it," he asked as he continued to grind into her body.

Her eyes were closed, brow furrowed in hedonistic decadence. "Please," she begged. She moaned again, when his cock slid at the perfect angle, knocking against that spot, making her walls clamp down on him, a vice he didn't want to break free of.

He could feel his own climax coming. He turned them over, reversed their positions until she was seated in his lap.

"Take what you want," he commanded.

She went to work without hesitation. Her hips were moving in an impossible rhythm at an even more incredible pace.

Where the fuck did she learn how to move her hips and waist like that? There couldn't be a class for that; it had to be all natural. He paid homage to whatever deity blessed her with this ability because the truth was he'd never felt anything so wonderful sitting on his cock.

The spasms in the confines of her pussy were increasing in pace and intensity. She was riding him hard and wild. Head dipped back on her shoulders as she ground her hips into his. He secured rigid fingers around her waist and met each snap of her hips with a hard thrust of his own.

She tried to hold out, but the force of his thrusts forced her to relent. She planted her sharp nails into the flesh of his thigh, just as a scream tore through her.

"Fuck," was all he managed. It was the only word that accurately expressed the powerful surges of pleasure he felt twisting in his sack, spiraling up his spine, and blasting through the slit of his cock into the condom.

His body seized in tandem with the pulse of each spurt of his cum. He was grateful for the bed beneath him. He wasn't certain he would've been able to stop himself from crushing the woman still in the throes of her own shattering orgasm, still riding his cock, pulling every drop of cum his balls contained.

She finally collapsed and he encircled strong arms around her, catching her, protecting her. He ran delicate fingers over her back, stroking her, the petting motion calming the last of the spasms still wracking her body.

She burrowed inside of the cocoon his arms created, and warmth spread through him. He'd always known that sex between them would be a powerful experience, the last five years of foreplay in the form of fighting was proof of that. But this connection he was beginning to feel with this woman could be dangerous for him. Being this attached to someone like A.J. Tenetti could prove to be a problematic situation for him, one he wasn't so certain he wanted to find himself in.

CHAPTER 12

Alan headed straight for Kenneth's office when he walked into the building. He needed to talk to his friend about this job offer sitting in his lap. He tapped on the door then stuck his head inside of the office.

"Hey man, you got a minute?" Kenneth lifted his head and waved Alan inside.

"What's on your mind?" Kenneth answered.

"I guess there's no other way to say this, but to come out and say it. Jeovonni Tenetti offered me the COO position at Tenetti Enterprises."

Kenneth pulled his attention from the work on his desk and gave Alan his full attention. "He what?" Kenneth asked.

"I went to T.E. to bitch at A.J. for blocking a deal while you were..."

"...Laid up recovering from a bullet wound that some maniac put in my gut? Was that the phrase you were looking for?"

"Not verbatim, no, but the meaning is pretty much dead on. After she and I finished having it out I ran into her dad in the corridor. We chatted for a bit and he invited me to dinner at their place. During dinner, he offers me the COO position," Alan added. "Apparently he's been researching me, knows all about my credentials and capabilities."

"Let me tell you something about Jeovonni Tenetti. He doesn't ask anyone anything. He just does what he wants. The fact that he asked you, means he really wants you. Take the job."

"Kenneth, you just got back, I can't just abandon you. Especially not after everything you've done for me."

Kenneth shook his head. "This is business, man. This is an opportunity that you will never get again. You could dominate the global market in a major way. Change business practices for the better around the world. That's what you've always wanted."

"I know that, and I'm tempted, but I'm just concerned. You know how manipulative A.J. is when it comes to business. Working under her, working for her father, is it just going to be more of the situation I left in California?"

Kenneth moved from behind his desk and stepped in front of Alan. "Alan, you know I think your grandfather was a piece of shit for treating you the way he did, for the way he fucked over Beth. I'm also still pissed at the fact the rest of your family sat back and allowed that shit to happen. But believe me when I tell you, the Tenetti's are not your grandfather."

"You sure about that?" Alan asked. "Some of the shit I've witnessed A.J. doing makes me question the validity of your praise."

"A.J. is a master of manipulation, but she does not set out to fuck with people for her own purposes. It may seem that way, but she really does care about those around her. Not to mention, she's fiercely loyal and protective of those she loves and serves. If you take this job, you'll be working with a different breed of people than your grandfather. Jeovonni is all about ethical business practices, you can't believe in that, practice that the way he does, and not have some kind of concern for the world and its inhabitants."

Alan stirred all of this information around in his head. He was certainly interested in this proposition, he just couldn't shake this feeling that he was getting in bed with the wrong people.

A.J. dropped her briefcase at the door, making her way down the hall to the family room. Her mother was sitting on the sofa with her legs extended across its length and her tablet in her hand.

"Hi, Mamà."

"Hey, baby," Gracelyn's face blossomed with a flash of excitement.

"Where's Papà?" A.J. asked.

"Working in his office in the back. He said he needed to do something to settle himself. You know how he gets when your brother first leaves for a tour."

She bent down to place a kiss on her mother's cheek and sat down beside her.

"How are you, baby?"

There was something in the way she asked that question. The sentence may have been phrased as a question, but those words were filled with so much knowing, as if she was just waiting for A.J. to confirm information she already possessed.

"I'm fine, Mamà," A.J. answered, hoping her voice didn't sound as feeble as it felt inside. Weakness wasn't something she could afford now, not in front of Alan, and especially not in front of her family. There was just too much going on. She needed to be able to deal with the craziness surrounding her, or they'd all suffer. She couldn't be the weakest link in their chain again.

She kissed her mother's cheek again; needing more of the comfort the feel of her always offered A.J. No matter how old you were, Mamà always made it better.

She walked down the hall and knocked on the door as she opened it. "Can you spare a moment?"

Her father looked up from his laptop screen and waved her in. She stepped inside the office and made sure the door was closed behind her. Once she was seated, she jumped directly into her topic.

"I'm tired of hiding; I've decided I'm not doing it any longer. I've talked to Teague, we've settled on a course of action. We're taking the fight to Reign."

Jeovonni said nothing, simply continued to look over the top rim of his glasses. She almost laughed at the picture he made. Not because it was the least bit amusing. Her father was quiet, but like her, quiet meant deadly. She'd never thought about how much she was like him. But sitting here now, his gaze bearing down on her, she could see where she'd acquired her death stare from.

He slid the glasses off his face in one smooth motion and rested them on his desk. "Just to make certain I have all the facts you're presenting, let me recap for a moment. You, my daughter, the princess or our homeland and Teague Maher, the agent who's been charged with our protection while we rest within the borders of this country, have decided on a course of action to deal with the war lord, Reign, and that course of action somehow involves you no longer hiding from my deranged brother?"

As an officer of the court, A.J. stood before everything from Judges, to criminals, and she never once felt the slightest bit of unease. Why should she? She was talented, and skilled, and completely aware of her capabilities in the courtroom. As a CEO, she gave no concern to the people she stepped in front of in the boardroom. She owned the boardroom just as completely as she did the courtroom, but sitting here in this man's presence with his quiet strength, she fought to keep the slight shiver of anxiety rattling inside her chest camouflaged.

"Yes," she answered.

He let another few moments pass before he spoke. "Well, I'm thrilled that you and Teague have decided to handle this little problem of ours on your own, without consulting me. However, there's only one problem with it."

"What's that?" she inquired.

"I won't allow it," he answered with finality.

She opened her mouth, but he stopped her with one wave of his hand.

"I am your sovereign, not the other way around. You don't get to make decisions like this without consulting me."

"Papà."

"Ilaria!" he bellowed, the sound shaking her from the inside out. It'd been so long since she'd heard the sound of her given name. Even the sound of it drenched in her father's anger was so sweet she almost forgot the reason for his use of it.

"I have sacrificed too much to protect this family; I will not have you putting yourself in danger."

"I can't live like this any longer."

"Why?"

Her courtroom persona threatened to take over, if she stumbled now she'd never get him to understand. An exhausted tuft of air left her mouth. How could she really expect the king to understand when she could barely wrap her mind around it herself.

He was her king, he did make the rules, and she was out of line for going behind his back and going to Teague without his knowledge. Listing the ways in which she'd crossed the line did nothing for her confidence. But then she remembered he was her father. Maybe that was who she should be appealing to, not her king.

"I've been seeing someone, Papà, someone very important to me."

She watched the edges of the firm angles of his face relax in front of her. "Who?"

"Alan Quillen."

"How long has this been going on?" he asked.

"If I'm honest, this began five years ago when he stepped into my office for the first time. But neither of us acted on the attraction until that day you invited him to dinner with the family.," she answered.

"He treats you well?"

"He does."

"Well, the fact that you were willing to tell me about him tells me you're serious about him."

"I do have strong feelings for him, but I don't know that they can truly go anywhere. How can I build a future with him, when I can't tell him the truth of who I am? Papà, please, a man like Alan will never accept the lies and deception. Please, I need this to be over, need to find normalcy in my life. I—I don't want to lose him."

Her father stood up, walking around to where she sat, and pulled her to her feet. There was so much concern swimming in his green eyes. He gently passed his thumb across her cheek. It wasn't until he pulled his hand away that she realized she was crying.

When had that happened, when had Alan Quillen become so important that the thought of losing him caused her tears? Yes, she'd known from the first night he'd found her on the bridge that she'd be irrevocably tied to him, but nothing mattered so much to her that she would cry in front of someone else. Except here she was, standing in front of her father as he ran comforting hands up and down her arms, allowing tears to slide down her face as the thought of losing this very special man shook through her.

"*Mia figlia*," he whispered as his lips kissed her forehead. "We will figure out another way, *Cara*. I can't let you do this. As your father, as your king, I cannot let you do this."

He returned to his chair behind his desk, sat down, and slid his glasses back on his face, indicating the conversation was over. She gave a slight nod of her head in deference to her father and walked out of the room closing the door behind her.

Standing there, her heart sank as she asked herself one question. *Is it better to defy your king or your father?*

CHAPTER 13

A.J. fumbled with two large grocery bags in one hand and her key ring in the other. She turned the key ring this way and that with one hand until the key she was looking for appeared. The key was instantly recognizable to her. Alan left it next to her phone with a note one morning with the words, "So you don't have to keep waking my ass up when you're sneaking in and out of here at all ungodly hours of the day and night."

She'd laughed at the note then, but later thought there might be more to the key than convenience.

Things were moving fast with Alan. It was as if after five years of foreplay, they just bypassed the normal fundamental parts of dating, and skipped right to the part where they just couldn't get enough of being in each other's presence.

She slipped the key in the door, and let herself inside. "Alan," she called, waiting for an answer, but receiving none. She locked the door behind her, and sat the groceries on the counter. She walked to the back of the apartment and stripped in his bedroom. She took a quick shower, then found one of Alan's old T-shirts to put on.

She smoothed the soft cotton material over her frame and shivered with excitement. Usually one single look at her in one of his A-line t-shirts and he couldn't stop himself from touching her. That's exactly the response she was going for tonight.

She quickly set about preparing their meal and setting the mood. She lit candles and placed them in the middle of his coffee table. She opened a bottle of his favorite wine, and placed it on the table as well.

Soon place settings were arranged, and the timer on the oven was dinging. She plated up the roasted Cornish hens, the garlic potatoes, and the steamed asparagus in two plates and rested them on the table.

She'd just finished dimming the lights and poured the second of two glasses of wine when she heard his key turning the lock.

"Damn it smells good in here." He moaned as he walked into the apartment. He locked the door, and turned around. She noticed the moment he laid eyes on her. His blue eyes brightened and an easy smile spread across his face.

"What's all this?" he asked as he stepped closer into the living room, and took the wineglass she held out to him.

"It's my way of telling you I missed you. We've both been working a great deal, time has been fleeting. I wanted you to know I was thinking about you."

"So is it safe to assume that every time you miss me I'm going to find you waiting for me at home in nothing but my undershirt with dinner and a glass of wine waiting for me?" He smiled again and raised the glass of wine to his lips and took a sip. "Mmm, and good wine too. You really outdid yourself tonight, Ms. Tenetti."

"I outdo myself every time, Mr. Quillen. Don't forget that."

"You do indeed," he answered. He took a seat on his sofa, settled his glass of wine on the side table, and pulled her onto his lap. He ran long fingers up her thigh, up the curve of her ass, up the curve of her back, and into the bound tresses of her hair. He removed the pin restraining the strands and watched the long strands spring free.

She'd straightened today. A style she didn't often wear just because it took too much effort to go from curly to straight, but today she'd woken with a desire to wear a bone-sleeked bun.

She loved how he loved her hair, he was always running his fingers through it, always worshiping it, always making her feel like it was a crown that adorned her head. She languished in the way his fingertips lightly scrapped her scalp when she felt his lips touch that stretch of skin just under her earlobe.

"This is different," he uttered.

"Different good, different bad?" she asked.

"I don't know that it's either, only that I love your hair. Doesn't really matter how you choose to wear it, as long as I get to bury my fingers in it, I'm happy."

She answered him with a smile and a nod. He pulled her to him for a quick kiss before raising his eyes to hers. "I would love nothing more than to let things move along just as they are. But I'm starving, and that food smells amazing. Feed me, baby."

And there it was, his usual goofiness that kept her exercising whichever muscles were responsible for rolling her eyes. Somehow, no matter how goofy he was being, she never seemed to mind it. If she were being completely honest, she actually liked it. But he didn't need to know that.

She climbed off of his lap and settled next to him on the couch while he stretched his legs out and his arms across the back of the sofa. She pulled a cloth napkin onto his lap, then handed him his plate, followed by his cutlery.

They ate in silence, only low murmurs breaking the silence throughout the meal. When they were done, she cleared away their dishes, and stacked them in the dishwasher. When she was done she felt a wall of hard flesh behind her.

"You need help?" he asked.

"Loading a dishwasher? No, not really." She turned around and he pressed her against the sink, his arms surrounding her on both sides.

"You are so short," he chuckled. "It really is amazing how tiny you are in your bare feet. You're what, just barely five feet?"

"No, I'm actually about five-six, it's just that freakishly tall men such as yourself think everyone else is little. Size is relative."

Before she began to process what he was doing, he'd hoisted her up so they were chest to chest. She wrapped her legs around his waist to keep her balance, as his large palms covered both hemispheres of her ass. He walked her into his bedroom and eased her down onto the bed. The sheets were cool against her skin, and a vast contrast to the fire she felt burning within.

He went to roll off of her, but she clasped her legs around him tighter. She needed him close, loved the feel of him pressed against her. His body always made her feel safe. Safety was something she ached for, but in her experiences, it was an illusion, something that was here one moment, and gone the next. The weight of him, the way his body pressed tenderly into hers made her feel protected, sheltered from whatever harm awaited her in the real world.

"Baby, I need to get a condom, or all this isn't really going anywhere tonight."

She nodded her head, but when he tried to move again she closed her arms and legs around him tighter than before.

Concern filled his eyes, they moved over her face, silently asking if something was wrong. When she didn't answer he leaned down and kissed her gently, reassuring her that he was there, that he was there for her. He lifted her again, walking them as one body to the opposite side of the bed. He laid her back down again, covering her with his body again, and reached into the drawer of his nightstand for a condom.

"Lexie, you okay?"

She smiled at the sound of his nickname for her. It was something she'd never experienced before. In most situations she was either being addressed by her full name or her surname. Always so formal and business like. But Lexie, that name always made her feel vibrant and colorful, like she was alive and thriving whenever he spoke it, breathed life into it.

She ran a finger over his lips, loving the feel of them against her skin. "You're an amazing man, Alan. You have no idea how I admire that."

He pressed a gentle kiss to her fingers. "Good. Hopefully that admiration will get you to consider stepping into the light with me."

There it was again, that one crack in their otherwise smooth relationship. This wasn't the first time Alan mentioned wanting more between them than the stolen moments they shared in his apartment.

"I'm not hiding you, Alan."

"It really does feel that way. You haven't told anyone about us."

"I told my father, and immediately after that I told my mother. John and Maxine don't know, but my parents do."

He wasn't expecting that. The widening of his crystal blue eyes, the slight slackness to his jaw expressed his thoughts clearly.

"Then why are we always shut up in my place if you aren't hiding me?" he asked carefully.

"I'm just not ready for that, for the expectation that will follow once we announce this. We lose this, the ability to just be us, to just connect the way we do without interference from anyone else. I'm just not ready to share you with everyone, Alan."

She could feel his frustration pulling his body tight. There was so much he didn't understand about her world, so much she couldn't explain. But she knew she needed to find some way to tell him the truth, without actually telling him her truth. He deserved that much at least.

"It's not about what others think, Alan. You should know me well enough by now to realize I don't give a fuck about what other people think of me." She ran her fingers through his tapered blond strands and smiled. Everything about this man was bright, sunny, life affirming. Such a stark contrast to what she was, both inside and out.

"Life has taught me that when you have something good, something that you've always wanted, but never thought you'd have, that you should hide it from the world. Let's just say in my experience, when people see you with something good, they do everything in their power to take it from you."

She closed her eyes and saw the flashes of moments she'd fought too hard to forget over the years. Angry snarling faces bearing down on her, the piercing sounds of fear she made each time another blow rained down on her. She felt the cold spilling inside her again, the numbness that began to spread after what felt like an endless amount of time being bludgeoned over and over again. Her body too limp, too broken to even respond with the slightest flinching motion to attempt to protect herself.

She felt the heat of her tears slide down her face and felt the gentle press of his finger against her skin as he chased it.

"Lexie, what's wrong? What's going on?"

The sound of his voice lulled her out of her past, and pulled her gaze to his. His brow furrowed, his eyes darting back and forth looking for answers.

"Lexie—"

"He said no one would ever want me. Said no one else would ever willingly love me. Said I should have known from the moment he asked me out that it was all a rouse."

"Who?" he asked.

"David..." she licked dry lips before she continued. "Upton. A man I met and dated my first year in law school. I was young and sheltered. I had no experience with men. He was my first taste of love. Or at least I thought he was until I walked into his home and found him having sex with someone else."

"Lexie, guys that young, they think with their dicks. Don't dwell on a prick like that."

There he went again, setting out to take care of her. The novelty of that feeling, of being catered to and worried about, it would never grow old.

She found his hand on the bed and linked her fingers with his. The lattice work of their digits was unbreakable as long as neither of them let go. She opened her eyes and saw such genuine concern filling his gaze. She blinked the tears back and opened her mouth. She attempted to correct him and her words caught in her throat. If she allowed these words to escape, once he knew the details...she couldn't. Once again, her truth would only destroy what she wanted.

"Sharing my world with people has always brought hardship, for me, for them, it just never ends well. I always lose when I attempt to bring what's meaningful in my life into the world."

She could see understanding begin to knit together in the lines of his furrowed brow. "You're afraid of losing me?"

"Every beautiful thing I've ever possessed in my life has been destroyed the moment I took it into the light. The moment I pulled it from my hidden treasure space to show someone else, to share with the world, it's been broken, sullied, destroyed. You're the most beautiful thing I've ever been granted. I'm just not ready to risk losing you yet by sharing you with the rest of the world."

He leaned down, placing a long and languid kiss on her lips. It wasn't about passion, but reassurance, a reminder that it was something to always expect, to be comfortable with.

He tightened his grip on their woven fingers. "Lexie, why are you so worried?"

Because I don't want you to die, because the same man that sent David to kill me will send someone to kill you to get to me. "Please, Alan, I just need a little bit longer. Please, I just need this to remain between us. Just us."

He kissed their linked hands, the warmth of his kiss chasing the remnants of her memories away. "I'm not going anywhere. As long as you want me, I'm here."

What she wouldn't give for that to be the truth. But like always, she knew the moment her real life intruded upon the one she was building with Alan, he was going to walk away. He would have no other choice, because she would have no other choice. Her first and only choice was always going to be survival, and she couldn't toss that aside, not even for him, no matter how she felt about him, no matter how he made her feel.

She snaked her hands up the firm ridges of his back, pulling him closer to her, needing to feel more of that reassuring weight covering her, keeping her safe from the outside world. He pulled her hands from his body, reached between them, and unbuttoned his slacks. He placed the opened condom in her hand as he pulled back the flaps and reached inside to pull out his rigid cock.

He took her hand, wrapped it around the pulsing heat of his flesh and pushed it downward for a slow stroke. By the time her hand was moving back up his length, he'd removed his hand and let her take control.

She smoothed her thumb over the tip, feeling the glistening drop of pre-cum spread over the stretched cap.

One of the things she loved about their sex was the foreplay, Alan was a man that believed in foreplay, believed in getting her off as many times as possible before he ever joined his body with hers, but tonight she didn't want foreplay. She just wanted to be joined with him, to be a part of him, if only for this passing moment in both their lives.

She rolled the condom on him, and guided his cock to the aching folds of her flesh. She pulled him down into a kiss as she positioned him just at her entrance. When he was positioned just right, she slid determined hands to his ass cheeks and pulled him as she raised eager hips. The result was a delicious glide that buried him fully sheathed inside her trembling walls. The maneuver was moan-inducing, on both their parts.

He let her hold him there for another moment before he took control of the situation. Placing a firm hand on the back of her knee, he pressed it to her chest, splitting her to make room for him. He rolled his hips in a slow and sensual move that seem to scrape her tingling flesh in all the right places. Electric sparks danced behind closed eyes with every slide of his cock inside her. His movements still painfully slow, but so intense. She was already on the brink of coming, already at the precipice.

He changed his angle slightly, rubbing over that electric spot inside of her, her body convulsed, edging her closer to completion. He was so in tune with her body, he always seemed to know what would bring her crashing over that pleasurable cliff. He kept up the slow pace, hitting that spot directly, with more determination. Once, twice more, and she was spilling over that ledge into a soul-deep orgasm that stopped her mid breath, locking all of her muscles in one giant spasm.

"That's it, Lexie, let it go," he whispered in her ear, still sliding so tenderly in and out of her. Holding her so carefully, as her body broke apart underneath him.

She held onto him as he rode her through the longest and most intense orgasm she'd ever experienced. He was her anchor, if she let go of him she knew she would drown, the undercurrents of the spasms too powerful to stay afloat on her own. She kept holding him until she felt the rhythm of his strokes stutter into his own climax.

When they finished, he moved aside and removed the used condom. He tied it off and dropped it into his bedside trashcan. He turned back to her and smiled. "That was fantastic, if we could manage to take my clothes off prior to the main event, that would just be like whipped cream on my dessert."

She mustered up just enough energy to laugh. "Stop being so sexy and I wouldn't have to destroy your clothing just to get at what I want."

"Sorry, my sexy is natural. You're just gonna have to deal."

She rolled her eyes again; this man was walking sex, but still managed to be so corny at the same time. Strangely, it still didn't piss her off as much as it should. Corny had become her new thing.

CHAPTER 14

A.J. walked into her office, heading directly for her desk. Her father was arriving shortly for a meeting with her and she needed to be prepared. Her father might not run the day-to-day operations of T.E., but monthly he scheduled time with her to keep him abreast of all the goings on in the company. He was her father, but he was a task master and he didn't allow her to get away with shit just because they were related. If she wasn't doing her job, he'd toss her ass, and replace her just like any other non-related employee.

When she walked in the office she found a small black chest with a note taped to the top. She pulled the note off, a metal engraving of a heart-shaped heraldic coat of arms with two great elephants protecting the crowned female resting in the center of the heart. A ribbon on the bottom read the Latin words, *"Verbo et Factis."*

She smiled at it, ran her fingers over it gingerly. The engraved image and words told her who the item was from, but she went on to read the folded note anyway.

"So proud of the work you're doing. You serve by word and deed."

She put the note down and lifted her eyes as the giver of her little surprise walked into her office.

"Grazie, Papà," she beamed.

Jeovonni Tenetti turned to close the door. "Not that I mind my daughter greeting me with 'thank yous,' but it would be great to know what I'm being thanked for."

"Papà, the gift is beautiful."

"Gift?"

"I know it was you, Papà, the jewelry box is beautiful." She picked it up and ran gentle fingers over it.

"Jewelry box? A.J., I—don't," he exclaimed as she lifted the lid to the box. A cloud exploded in her face covering her in a white substance. She coughed, trying to clear her airway of whatever was floating around her. Soon her lungs burned and her breath was coming in short painful gasps.

She heard her father screaming at her secretary to get help. He was running toward her, but she held up a hand to halt him. She didn't want him breathing in whatever this was impeding her breath. If this substance killed her, she couldn't let it kill him too. One of them was needed to live. She crawled out of the cloud that lingered around her desk and made it as far as her door, where she felt her body being pulled out of the office into the hall.

Her father turned her over onto her side as she continued to cough adding a minimal amount of relief to her agony. She turned her head to him, needing to memorize his features. They were marred in concern and angst, but beneath the fear and worry was his love. The one good constant throughout her life, it was the one thing she'd always depended on. If this was the last thing she would see, she would focus on nothing else except the father who showered her with love since before he held her in his arms for the first time.

Soon darkness came, she fought it, gave everything she could to keep her eyes opened, and her father's face in view. But soon, the darkness won out, and inch by inch the darkness bled in from the sides until there was only a small tunnel of light left. And then it was gone.

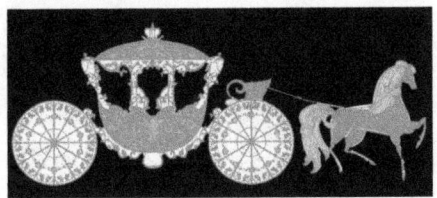

A repetitive beep was the first thing she noticed. It was constant in tone and frequency. The same sound over and over again. Wherever she was there was no light. She tried to open her eyes, but they were so heavy.

"*Cara? Sei sveglio?*"

Her father's voice penetrated the darkness. She swallowed, her dry airway protesting the idea of her talking. She squeezed her eyelids, and then willed them to open. They peeled apart slowly, allowing at first only a sliver of light.

"Pa-pà," the word so small, but taking so much effort to produce. "What happened?"

A shocking slip of red hair entered her field of vision. "Teague?" she said as the face came into focus.

"Yeah, it's me," he said, a rare smile coloring his usually stiff features. Then he changed the direction of the conversation when he stated, "Apparently Reign sent you a gift this morning."

"He knows who I am, where to find me, where to find us?"

He nodded his head. "I'm afraid so, A.J., but all isn't lost. My team has been able to infiltrate the part of his organization that's here in the states. We're working on this."

She saw his statement for what it was, a non-promise. Teague Maher was an FBI agent that was assigned with the task of keeping her family safe while they lived in this country. The fact that her pursuer was able to get this close to her said one thing, Teague couldn't promise her safety. He'd try, but Reign had just proven that Teague's attempt just wasn't good enough.

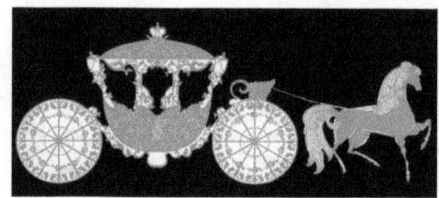

*A*lan looked at his phone again. He'd been staring at it every few moments for the last few days. He hadn't spoken to A.J. in nearly a week. They didn't speak every day, but at least every other day one of them contacted the other. His skin felt itchy with worry, something wasn't right and he needed to find out what it was.

Not really wanting to raise an alarm, but afraid that something tragic might have happened to her, Alan scanned through his contacts until he found the number he was looking for.

"John?"

"Hey, Alan," John responded. "What's up?"

Alan relayed his worries about A.J., apologized for interrupting John on his tour, but pleaded with John to confirm that A.J. was indeed away on business. When John became quiet, the pause between question and answer being too pronounced, Alan knew something was wrong.

"What's going on, John?"

"Alan, I know you and my sister are seeing each other."

"John—"

"Alan, don't try to deny it. Remember when we all took a soak in my hot tub? Max found A.J.'s bikini top wedge precariously between the bed and the headboard when she went to clean up after you left."

They were busted. He took a deep breath and forged ahead. "Okay, you found us out. What's that have to do with what's going on with your sister, John?"

"My sister is going to kill me for telling you this, but I know she's too proud to talk to you about this. Someone decided to play a prank on my sister. They left a jewelry box on her desk and made it seem like it was from our father. When she opened it, a powder capsule exploded and she breathed its contents in. The powder turned out to be nothing, and it didn't cause any permanent damage, but she wound up having some sort of breathing difficulty because of it. She was forced to stay in the hospital for a few days behind it."

Alan tightened his fingers around the steering wheel as fear tore through him. "Where is she now, is she all right?"

"She's home with my parents. She's fine from what they tell me, but I'm not there, and I'm afraid my family may be minimizing her condition because they don't want to worry me while I'm on tour. I'll be home for a few hours the day of the charity event at Mac's Place. I'm literally dropping in for the event and leaving right after in order to stay on track with my tour dates. Can you check on her for me, make certain everything is cool and let me know. Otherwise, I'm gonna have to cancel tour dates to come check on her."

Alan could hear the worry in John's voice for his sister. Hell it matched his own. "No worries, I'll take care of it and get back to you. She's supposed to be at the center today, I'll catch up with her there. If she's not there, I'll head straight for your parents' place."

"Thanks man," John said, and he ended the call.

Alan pulled his phone from his ear and threw it into the passenger seat.

"That fucking woman!" he exclaimed loud enough to draw strange looks from the woman loading groceries in the backseat of the car next to him. Without a second glance, Alan put his car in reverse and headed for Mac's Place.

*A*lan waited in his car, tapping the wheel, the console, whatever would keep him from charging inside of that community center and grabbing A.J. by her shoulders in front of a crowd of witnesses.

He saw a few kids of varying ages walk out in small groups. He figured they must be the group A.J. came to work with.

When he pulled up into the parking lot he'd seen A.J.'s tiny red car there. He parked right beside it, leaving her no chance to escape when she finally exited the building.

Soon he watched her open the door and head toward her car. He was angry; at least he had been the entire time he'd been stewing in his car, thinking about all the things he wanted to scream at A.J. once he got the chance. But seeing her, knowing she'd spent several days sick enough to be kept in a hospital turned his fear into concern quickly. She looked all right. There was nothing amiss about her appearance that should cause him concern. There was nothing that said, "I'm sick, I'm weak, I'm fragile," about her. Her spine was still ramrod straight with confidence. Although dressed in jeans and a fitted ladies tee, those damn heels she always wore made her look like she'd just stepped out of a designer fashion store. Her hair was pulled back in a severe bun and her face was artfully covered in pristinely applied makeup.

This was his A.J., always ready for the world, never to be seen looking amiss. She almost had him fooled until he caught sight of her eyes. Were there bags or shadows? No, but the usual bright flame of her amber-colored eyes was dimmed to an almost dull brown. When he saw them, he moved without thought, stepping out of his car and directly into her path.

"What the hell are you doing here, Alan?"

"I could ask you the same. Aren't you supposed to be in Europe dealing with some sort of business crisis?"

She slipped a large pair of sunglasses on her face before facing him again. "I did, I just flew back last night."

He snatched the glasses off of her face and threw them against the side of the nearby building. They cracked upon impact.

"Do you know how much those sunglasses cost?" she screamed.

"I could give a fuck," he answered. "If you're going to lie to me, at least have the decency to look me in the eye when you do it."

She was busted and he was pissed. She held her hand palm side up in the air. "Alan, what's going on here? Why are you so angry?"

"Is everything okay here, Ms. Tenetti?"

A.J. looked around a saw a familiar face standing at the gate of the parking lot. Carla greeted A.J. with a terse stare, her usual high-energy smile pulled into a sharp flat line across her face.

Carla moved cautiously toward the spot where A.J. and Alan were standing. Carla watched Alan carefully before landing sympathetic eyes on A.J.

"You okay, Ms. Tenetti?" Carla asked while she stared at Alan with an exaggerated up and down motion of her head. "He ain't botherin' you, is he?"

Shaking his head with bright eyes and an open mouth, his particular version of a, "what the fuck," face, Alan folded his arms across his chest. "Who are you?" he asked.

"Na, who the hell is you?" Carla asked in return.

It was almost amusing. Carla was probably an inch or two shorter than A.J., yet she was pushing up in Alan's face, a man who towered over both of them, as if she was ready to tumble in the streets.

A.J. placed a gentling hand on Carla's arm. "It's okay, Carla. This is a good friend of mine, we were just having a heated debate. Nothing to be worried about."

"He ain't like Nico, right? You know what happened when Nico and me got into heated debates."

A.J. shook her head. She knew all too well what Carla was talking about. She'd met Carla after one such debate. The woman's eye was purple and swollen, and her lip didn't appear much better. That last encounter with Nico had landed Carla in the hospital with multiple contusions on her body.

"Carla, I promise you, nothing like that is going on. Alan and I really were just having a heated discussion."

Carla gave Alan one more cautionary look and then nodded her head. "I'mma be next door at the counseling center if you need me, Ms. Tenetti." She walked away, paying several glance back over her shoulder as she exited the parking lot and made her way into the counseling center.

"What the hell was that about?" Alan asked her.

"Nothing I can really get into. Carla is a client of mine."

Alan stuck his thumb behind him in Carla's direction. "You're really trying to tell me that woman can afford your retainer?"

"Quillen, please. You can't even afford my retainer. I do some *pro bono* work at a women's shelter," she answered. "I've had occasion to help some of the women out that I've come across in my service there."

Alan opened his mouth to say something then shook his head. "You know what, forget it. Back to the important shit," he ground out through his teeth. "You disappear on me for a fucking week. No calls, nothing, except some bullshit line your secretary is running and you want to know why I'm mad? I'm mad because I know you've been laid up in a damn hospital for the last week, and I can't figure out for the life of me why you would keep something like that from me."

She swallowed carefully. "How did you—"

"Know? I knew because your brother didn't believe the bullshit you were feeding him either and asked me if I would check on you and report back to him."

She leaned back against her car as she digested his words. "I don't think I really want to talk about this right now, Alan."

"I don't really care what you want to do; I'm telling you I'm not putting up with your bullshit anymore. You either come clean right now about all of this shit, or I'm done, A.J."

She slid a practiced hand across the top of her head. "My brother had no right to give you that information, Alan. It was my business, not his, so back the hell off."

"It was something I shouldn't have had to find out from him," he barked. "I'm not fucking him, A.J., it should have come from you!"

"Why would he have even discuss this with you? As far as he knows we work together occasionally for Kenneth. Why would he trust someone he barely knows with this kind of information?"

"Probably because his wife found your bikini top wedged in the headboard when she was cleaning. They've known about us since John left for the tour."

"Bullshit," she exclaimed. "I swept that carriage house like a fucking pro. No way was any evidence of you and I sexing left behind. If my brother told you that bullshit, it was because he was guessing, and you just clued him in."

"Big Willie, bring your ass on if you don't want to get left," they each heard Heart's voice call out from a distance. They stepped apart, and each attempted to put on their publicly calm faces.

Heart busted out of the door and acknowledged both of them "Counselor?" Heart addressed A.J. first. "You're still here?"

"Yes, Alan needed to drop off some contracts for me from Searlington Realty."

"So he came all the way over here instead of seeing you at the job tomorrow?"

Alan ran a hand through his blond locks and scratched his scalp. "It couldn't wait until tomorrow. You know we're always about making your man money."

Heart let her eyes pass back and forth between the two of them. Big Willie ambled not long after her and met up with the gathering crowd. He exchanged salutations with A.J. and Alan and motioned for Heart to head to her car.

"Bring ya' ass, MacKenzie," the older man grumbled. Heart waved a hand at them both and hopped in the car with Willie. A few moments later and they were gone.

A.J. felt Alan returned his gaze to her as he stepped in her personal space. "You have no fucking idea how worried I was all this week, how scared I was that something happened to your ass. I was afraid that once again something terrible happened to the woman I loved and I wasn't there to protect her!"

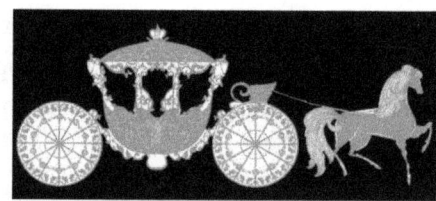

A.J. moved closer to Alan. His chest was still heaving with anger, there was so much pain swimming in his blue eyes. She stepped carefully toward him, slowly closing the distance between them before she placed a gentle hand on his chest. She drew slow, soft circles over his skin, hoping to calm the raging monster that was controlling him.

"Alan, I'm sorry. I didn't know...I never thought this would affect you so much. I was trying to prevent you from worrying. Nothing happened; I just came in contact with something that caused some weird reactive airway response in my lungs. The doctors kept me on bronchodilators and steroids for a few days and then sent me home. I'm fine. I promise you, if I'd thought for a second this would bring back memories of what happened to Beth, I would have called. I thought the message I gave Carole would have been enough to keep you from worrying."

She felt the press of strong arms around her as he pulled her tightly to his chest. Her ear pressed just over his heart, she could hear its rapid drumbeat.

She circled her arms around his waist and the simple motion seemed to calm him enough that he was able to finally speak again."My reaction might have been because of Beth, but my worry, my concern, that was all because of how I feel about you."

She leaned back to look up at him. "So when you said, 'the woman you love,' you were talking about me?"

She shivered as he smoothed a thumb over the apple of her cheek and lifted a weary smile on his tired features. Something inside her tightened at the sight of that smile. She knew she was the cause of it. One moment sheappeared to be driving him insane and the next she could swear she was twisting him up in knots. She curved her lips into a lopsided grin, , that coy, alluring smile, the one that made him want to give her everything she could want, the one she knew quite simply made him melt.

"Am I right? Were you talking about me?" she asked.

"Yes," he answered. All of the fire and bluster pouring out of his mouth was replaced by a reverant whisper. "I was talking about you, A.J., I'm in love with you. I have been for a while, I was just afraid that you were too skittish to deal with it."

She laughed. He knew her well. If he'd told her this under any other circumstances, she'd have run as fast as she could in the opposite direction. Hell, part of her was still looking for an escape plan.

Before she could fully form one she made the mistake of looking up into those concerned blue eyes of his and instead of running, she was standing there listening to him say, "I know this was all supposed to be fun, but you have to realize it's turned into more. At least it has for me. This is more than a fling for me, A.J. I want more, I want exclusivity. When I thought something happened to you…I just don't want to be the person that no one knows to call when something is wrong with you ever again."

She opened her mouth to respond, but he stopped her and continued.

"I don't need dying declarations from you to know you care about me. I just need to know I'm not in this thing by myself, that you want the same things I do. I need to know you're not keeping me out."

"Alan, I don't know if even a man with the saint-like qualities you possess could deal with me and all my bullshit," she muttered. It was true, Alan wanted her, but he didn't' really know who she was. He didn't know the truth of who she was behind the façade she kept carefully in place every day.

"I can deal with anything you can throw at me, except for this manipulation bullshit you fall back on when shit goes crazy. I really can't deal with the walls you put up when you're afraid. When you're afraid, that's the time for you to lean on me, I promise, I can take it. You don't have to be afraid to lean on me."

There was so much hurt, and fear behind his eyes, and she'd put it there. She'd done her best to protect him, but instead she'd just caused him more pain. She stepped back into his embrace and held him with all the strength her arms could generate.

"I promise I'll never make you worry again, Alan." It was a lie; she'd known it was a lie before it crossed her lips. But sometimes, sometimes the truth did more harm than good, and in those situations, whatever hurt less was the right choice.

"I know you won't," he answered. "You're brother told me all this shit happened because someone thought it would be funny to play a sick joke on you. I can't have shit like this happening to you. I need to protect you."

"Protect me? You can't be with me every day. There's no way you can be with me every second of the day to prevent something like this from happening."

"Yes I can, especially now," he answered.

"What do you mean?" she asked.

"I took your father up on his job offer. In another week, I'll be working right beside you as your new COO."

CHAPTER 15

A.J. looked at the pile of props left over for the kids' performance and knew she was screwed.

"No way is this fitting in my baby." She looked around the auditorium at the dispersing crowd and spotted Kenneth. She made her way over to him and tapped him on his arm.

"Hey Kenneth, you have a minute?"

He nodded and gave her his attention.

"I need to borrow your truck tonight."

"The fuck you say, nobody drives my baby but me."

"Come on, Kenneth, it's for a good cause. The person who was supposed to take this stuff back left to deal with an emergency. I need to clear this stuff out before Willie has my ass, you know how he is."

Kenneth squinted his eyes, whether in disbelief or annoyance, she wasn't quite certain, maybe it was a mix of both.

"AJ, can't your brother take you?"

"No, John left," she answered. "He has to get back to his tour. He only dropped by to do this favor for the kids."

He looked around the room for a moment and said, "Let me check with Heart first. We came in separate cars. She may need me to take the baby home if she has to stay behind and finish up some administrative things."

A few moments later, Kenneth came back to her with his keys in hand. "Not a fucking scratch, Tenetti, or your ass is mine."

She nodded her head and gave him her keys in return. She wrangled some of the older kids and Alan to help her pack Kenneth's large cargo area. When they were done, she and Alan slipped into the truck and she made her way out of the parking lot and onto the street.

Aside from veering through weekend traffic on Atlantic Avenue, they made quick work of delivering the items to the prop company and headed for Alan's apartment in Williamsburg. Tired and more than ready to crash, she climbed onto the couch and stretched out lengthwise on it.

"So I guess I'm not supposed to sit down next to you?"

She managed to sit up just enough that he was able to sit down next to her. As soon as he was comfortable, she laid back down, resting her head and shoulders across his lap.

"I'm such a sucker," he whispered.

"You were the one who wanted to sit down next to me," she laughed. The sound of her cellphone interrupted the moment. She sat up and reached for her purse perched on top of the coffee table.

She saw an unknown, but familiar number flash across the screen. "Hello?"

"A.J., this is Kenneth. I'm at the seventy-fourth precinct. Three black SUV's just chased me down from the Belt Parkway to the Cross Island."

"Are you alright?"

"Yes, Heart and her officers were able to intervene. The police are about to question me and I'd really appreciate it if you'd come down."

"On my way." She stepped over Alan and walked into his bedroom. She headed for the closet. She kept extra clothing at his place, and found a quick blouse, skirt, and shoe combination that would work for the occasion.

"What happened?" Alan asked as he entered the bedroom.

"That was a client; I have to meet him at the precinct."

"You still take on criminal cases?" he asked.

"Sometimes, on occasion, if only to keep my experience current," she answered as she tucked her blouse in her skirt.

"Want me to come with?" he asked.

"No," she quickly shook her head, "I don't know how long this could take. Just relax; I'll come back when I'm done."

She went to rush past him, but he snaked out a hand and wrapped it around her waist. "Be careful out there," he said, gifting her with a warm kiss that promised so much more if time permitted. "I love you, Lexie."

Every time he said those words, warmth spread through her. Those words should make her scared, should have sent her running in the opposite direction, but they didn't. Probably because she felt the same, a fact she'd been remiss in making him aware of. She was going to fix that tonight. As soon as she dealt with this situation with Kenneth, she was going to run back here and tell Alan everything, all the things she'd been so desperate to keep secret. Of all the things she needed to protect, Alan's place in her life was it. Tonight, tonight she would make things right so they could move forward without anything holding them back.

"Keep my side of the bed warm for me," she said as made her way out the door. Within moments she was in Kenneth's truck heading back to the other side of Brooklyn.

Once inside, she was taken immediately to Kenneth. She hadn't realized how worried she was about him until she released the breath caught in her throat. He looked fine, looked as if he'd suffered no harm, save for the anxiety he seemed to be wearing like a coat.

Her stomach sank as she listened to the details. Three cars followed Kenneth in her car after he'd left the community center tonight. Those men chased him down on a parkway and shot at the vehicle he was driving. At her car, they'd shot at her car, those bullets were meant for her.

She excused herself when Kenneth was finished giving his statement. She needed to call Teague; he needed to know what was going on.

"He came for me again," she whispered. "Kenneth was driving my car, and three goons tried to kill him on the Belt Parkway."

"I know, I was there," he answered. "I'm on my way to the precinct now."

"Enough, Teague. We have to tell Heart. He could have died, again. This time I know for certain the target was me. I know this is Reign's work. I have to say something."

"You keep your mouth shut, A.J. I am on my way, and I will handle it."

He disconnected the call. She was standing in the middle of a precinct, surrounded by officers, and yet she knew there was no safety here. Her world was on the verge of exploding, and there was nothing any of these officers could do to stop it.

CHAPTER 16

"Are we completely certain that Reign is after Kenneth?" A.J. felt the words leap out of Heart's mouth and smack her in the middle of her chest. "I have an alternate theory; I don't think they were after Kenneth at all." Heart finished, her face turned to AJ's, she slid her hands to her thighs and bent down so that she and A.J. were at eye level. "I think they were after you."

A.J. fought against every nerve and muscle in her body. She could feel the tremors attempting to break through her protective wall. They came from the bottom of her soul, trying to make their way to the outside where the inhabitants of Heart Searlington's office could see them.

She stiffened her spine, reciting in her head the words she'd been taught as a child, the words that were meant to remind herself and others the power that came with her heritage.

I am the crown Princess Ilaria Noemi Casa di Barca, heir to the throne of Azuria. I bow before no one but God and my king. Regnaba verbo et factis, I rule by word and deed.

It was a litany, something that gained strength over the ages, whose power grew more infinite with each utterance. She was second in line to the throne of her kingdom. If her words did not evoke strength in her, then what of her people?

Feeling some of her control trickle through her vessels she returned her eyes to Kenneth Searlington. The man who offered her family his friendship, and in return they'd offered him betrayal. It hurt to look at him, his bright blue eyes sullied with just enough anger to cover up the pain.

She wanted to make this right with him, but the truth was there was no way to make this right. How do you fix it when your family's demons almost cost a man his life? How do you make him understand that you had no other choice, that the last thing you wanted to do was bring harm to him? But seeing him like this, knowing what she'd done to make this happen, she knew there was no way to explain her actions.

"How?" he croaked, licking his lips in an effort to moisten their suddenly dry skin. "How are the Tenettis involved, A.J.? Why would someone want to kill them?"

A.J. sat fixed to the chair with her shoulders back, Teague's command to say nothing still ringing in her ear.

"Because her father and mother are the King and Queen of Azuria," Heart uttered as the final pieces to the puzzle all dropped into place. "Kenneth please meet your bestie, Her Royal Highness, the Princess of Azuria."

The world began to tilt and she held onto the arms of her chair to keep herself from falling over. She couldn't exactly say what happened after that. She was too busy watching the pain etched on Kenneth's face spread wider as it covered him completely. By the time she took her eyes off of him and focused on the rest of the room, Teague was standing in the middle of the room going head to head with Heart.

"I'm sorry, Kenneth," A.J. whispered hoping those words would ease some of the pain she'd so obviously caused. "I didn't have a choice."

"I'm so sick of the people that I love telling me there were no other alternatives but to lie to me. The truth is that you sacrificed my family for yours A.J. and I can't accept that. And I damn sure can't accept the lame ass excuse that you didn't have a choice, because there's always a choice. You had a choice and you chose wrong."

Kenneth's cold gaze was enough to shake the ground they walked on. If her years at court in her kingdom and the years she'd spent as a litigator hadn't prepared her to master her reactions, she'd have crumbled into a brittle mess right at his feet.

It would serve no purpose anyway, even if she did bow to Kenneth's feet, he would never forgive her for this. With each passing moment she could see the soft spot he'd always carried for her crusting over with one layer of granite after another.

He took one final look at her, then turned to his wife. "I'll be waiting for you in my truck," he stated plainly to Heart. "All this bullshit polluting the air is fucking with my allergies."

The soft click of the closing door rang in the silent room like a deafening boom. She sat still, waiting for Heart to continue her earlier assault. It took her more than a moment to realize Heart was sitting against her desk, calm filling the tense lines that pulled her face into sharp contours earlier.

"It should go without saying that every word that was said and heard in this room is never to be repeated," Heart uttered. "If you don't fear losing your jobs and pensions, you'd better fear me. Not one single word to anyone. Copy?"

There was a collective, "Yes Captain," that softly filled the room. Seemingly satisfied by the response, Heart nodded her head as she sat atop her desk.

"Dismissed," she uttered. Her voice was barely above a whisper, and yet her staff responded instinctively to it and Heart's authority. It was the mark of a true leader. Only those with true power, power that lived within, understood this. When you were a true leader, you didn't have to scream to make your subordinates follow; they would instinctively follow where you led.

In a matter of moments, the room went from packed to overflowing with space. Only the two women remained.

A.J. always knew it would come down to this one day. She and Heart pitted against each other, going head to head over Kenneth's broken heart. Selfishly, A.J. believed Heart would be the perpetrator in this scenario. Despite all her sins, she'd never once thought that she would be the one to hurt her friend.

She'd fought tooth and nail over the years to protect him from every enemy, even himself. But she'd never in all her imaginings thought Heart would need to protect Kenneth from her.

"You hurt my husband," Heart voiced. "I've been willing to kill people for less."

A.J. wasn't at all surprised by Heart's statement. She didn't take it lightly either. There was a lethal aura the young captain wore proudly. She was a predator, and she had no problems with destroying anything that was a threat to those under her protection.

"I don't doubt that, Captain," A.J. responded. "But unless you want to start an international incident, I'm sure you have no intention of murdering me in your office."

"Don't," Heart cut her off. "No jokes, no slick ass remarks, none of that shit. You hurt my husband. You put my child and my husband in danger. My lieutenant almost died, A.J., you don't get to sit here and talk to me like that doesn't mean shit."

A.J. nodded her head, Heart was right. There were too many innocent lives being affected by her past coming to life.

"As I see it, there are two ways this situation can end, A.J.," Heart stated. "You can keep up the same shit you've been doing, and I walk out of here and tell my husband to wash his hands of you and your fucking family."

"Or?" A.J. questioned.

"Or you can look me in my eye and tell me if you really were attempting to sacrifice Kenneth for your family and a title or not."

"What happens if we walk through door number two?" A.J. probed.

"You convince me that you weren't out to get him, to get us, and I do what's best for my husband."

"Which is?" A.J. asked.

"Convince him to forgive you and yours."

"Why would you do that for me, Heart?"

"I wouldn't do it for you, but I'd do anything for Kenneth. I may not like it, but he needs you. Losing you like this would be more of a punishment for him than you. So come on with it, counselor. Tell me the real deal, not the feds' version, of the truth."

A.J. watched Heart for a brief second. They'd rubbed each other the wrong way from the moment they laid eyes on one another it seemed. But here she was, setting all that aside to help the man she loved.

A true leader.

"I've done a lot of shit I'm not necessarily proud of, Heart. Many of those things were done intentionally. I knew exactly what I was doing when I was executing them. But I promise you, putting Kenneth in harm's way, putting you and Amare in harm's way, no that was never my intent."

Heart nodded. "I noticed you didn't say hurting Kenneth, but that you hadn't intended him to be placed in harm's way. You're a word-smith, A.J. Why those words?"

A.J. gave it to the woman. She damn sure was perceptive. "Because I'd be lying if I never considered that Kenneth could end up hurt because of my secrets. No, I never wanted his feelings hurt," A.J. answered. "However, I'd rather him be upset with me for keeping my secrets from him and alive than be aware of my lies and die because of that knowledge. I really did believe I was doing the best thing for everyone involved."

A.J. was right; Heart really was a leader, only a leader could put aside their own shit to help those they'd been sworn to protect and love.

It was time for A.J. to start doing some of that. Setting aside her shit to protect those she loved. She couldn't consider the consequence. It was her obligation, that's all that mattered. She would be queen one day, better to learn this lesson now, than when she was sitting on the throne.

She'd told Kenneth and Heart her truth, now there was one other person remaining. The person she needed most, the person that would more than likely walk away when he learned what she'd done.

She needed to tell Alan.

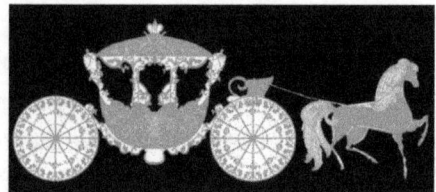

Teague parked his car in front of the familiar two-family home on Crescent Street. Twelve years had passed since he'd stood in front of these doors. He checked his service weapon, and the backup he always carried strapped to his ankle. If he was smart, he'd have an army behind him walking into this deathtrap.

He walked up to the door and rang the bell. It took a minute, but soon the door opened and Teague was face to face with his former commanding officer, General Hunter Amare.

"Maher, you sure you want to do this?"

"I don't really have a choice, sir. Someone's got to stop Reign, and quite frankly, there's no one else good enough."

The stoic army general nodded his head, and stepped aside allowing Teague's entry into the house. Teague headed straight, assuming they'd be taking this meeting in the hidden citadel beneath this house. A slight nod from Hunter stopped him and he turned toward the stairs that led to the family residence on the second floor.

Once he reached the top of the landing, he stepped aside and allowed Hunter to step in front of him. At least this way he would probably avoid catching a bullet in his chest with Hunter as his shield.

"Pops, who was that at the door?"

He could hear the smile in her voice before he saw her. It was a special bubble of excitement that was only present when she was addressing someone she possessed great admiration for.

He'd seen her briefly a few hours ago immediately after the car chase that nearly landed Kenneth Searlington in a body bag. When she'd realized it was him, when she'd been confronted with the lie of his supposed death, her voice was filled with cold precision. Hearing the warm greeting she now addressed her father with nearly tore a hole in him.

She was standing at the stove, stirring something with vigor. Actually, it kind of looked as if she was attacking it, and knowing how she loved a good fight, he was certain she was enjoying beating the hell out of whatever was in that pot.

"Hello, True," was all he said before the genuine smile slipped from her face and the banging at the stovetop ceased. She hadn't even looked up and she was already closing herself off into her protective gear.

"What the hell do you want, Teague? Why are you in my father's house?"

"Is that any way to greet an old friend, True, after all we've meant to one another?"

He moved just in time for the knife that flew from her hand spinning in his direction. A millimeter in the wrong direction and she'd have nicked the side of his face or ear. Instead, the expertly thrown weapon continued its travels unabated until it buried itself in the wall behind him.

He stared at the knife, a beautiful piece of steel that he'd given her twelve years ago when he'd taught her how to knife throw. Since he'd placed it in her hand and helped her perfect her technique, True didn't miss. The fact that it hadn't landed in his head or his chest meant one thing. She was actually ready to listen to him, otherwise, he'd never have seen her aim the knife, let alone been able to avoid it.

"You've got five minutes, Maher," she growled. "Five minutes; after that, I'm not responsible for what I might do to you if you're still in my presence."

"I won't take that long," he answered. "The Azurians need our help again. Are you and your team up for the challenge?"

CHAPTER 17

A.J. slipped the key inside the lock with little effort. After using it in mostly nighttime hours with barely any light, she was certain she could get the small sliver of metal inside the lock even if she threw it from across the hall.

*A*gent Maher told her to stay close when she'd left Heart's precinct, with an edict like that, it was very plausible that her plans for the near future were indefinitely fluid. Whatever Teague Maher decided on the Tenetti family's future would determine if she was able to live out the rest of her days here in relative peace and comfort. In Alan's arms, or if she'd be returned to her homeland, unprotected from a crazed maniac intending to usurp her claim to the throne by murdering her and her family.

She turned the knob and tapped in the disabling code on the security pad. Once inside and the door locked, she rearmed the alarm and stepped inside the foyer. She rested her briefcase down on the floor by the hall closet and removed her heels. Barefoot, she walked soundlessly through the darkened hall until she stood in front of the bedroom door.

She twisted the knob, and padded across the room until she stood near the bed. The moon crept through the blinds, highlighting the prominent cheeks, and sharp cut of his jaw line. His short and neat blond hair lay flat against his head, still damp from his usual shower just before he climbed into bed every night.

She stuck out her hand to touch him, wake him in order to have this very heavy conversation but her hand froze. She needed to talk to him; he needed to know the truth. But watching him, relaxed, no cares or troubles, beautifully at peace, it hurt to know that she was about to destroy all of that.

She withdrew her hand, clutched it over her mouth to stem the aching moan she so desperately wanted to release into the air.

I can't do this, not yet, not until...

She released the single button on her blazer and let the material slide down her arms. She folded it neatly. She stepped quietly from his side of the bed and walked to the foot of it. Gently resting the blazer, followed by her skirt and blouse on the bench positioned at the footboard.

A few more steps and she was on the side of the bed that she'd come to think of as hers. She lifted the comforter, carefully climbing in, trying her best not to disturb the sleeping man.

She inched closer and closer until the warmth radiating from his solid form began to sear the first layer of her smooth skin, slowly working its way inside to the layers of frigid fear that were plastering her insides.

When she lay her arm around his narrow waist and let splayed fingers travel up to his chest, she felt the shift in him as he climbed from slumber to wakefulness.

He caressed her hand, bringing it to lips she knew were soft and talented. He turned, pulling her flush against his chest, as his hands found the curve of her ass, letting palms caress and handle it.

"Mmm, baby," he murmured.

"Shhh," she whispered. "Go back to sleep."

Blue eyes slowly opened allowing the fog of sleep to fade as he focused on her face. "The sexiest woman on the planet sneaks into my bed and you think I'm just going to roll over and go back to sleep?" he asked. "Not in this lifetime."

Warm lips found hers in the darkness. They were sure, certain of both their destination and their reception. Since that first time she'd learned just how glorious his skin felt against hers, she'd never refused the opportunity to experience him, his touch.

The idea that this could be the last time, that she might lose the allowance of touching, tasting him whenever she wanted, sent a frightening slice of pain through her heart. The anticipation of loss filled her with desperation. An emotion she'd never known until she'd allowed Alan beyond her borders.

He rolled her onto her back and settled between her thighs, spreading her. She ran eager fingers down his back to his bare ass. She'd always loved the fact that he slept in the nude. Another tug on the hard muscles of his ass netted her the blissful sensation of the heavy flesh of his cock pressing against her plumping clit. He rolled his hips dragging his length against her lace covered folds.

Too eager to feel the delicious fullness that always came once his cock filled her, she pulled the seat of her lace panties to the side and grabbed his rigid flesh. She gave it one long tug that resulted in his head lolling back on his shoulders. She ran her thumb across the tip, allowing her fingernail to briefly graze the tender flesh. He shuddered, calling out her name into the silence of the room.

She pulled him closer to her, and placed the pulsing cock in her hand to the entrance of her dripping cunt, raising her hips capturing it one quick motion.

"A.J."

She felt his body stiffen, felt terse fingers grab her chin forcing her gaze to meet his.

"A.J., what the hell are you doing? I'm not wearing a condom."

She could feel the tiny tremors in his body signaling the effort he was executing to keep himself from moving.

"We exchanged test results a while ago. We agreed to exclusivity, unless you've changed your mind, there's no reason we can't."

She ran her fingers down the trembling muscles in his arms while she contracted the walls of her pussy around him.

He shuddered again, stronger than the last time, his resolve ebbing away quickly. "Contraception?" he questioned between clenched teeth.

"I.U.D. I can almost guarantee we'll not be creating any offspring tonight."

He paused a moment, blue eyes carefully considering her. She wasn't lying, wasn't manipulating him. There was nothing about that statement that was even possibly untrue. There would be no reminders of this night except for those that lived in her heart, mind, and soul.

"Alan…please?"

Her voice broke, the fear she'd been holding inside began to spread through her. The moisture collecting at the corner of her eyes spilled down the sides of her face and onto his sheets.

"Baby, what's wrong?" he asked as he gathered her into his arms.

"Please, just make love to me," she begged. Leaving the unspoken —*for the last time*—floating in her mind.

His brow creased with concerned lines marring his golden perfection. For a moment she thought he would refuse her until he lowered his body on top of hers, covering her completely like a strong, beautiful blanket.

He rolled his hips again, and she locked her legs around his waist to keep him buried inside her. He kissed her hard, forcing her lips to open to him, planting his tongue fierce and deep inside her mouth as he thrust inside her.

Each glide of his cock scraped against her walls, bringing the tingle of her arousal to a fevered burn.

"So hot and tight," he growled in her ear as he snapped his hips. His heavy balls smacking against the puckered crease of her ass igniting the sensitive flesh there, adding to the crest of sensations that were assailing her.

He sat on his haunches, placed firm hands behind her knees and bent her body in half. The angle allowed for deeper penetration. She felt all of him, everywhere. There was no place to hide from the sizable cock buried to her hilt, splitting her tender flesh at the seams.

He dropped one of his hands to her mound, using his thumb to strum the perfect rhythm against her throbbing clit. It felt like fire slicing through, drawing her closer to her peak. It was happening too quickly, shaking her head back and forth, trying to stave it off.

"Give me what's mine," he insisted.

She held on for a few moments longer, but the longer she held out, the harder he pounded inside of her. He demanded her climax as if it were his property, like he owned it. Her walls were beginning to convulse now, a precursor to the total body spasm she knew was coming. The more her pussy quivered, the harder he used her, plowing her like his cock was some sort of tool to punish her insolence.

She knew the moment her resolve slipped; she felt that last swell of fire blossom from her cunt, spreading throughout her body. A loud moan climbed from her throat, its volume and force leaving her raw.

When her body began to seize with her climax, Alan continued his assault, continued battering her cunt with his cock, keeping her on the crest of her climax.

"Fuck, yeah," he muttered as she came. "It's mine, I want it all."

He was right. It was his; everything about this orgasm ripping through her body was his. Hell, the truth of it was everything about her belonged to him. She was his, had willingly given herself to him so long ago, even if she couldn't say the words, she was his possession.

He held her suspended in the middle of her climax for what seemed like an eternity. She couldn't tell if she'd come multiple times, or if this was the same peak continuing from the moment he'd demanded it.

It didn't matter, her walls clamped down tighter on his cock, her body jerked harder, her screams became louder. And just when the rainbow colored flashes of light began dancing behind her closed lids, she felt his pace falter, stuttering as he attempted to exert control over his impending release. He managed two more staccato pumps before the hot splash of his cum painting her arousal-slick cavern signaled his release. The surge of each jet of his spend coincided with her spasms, her cunt milking him for each drop he possessed.

He collapsed against her, holding her to him, the sweat covering their bodies acting as a seal between them. She held tightly to him, preventing him from separating their bodies, refusing to lose even a millimeter of his skin.

Their heart rates settled, and their skin began to cool, but she still refused to let him move even an inch. Realizing she had no intention of letting him go, he finally settled long enough for sleep to pull them both under its dark blanket. They were together, sealed by passion and their bodies. If only she could somehow prevent that seal from ever being broken, keep it intact for all eternity. If only…

A.J.'s mind crept slowly back to wakefulness. She savored the pleasant ache in all her limbs, especially the tender flesh of her feminine folds.

The flashes of memory from the night before etched a sinful smile on her face. Last night Alan took her to heights she hadn't known were possible and she'd be more than willing to let him do it again this morning. She turned over to nuzzle up against him, reaching and expecting hand toward him, but met nothing but cool sheets and bedding.

His absence pulled her from her semi-awake state. She sat up quickly, looking around the room for signs of his presence. She saw nothing, she heard nothing, but silence, and an empty room save for the furniture and herself.

"Alan?" she called out. Her voice returning void to her made panic begin to rise quickly. She'd failed in her original intent. She was supposed to have talked to Alan.

"You were supposed to tell him the truth before anyone else could," she mumbled to herself.

She turned to get out of the bed and saw her cellphone resting on the nightstand. Alan must have placed it there. It was probably ringing in her bag when he left the bedroom. When she her fingers touched it she found a piece of notepaper stuck to the screen covered in his neat block letters.

Had to go in for my exit interview at Searlington.
Stay, we need to talk.
No regrets about last night.
A

She pulled the note off her phone and swiped the screen to try to make a call. If she were lucky she could catch him just before he made it to Kenneth. This wasn't the best way to clue him in, but she needed to reach Alan first. She was about to tap his icon on her favorites list when she saw an unread text message from him.

Don't fucking move.
Keep your ass right where I left you or I promise there will be hell to pay.
I'm on my way back now.

It appeared her luck just ran out.

The message screen blacked out and was replaced by Teague's flashing name and number. She hesitated a moment before answering. Whatever he had to say probably wasn't what she wanted to hear.

She let one more beat pass before she swiped her finger across the screen and answered, "Yes, Teague."

"A.J. I told you to stay close. Where the hell are you?"

She took in a deep breath, too tired to play games with the agent on her phone. "Teague, you know exactly where I am of every moment of every day. Please, let's cut the bullshit, it will save us both a great deal of time and energy."

"Did you tell him?" he barked.

"I wanted to, but I didn't get the chance. As soon as he comes home I'm going to tell him everything. I'm tired; I can't do this to him anymore."

"Princess, I don't care how fucking sweet you think his dick is, don't utter a damn word. I'm tired of cleaning up this mess. The more people that know, the messier it gets. Leave the boy scout out of it or I pull back my government's support."

His razor sharp voice cut through her. Over the years, she'd learned to gauge just how far she could push Teague before he was at his limit. The angrier he was, the sharper his pronounciation became. Loud and overbearing on most occasions, whenever the timber of his voice dropped to a quiet yet hard whisper, she knew all bets were off. Teague was serious.

She sank under the covers and rubbed shaky fingers against her forehead. Once again she was being forced to choose between her duty and her heart.

A.J. awaited Alan's arrival with a heavy rock in the pit of her stomach. Her skin felt tight with anxiety, uncomfortably stretched across her body, creating the need for her to scratch and rub her limbs.

This wasn't going to be pretty. Alan was angry; their time together taught her Alan didn't wear anger well.

She sat back on his couch with a cup of tea and let her mind wonder back to the beginnings of this clandestine relationship. If her memory served her correctly, and it usually did, they hadn't really started off in a good place either. They were both drowning in their own pain individually. Two people raw with hurt should never have attempted to bond over their individual and mutual pain. Too bad neither of them thought better of it then. Perhaps if they had, she might not be sitting here waiting for Alan to rip her heart out.

CHAPTER 18

Alan tapped a rhythmless beat against his thigh. It was the only outlet for his boiling temper that wouldn't get him tossed out of this cab and possibly arrested for threatening to choke the nearest body out.

"When I get my hands on her," he muttered through his teeth.

"Did you say something, sir?" the young cabby asked as his eyes glanced up quickly in the rearview.

Not trusting himself to speak, Alan just shook his head and went back to thinking about earlier events of what started as such a wonderful day.

He'd awoken this morning with A.J.'s warm body pressed beneath him. She'd clung to him last night during and after their lovemaking, a moment Alan would treasure for the rest of his life.

After five years of fighting, after three months of carefully stepping through her emotional minefields, he'd hoped last night was proof that he'd finally made it beyond her barriers.

But after meeting with Kenneth, he now wondered if last night was just another manipulation ploy in her arsenal.

There were too many unknowns running through his mind right now. Kenneth hadn't given him any details, he'd simply told him he was terminating A.J. as the attorney of record for Searlington Realty and wanted him to deliver the forms to her directly. Alan attempted to ask his friend why he was doing this, but Kenneth just raised his hand and replied, "Because I said so," before motioning for Alan to leave his office.

That wasn't Kenneth, and that especially wasn't the way that Kenneth treated him while he was a respected executive in his company, nor as a friend. He knew right then and there something was up, A.J. somehow drove Kenneth beyond his edge yet again.

When the cab stopped in front of his apartment, he grabbed his billfold and handed the cabbie more than enough money to cover the fare. He stepped onto the sidewalk, quick, angry steps taking him to the entrance in a matter a seconds. He raised his hand to snatch open the door, but stopped himself.

He needed a moment. If he went upstairs with his emotions raging, he wasn't sure he'd get what he needed. A.J. was often like a caged animal. When she felt cornered, she didn't back down or submit, instead she came out swinging hard.

"Get it together, Quillen. Don't let her manipulate you. Control yourself."

He whispered those familiar words over and over again. It seemed like he was always reminding himself not to let A.J. play him, not to allow himself to be pulled into her games. He'd been dodging her games for five years now; he mistakenly believed everything was under control.

Unfortunately, his encounter with Kenneth this morning gave him the distinct impression that his assumption was wrong. *Could she really have been playing me all this time?*

Just that quickly his anger began to boil again and he remembered the last time he found himself standing outside of a building trying to control his damn emotions.

"Are we really back to this shit again?"

CHAPTER 19

Alan stepped inside of his apartment to find A.J. standing at the kitchen counter with a cup of tea in her hand. She eyed him carefully; he could see her attempting to assess him. What else had he expected? This was A.J. Tenetti; she was a tactical planner in intellectual warfare. No way was she walking into a potential battle without preparing on some level for the enemy.

"What did you do?"

She took a painfully slow sip of her tea before carefully setting the ceramic mug down safely on the counter.

"I'm not really certain I know what you're talking about. You'll have to be a bit more specific."

"A.J., I'm not about to stand here and do this back and forth verbal tennis with you. What the hell did you do to make Kenneth so angry that he'd slap these papers in my hand and tell me to deliver them to you personally?"

He handed her the courier envelope and watched as she opened it and quickly skimmed the documents. She stood unfazed as her eyes passed quickly from line to line and her fingers flipped from page to page. It wasn't until he saw a brief twitch of what looked like discomfort on her otherwise unmarred face that he actually believed she'd processed what he'd handed her.

"It appears I no longer work for Searlington Realty."

He nodded his head in agreement. "Care to tell me why?"

"Alan, this is really a matter between Kenneth and me. You don't need to be involved."

"The fuck you say. Kenneth had murder in his eyes when he gave me those damn papers. When my best friend seems to be contemplating killing the woman I'm currently sleeping with, I think I deserve to know what the hell the problem is. What happened, A.J.? What the hell did you do?"

A.J. felt those words pierce her as surely as a sharpened blade. Those jagged edges of those words ripped at her heart. She could see his mistrust of her so clearly painted across the surface of his anger-filled face, in the stiffness of his rigid body, in the piercing harshness of his barking voice.

"Amazing how you jump to the automatic conclusion that I did something to create whatever scenarios you're running in your head. I'm the one you've spent the last while fucking, but Kenneth is the one whose innocence you presume."

His eyes narrowed and he crossed his arms over the broad expanse of his chest. "Deflection, huh?" He tilted his head to the side as if to get a more perceptive look at her. "I read that part of the how-to-get-out-of-shit-when-I-know-I'm-caught manual too. Please do us both a favor, don't waste our time on this elementary bullshit, at least take me seriously and come with something a little more difficult on the defense mechanism scale. What happened, Alexis-Jeovonni?"

She opened her mouth, but nothing came out of it. She just stood there, feeling as if she were stuck in something. Her chest hurt and her muscles seized, making it difficult to drag in a breath. There were a million different ways she could get out of this predicament without admitting a thing. She knew that, and so did he. But the smooth skin of his face was marked by a mixture of pain, anger, and loss. An expression she'd only witnessed once before, the morning he'd told her about his dead wife.

She remembered how broken and crippled he'd appeared when he'd told her his story, how sick he was with loathing for his family, especially his grandfather.

In that moment she'd wanted nothing more than to protect him from that pain. They'd been almost inseparable since that morning; he'd burrowed under her skin and into her blood.

She could lie, she could twist this until things worked out in her favor, but he would never trust her again if she did. Somehow, that fact was unacceptable to her. But then she realized why. Alan refused to be party to the games she'd played for years, and even when he'd known that she wanted him, he'd refused her because he didn't trust her. And now, standing here watching the weight of his fiery gaze bearing down on her, she knew one thing to be true. If Alan believed he couldn't trust her, he wouldn't hesitate in walking away from her.

Out of every concern she carried across her shoulders, that particular one seemed too heavy a burden to sustain.

"A.J.?" he asked her again.

"I nearly got him killed," she blurted out. "I literally almost got Kenneth killed."

"What do you mean?"

She walked over to the chaise lounge to sit down and motioned for him to sit down across from her on the sofa.

"I opted to keep some very sensitive information from Heart because of a legal situation that precluded me from revealing said information to Heart. Because of that, Kenneth ended up in a very bad situation where he was nearly killed."

The banging of his heart was so loud he could hardly hear surrounding noise. He stepped closer to her, stopping close enough that he was almost touching her.

"You're telling me you purposely withheld information from the police that almost got Kenneth killed? Is that what you just said?"

"Alan, there is more going on than you know, more than I'm at liberty to explain. I could not help it; my hands were tied, by the law."

"Fuck the law, he's our friend, how could you put him in danger?"

"You don't understand, you couldn't, and I can't explain it to you. I did not have a choice. There was nothing I could have done differently. I went to the only person that would have been able to help as soon as I realized there was a problem. I tried, Alan, I tried. I did the only thing I could and it failed."

He grabbed her by the shoulders, wanting so badly to shake her. "Why didn't you come to me? Whatever it is you're mixed up in, I could have helped you, I would have helped you."

She shook her head and closed her eyes. "I couldn't Alan…I couldn't."

"What the hell are you caught up in, Alexis-Jeovonni? I want to know what's going on right now!"

She held the lids of her eyes tighter. Refusing to see him, refusing to face his anger.

Their time together had lulled him into a false sense of security. He'd thought they'd moved beyond her secrets and manipulations, beyond her need to control everything and everyone.

"I am so sick of…" The words caught in his throat. He was burning with frustration, so angry that she'd once again chosen to play chess with people's lives rather than trust someone, trust him.

He knew she loved Kenneth, he knew whatever this situation was, she didn't want Kenneth to be harmed, but she'd let things get so out of hand because she couldn't reach out for help. In all this time, she still didn't believe she could trust him. That pissed him off more than anything else in this entire fucked up scenario.

He gave her arms a hard tug until she collapsed against him. She was involved in something dangerous, and from the nervous attempts at deflection he'd seen earlier, she was scared. He didn't like her being afraid. It didn't seem natural, wasn't something that should be a part of this confident woman's make up.

She needed help, even if she couldn't see that, he did. He was determined to help her, even if it meant breaking her to protect her. He needed to help her; needed to be the one who provided what she needed, him and only him.

He planted firm lips against her, forcing her lips to open and make way for the harsh strokes of his tongue. Trying his best to not think about why this unusual protective streak was raging through him right now, he walked her backward until they tumbled onto the chaise lounge in a tangled heap. He wasn't particularly concerned about how smoothly this happened. This wasn't about finesse, this was about showing her who he was, and what he was to her. Or more importantly, what he wanted to be to her.

Alan took a moment to stare down at the body lying beneath him on the chaise lounge. A perfect mix of brown and blonde curled ringlets fanned out across the silken fabric beneath them. Hazel eyes with flecks of emerald fire sparkling in the dim light of the living room. Full lips that made his dick jump just with thoughts of them around the rigid flesh of his cock. Smooth honey-brown skin lay taut over tight, deep curves.

God this woman was as tempting as sin itself and far more dangerous than Satan could ever be.

She must have felt his mind pulling him out of the moment because she snaked slender fingers around the base of his neck and pulled his lips back down to hers. One press, just the briefest touch with the slightest pressure and he was falling into the lure of her desire. Burning with the need to slide between the heat that was all too familiar to him now.

He pressed deeper into the kiss, demanding more of her, needing to fill his mouth with the sweet taste of her, a mix of mint, heat, and some unnamable flavor that he simply called A.J.

Who would have thought it? When he arrived in New York five years ago at the behest of his friend Kenneth, Alan believed he'd spend no more than a year here, helping his longtime friend, Kenneth Searlington, balance his work and family life. He'd needed the break. He'd needed to put distance between himself and the pain of loss and grief that surrounded him in his home like a damp, musty blanket. Coming to New York was supposed to be temporary, a change of scenery to help him hold on to his sanity, help him recharge, rebuild.

It was not supposed to turn into a semi-permanent vice presidency at one of the largest real estate firms in the world. And it certainly wasn't supposed to morph into this…this…whatever this was between him and his best friend's lawyer, Alexis-Jeovonni Tenetti.

His tongue slipped into her mouth, licking, fucking, insisting that she relent to him, give him everything he demanded and more. She melted into the kiss, bowing her body, curling her short sexy legs around the backs of his thighs, letting pointed toes glide down the curve of his muscles.

His hips instinctively bucked against her, wedging the ridge of his thickening cock between her silk covered pussy lips. He started a slow grind that made sparks dance behind his closed eyelids. Damn, he hadn't even managed to get either of them naked yet and he was sure he could come from this alone.

She began to match his rhythm, stoking the fire that had his balls hanging so heavy, aching as they inched up closer to his body, begging for release.

"Shit," he hissed as he pinned her hips to the chair with a fierce grip. "You're killing me, woman."

He quickly pushed the pencil skirt that was currently resting just beneath the curve of her ass up around her waist. He then wrapped eager fingers around the thin material of the panties separating him from the release his body was craving.

With no time for niceties, he gave the material a firm tug. The cleaving sound of splitting thread filled the air as the silky lingerie fell in tattered pieces directly through his fingers. Just as the last sliver of fabric ghosted across his fingertips, his hand was reaching for the only thing that would stop the relentless ache that seemed to be strangling the shit out of his cock and balls.

He didn't ask permission. They'd come to know exactly what the other needed, and anytime he was this turned on, it was because she needed release just as badly as he did.

A single finger circled the mouth of her cunt, the pooling slick of her arousal providing a smooth glide in to the second knuckle. Her excitement evident, he quickly added a second finger, causing her breath to hitch in her chest. He sawed his fingers in and out, making sure to apply consistent pressure to that sweet spot that made her hips buck in response. By the time he added a third finger she was clawing at the intricately woven design of the upholstery trying to gain enough purchase to fuck herself onto his digits.

He could feel her walls clamping down, her body so tight, so ready to break apart for him. He added pressure and speed to his hand movements, meeting her thrusting hips with each down stroke. She was there; he could see it in the tight lines of her face, in the way she was nearly biting through her bottom lip. He crooked his fingers forward, scraping the pads against that spongy bundle of nerves, and she splintered right before him.

When he pulled his fingers free of her grasp her release poured fluid from her like an erupting spring, spraying his hand, his pant leg, and the couch beneath them. He dipped a soft finger inside her still quivering flesh, swiveling it around, making certain he got it good and wet, then he removed it, painted her lips and tongue with it, and licked his tongue inside her mouth to taste that amazing flavor.

He would never tire of tasting her.

Before she could come down from the high of orgasm, he undid the buckle of his pants with one hand and managed to set the aching flesh of his cock free from his boxer-briefs. There was no finesse, no romance; there was only his need to plant himself inside A.J.

He ground himself inside of her in one swift shove, leaving the both of them gasping as he bottomed out balls deep inside the slickest, hottest piece of ass he'd ever experienced.

"Fuck, A.J.," he groaned. Her sheath was so tight around him it brought dancing white spots behind his closed lids.

"Please," she choked out, snatching his attention, forcing him to focus on the task at hand. At the moment that was one thing, bringing this pushy, aggravating, infuriating bitch to heel and giving them both unspeakable pleasure while he did so.

No small feat when dealing with a woman like A.J. She was difficult at best and purposely obstinate at worst. But the one thing he knew how to do was to stop that mouth of hers from running, and using it for more productive things like moaning his name in pleasure.

"Please what?" he asked, refusing to move until she gave him the answer he wanted.

"Please...Alan...fuck me."

A crooked smile curved his lips as he watched the last of her resistance fade away. She was his now, willing to do whatever he asked to get him to satisfy her.

"Be a good girl and turn over on all fours. I want that ass high in the air."

She did as he asked, legs spread wide in invitation, burying her head in the cushion and raising her hips until the round globes of her ass hung high in the air, waiting for him, inviting him to come in.

"So fucking hot...so sexy this way."

He shoved inside her again, wrapping strong fingers around her shoulder, pushing her down into the cushion, adding the force of his entire body into his strokes.

"Is this what you want?" he bellowed. "Is this what you were asking for when you were trying to piss me off?"

She didn't answer. He knew she couldn't. Every time she tried to draw in breath to speak he would plant himself into her again, stealing whatever small amount of air her greedy lungs attempted to snatch since his previous stroke. All she could do was moan, and that's just the way he liked her.

A.J. possessed a brilliant mind. She always had an answer ready for any question or remark thrown at her. She naturally thought circles around most of the population. But here, under him, under his power, she was reduced to rudimentary words and animalistic sounds to convey her needs. She was so intoxicated with desire that her mind couldn't string two coherent thoughts together if she'd tried. And that was a good thing, at least for him it was. Because when Alexis-Jeovonni Tenetti thought, she thought herself right out of feeling. And whether she knew it or not, she was never better than when she allowed herself to feel.

When she felt, all of the things she used to protect herself from the world faded away. When she was stripped clean of her defenses, beneath that hardened exterior was a vulnerability that made her irresistible, that made her human. That was the part of her that kept him in this constant fight-fuck-fight loop that he seemed to be on with her.

He leaned into her, putting all of his weight into his rapid thrusts. He could hear the legs of the chaise scraping against the shining wood floor, no doubt destroying its pristine glow. But A.J. didn't seem too worried about it, so damn if he'd let it keep him from fucking her through the damn chaise lounge if he could.

He felt her walls clamping down around him; she was close, damn if he wasn't too. He slapped a hard hand against an ass cheek and felt the ripple of the shiver that passed through her surrounding his cock. God, for someone with such a wicked disposition on most days, she damn sure had the sweetest box he'd ever had the pleasure of resting inside of.

"I swear to God, A.J., you are going to learn to fucking listen to me if it kills you." He slapped her ass again in the same spot, ripping another wail of pleasure from her. "I'm so fucking tired of your bullshit," he continued, following his break in speech with another hard hand across the now reddened skin of her ass. "This bullshit with you keeping shit from me stops now. Do you understand me?"

She nodded her head in response, but that wasn't good enough, so he smacked that ass again.

"Do you understand me, Alexis-Jeovonni?"

He changed the angle ghosting over her g-spot, making her quiver uncontrollably. He kept slamming against it, kept smacking her ass, until she was a crying mess and the only thing she uttered over and over again was one word.

"Yes!"

Her orgasm locking all of her muscles, causing her grip on his cock to contract into the tightest clasp he'd ever felt, pulling his release up from his balls, through his shaft, and into the blessed heat of her cunt.

When they were finally able to breathe and move, he pulled himself from her grasp and walked away to the bathroom. He quickly cleaned himself up and was wetting a clean washcloth for A.J. when his reflection caught his eye in the mirror.

He looked well-fucked. There was no other way to describe the mussed blond strands of his tapered hair, or the swollen redness of his lips, or the claw marks he could see just above the collar of his open button-down shirt.

The image of utter debauchery nearly made him smile until he looked into his own eyes. His eyes were blue, usually bright with the excitement of whatever the day offered him, but there was something else that appeared strange. Happiness, there was happiness there in his eyes and that above all scared the hell out of him. This wasn't supposed to have happened. Not to him, not ever again.

His life here wasn't supposed to happen, his job, and certainly not this crazy attraction he for A.J. But of all the unexpected things that should not have been happening to him at this very moment, happiness? No…it wasn't right…it just wasn't supposed to happen. Not to him…not again.

For him, happiness was the harbinger of death. It was the herald of bad things to come, and yet he'd let himself become so intricately entangled with this woman that he'd willingly walked into this situation with a blind eye.

What the fuck was he supposed to do now?

He stepped back into the living room finding her sitting on the lounge where he'd left her, covered in the afghan they usually curled up under when they spent late night vegging out in front of his television.

The sight of her, sitting there, looking so broken and afraid triggered every protective instinct he possessed. It would be so easy to go to her, pull her into his arms and forget about the reason they were here right now. She'd lied. Not just to him, but to everyone. She'd allowed their friend to get caught up in those lies, and even when she could have stopped it, she didn't.

Anger began to burn inside of him. Whatever game she was playing, whatever madness she was involved in, it very nearly killed Kenneth. Whatever her motivation was she'd obviously placed it at a higher value than the life of a man she claimed to call friend.

"I need you to explain this all to me. Help me to understand it, so I can get beyond this, A.J. As long as I've known you, you've used manipulation as a tool to get what you wanted. I told you I couldn't deal with that and be involved with you at the same time. You told me you were done with the game playing. And yet here we find ourselves, wrapped up in a ball of your secrets. So I'm going to ask you one final time. Explain this shit to me. Make me understand why you would place Kenneth in harm's way."

She closed her eyes and slowly shook her head. "I can't," she softly murmured.

"You can't?" he asked. "Well, here's the deal. If you won't explain yourself, then you leave me no choice. I'm leaving," he spat. "Be gone when I return. Don't worry about the items you have here. I'll make certain they're packaged and returned to you."

"Alan—"

He turned his back on her silencing her attempt to speak. "I'm tired of begging you to be honest with me. If you can't, then I can't. As of this moment, the only relationship we need to be concerned about is the one at work, because this one—" He stopped when reaching the door. He turned his head just enough to see the broken image of her sitting in his living room, shoulders slumped, arms wrapped tightly around herself. "This one is over."

CHAPTER 20

A.J. stepped off the elevator and onto the executive floor of Searlington Realty. A place that was always so familiar to her seemed different somehow. She hadn't been inside these walls since before Kenneth's run in with Reign's goons. That was the night he'd told her to he wanted nothing more to do with her and her family.

If anyone asked her, she would have guaranteed there was no way Kenneth would ever willingly allow her into these offices again. That termination of services document was legal and binding, having the same effect as a restraining order sworn out against her.

Kenneth knew the weight of that document, him signing it sent a clear message to her. They were done.

*A*bby greeted her with a generous smile and hearty handshake. "It's so good to see you here again, Ms. Tenetti. Things haven't been the same since you left."

She hadn't left, she'd been pushed out, but if Kenneth hadn't shared that bit of information with her, or if she was just kind enough not to mention A.J.'s termination, A.J. certainly wasn't going to correct her.

"Thanks, Abby, I've missed this place too. Is Mr. Searlington ready for me?"

"Sure, go right in."

A.J. forced a measured smile on her face and walked toward Kenneth's office door. She tapped lightly and waited for the stern, "Come in," from the other side of the door before walking inside.

Kenneth was sitting behind his desk. Thick, black hair captured in a neat ponytail making his features seem that much more stark and unsympathetic. When he finally raised his eyes to her, the frigid blue gaze cast out a chill throughout the room that hit her right in the middle of her chest.

He was still pissed, that was evident, but he asked her to meet him here, so she swallowed the hurt his cool demeanor inflicted on her and sat down in front of him.

"It's good to see you, Kenneth."

"Is it? I would think you would have been happy with the distance I put between us. One less body to protect with your lies, right?"

Anyone else and she would have read him, educating him in no uncertain terms about what kind of bullshit she wouldn't take from anyone. But even though his words hurt, they were true. A truth that seemed to paralyze her in regret and guilt.

"I'm sorry, I had no right, and I admit that. But this," she waved a hand back in forth between them, "isn't going to fix what's broken between us."

She readjusted her seat and eased back into the comfort of the chair. "You called me here, Kenneth. That tells me you're looking for something, otherwise, you wouldn't have dialed my number. I fucked up, we both know that. I've apologized for it; it's something I will regret for the rest of my life. But me constantly apologizing isn't going to help us in the long run. So please, let's drop the passive-aggressive jabs at me. Tell me what you want, and if it's within my purview, there's no question that you'll have it."

He seemed to be weighing her words, tossing them around in his mind and heart.

"You have no idea how angry I've been, how pissed I've been at you. There were only a few people in my world that I put my absolute trust in, and you used it to keep me in the dark about something that almost got me killed."

She nodded her head, what he was saying wasn't untrue. But there was a fine line between the truth he knew, and the obligation she was forced to bear by accident of birth.

"Were you using me and my family as bait, a moving target for Reign to aim at while you hid in the shadows?"

A.J. was never prone to fits of anger. She never allowed herself to get so far out of control that she'd allow anger to impede her thought process. But what he was suggesting, this man whom she'd loved like a brother for so many years, didn't just hurt her, it down right pissed her off. Her anger rose quickly, spilling out of her mouth before she had time to think better of what she was saying.

"What the fuck did you just say to me? You obviously have no idea how much of my life I've sacrificed to protect those I love, including your ass. What I still have to deny myself because there is a very real threat against my life out there. I never wanted you hurt, Kenneth, I was trying to keep you safe."

She grabbed the briefcase she'd placed on the floor and headed toward the door. When her fingers gripped the knob she heard Kenneth call her name.

When she turned around, he was standing at his desk with a set of documents in his hand. "I think you've forgotten something," he stated as he held the papers out to her.

She assessed him carefully and walked back to his desk to take possession of the legal-sized sheets of paper in her hand.

She pulled her reading glasses from her briefcase, and read the document in hand. She catalogued each sentence of legalese on the first page, and continued on to the subsequent pages to do the same.

She understood what she was reading, any first year law student could navigate through the contract she was reading, what she didn't understand was why Kenneth was giving it to her.

"You're reinstating me as your lawyer? Why?"

"Everything is not fixed between us, and for the last little while I've been vacillating between letting things remain as they are, or whether or not I even wanted to try to make things right. I don't know if we'll ever get back what we had as friends, but I do know we had an amazing work relationship. Maybe the way to fixing them both is by starting with the least complicated of the two."

She took out a pen, signed the contract, and smiled as she handed it to him. "So, whoever my replacement was, sucked, is that right?"

He didn't answer, but the way his eyes looked at everything else in the room other than her confirmed her suspicions.

"I told you no one can do what I do, Kenneth."

She watched him cross his arms over his chest, letting an exasperated tuft of air leave his lips.

"Too much, too soon?"

There was a small spark in his eye, just enough to let her know he was fighting to keep a smile off his face. She eased out of his office and waited until she was sitting in her car to let the bubble of hope inside her blossom into a wide grin. That contract wasn't an all's forgiven, but it was an opening, a chance to get back into her friend's life. A chance she wasn't about to pass up.

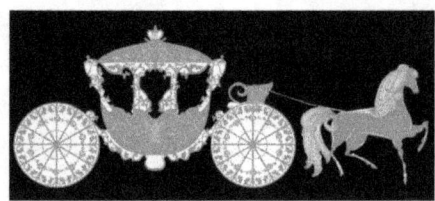

A.J. stopped in front of Carole's desk to pick up a stack of files she needed to start her day.

"You're meeting with Anna Shelton, the new Lincoln Industries exec at nine. At ten, you and Mr. Quillen are supposed to meet to discuss the plans on the Edison deal, and at eleven you're scheduled to meet with a Johnathan Garcia, lead counsel for Strands Incorporated, to finalize a deal for Searlington Realty. Seeing as Mr. Quillen is familiar with the deal since his prior employment with Mr. Searlington, I've asked him to sit in on the meeting."

A.J. nodded a thank you to Carole and continued into her office. She skimmed the files for her first meeting, having already read them; she made mental notes of the important sections that would need amending if the deal was to progress further. At precisely nine on the dot, the representative for Lincoln Industries walked in and the two women wasted little time beginning negotiations.

The meeting proved unremarkable, negotiations went as expected, and both A.J. and her visitor agreed to terms without much trouble. When she was alone again, she pulled up the files on her tablet that she'd need for her meeting with Alan.

When her father initially offered Alan the job she hadn't really been worried about if they'd be able to balance both their work and personal relationships. She hadn't honestly believed Alan would actually leave Searlington Realty in the first place.

Alan didn't like unexpected surprises or change. It was obvious in how he lived his life. In fifteen years he'd worked for only two companies before becoming COO at T.E., his grandfather's business, EAQ, and then Searlington Realty. Despite his refusal to sign on permanently at Searlington, without fail he signed his annual contract. He liked the predictability of being in the same place with the same people.

She'd been certain he was going to thank her father, and then politely decline. Without fail, above all else, Alan was always polite, infuriatingly so in most cases. When Alan actually accepted the position, that's when a little niggling of concern and anxiety began to grate on her nerves.

Although she watched her brother and his wife work well together over the years, she wasn't certain if she'd be able to maintain such close quarters with someone she was intimately involved with. However, in the time he'd been there, Alan put her concerns to rest.

He was an efficient COO; his implementation of ethical business practices into their policy was executed in an almost flawless transition. They wouldn't be able to see the numbers until the next quarter, but the projections for an increased profit margin was definitely expected.

She continued to prep for her next meeting when the office phone rang. "Yes, Carole?"

"There's been some sort of mix up. Counsel for Strand arrived early. Are you able to see him now?"

A.J. looked at her watch, then gave a passing glance over her calendar. "Send him in. Can you please have Mr. Quillen join us?"

"Mr. Quillen is still in a meeting with the branch directors."

"All right, just have him join us when he can."

Today, like most days spent behind this desk, was fast-paced, filled with spontaneous events that popped up without warning. Things like executives who either couldn't get their times straight, or were inconsiderate enough to believe their time was more valuable than hers.

She walked to the conference table and poured two cups of coffee. She'd worked with Mr. Garcia prior to this, and early morning negotiations with him always went better if she was well-caffeinated. Mr. Garcia was a lovely, older, Latino man who was a stickler for doing everything manually. He took his notes by hand and made all contract changes by hand. A.J. was thorough, but she believed in maximizing her productivity with tools designed to aid in her efficiency.

"*Señora* Tenetti."

A.J. smiled at the older man's greeting. In twelve years it remained exactly the same.

"It's been twelve years; you'd think you'd have found at least one occasion to use my first name by now."

She turned around, placed the cups of coffee on the table and then offered her hand to the older gentleman.

He shook it, and gave her a playful smile. "Ms. Tenetti, you know proper doesn't change. Until I learn that your designation in life has changed, you will continue to be Ms. Tenetti."

She took in the image of him, dark soulful eyes that shone a rapt intelligence that rivaled her own. The blue-black color of his hair was almost exactly the same as it was when she'd walked into his classroom on her first day of law school. Save for the slight sprinkle of gray at his temples, the man was still the same esteemed gentleman that intellectually challenged her throughout her law school education.

"All right then, Professor Garcia, let's get down to business."

He nodded his agreement and they began their work. Working with him was a welcome distraction. Johnathan Garcia was known for sending first years home in tears. If you couldn't pass his law and ethics class, then it was a forgone conclusion that your ability to be effective and honestly uphold the law was non-existent.

He taught students to do what was right for the clients, not because it was their job, but because it was the right thing to do.

His class was the most difficult class she'd experienced in her three years of study. Was the work difficult? Yes, but difficulty wasn't the reason she struggled. Her life, her family always taught her that duty was paramount. Wondering if she should do something never entered into the equation for her.

"Professor?"

He raised his eyes from the legal pad in front of him and removed his glasses. "Yes, Ms. Tenetti?"

"I have a question I need to ask you. How do you know when one should side with judgement versus duty?"

"I'm not really certain what you mean?"

She paused for a moment, twisting her pen between her fingers as she gathered her thoughts. "I have a client who is sworn to a particular duty because of the law. Keeping his duty placed someone he cared about in danger. He's lost some very important people as a result of it, but his hands really were tied by legal obligations."

"The law is not black and white, Ms. Tenetti. It is subject to those who are interpreting it. The question your client must ask is not whether it is right or wrong to keep or not keep his duty, but who will best be served by him keeping his obligation. Is he the only person to benefit, or is there a greater good that must be considered? And if there is a greater good, can that need be satisfied while some sort of compromise allows your client to attend to the needs of those that are important to him?"

Compromise, she'd never truly considered that there could be some kind of middle ground that could help her.

"You were always a bright student, smarter than any other student I've ever encountered, but there was always one flaw in your interpretation of the law. You never saw that both sides could win. You had to win and your opponent had to lose, there was no room for sharing the win. Find a way so that your client may share the win, and you will have solved his problem of fulfilling the law and maintaining his ethics."

Sharing the win? Was there a way?

Alan finished a long set of meetings and wanted nothing more than to recline on the couch in his office for the next fifteen minutes. The work he was doing at T.E. was everything he'd imagined work life should be like when he mistakenly took the position with his grandfather's company.

It was refreshing to work for someone like Jeovonni Tenetti who insisted from the beginning that his employees did it right the first time. He never made excuses, never looked for loopholes to mitigate his responsibility, he simply did right and expected those that worked for him to do the same.

It was perfect, a job he loved, a ridiculous compensation package, and he felt as if he was giving back to the world and their consumers by setting a code of business ethics that he was proud of. There was only one thing missing in the time he'd spent working for Tenetti Enterprises, the woman he loved.

Well, if he was honest she wasn't actually missing. She was actually in the office across the hall from his. He could see her anytime he wanted, he could talk to her any moment of the day. Except the only subject they could broach was work.

Every meeting he attended with her, every time he heard her voice felt like a hot blade sliding through his flesh. It burned him, seared his insides and flayed them open bare and exposed to the air.

Every time he sat across from her, his skin tingled with the need to touch her. It would be so simple just to reach across the table and take what he wanted. The quick glances she stole when she thought he wasn't paying attention told him any advances he made probably wouldn't be rejected.

Whenever he thought about bridging the emotional chasm that rested between them, he knew he couldn't. Why? He could see she still wasn't ready to give up whatever it was that she was mixed up in.

If only he had some inkling what it actually was. Talks with Kenneth and Heart yielded no return. Neither of them answered his questions when posed. In fact, it seemed the dynamic duo was very apt at deflection and redirection. Whatever it was, she was in deep if Kenneth, the man who almost died because of her secrets and his semi-violent police captain wife, were still protecting her secret.

A pinging sound coming from his phone reminded him he was supposed to attend another meeting in ten minutes. A meeting he wasn't really looking forward to. They scheduled monthly operations meetings where he reported to her directly on what was happening in the rest of the company.

He picked up his tablet, made certain the notes he needed were accessible and headed for A.J.'s office. Her door was ajar; he could see her sitting at her desk working on her laptop. One sexy curved leg crossed over the other, a sexy pair of black stilettoes adorned each foot.

"Hey, are you ready for our meeting?"

She waved him in, directing him to close the door behind him as he entered. He forced himself to keep his eyes off her legs. The sight of them would make memories of a not so distant past where they were wrapped around him, pulling him deeper into her sweet heat, arise. Just the thought made his dick start filling out. He bit down on the inside of his cheek, hoping to take some of the steam out of the semi-hard on he was sporting at the moment.

He moved directly to the conference room table. He wouldn't be able to see those legs from the table's vantage point, coupled with the added bonus of concealing his current state of almost arousal.

He sat down, taking a moment to discreetly readjust the weight of his dick. He took a few deep breaths, trying his best to calm the need to do something stupid like touch her, or kiss. In a desperate need to not look at her he glanced at the side of the table and saw several takeout cartons stacked on top of one another.

"You ordered takeout?" he asked.

She walked over to the containers and began opening them up. "No, I actually cooked. I've stayed late every day this week. My stomach threatened to protest if I ordered anymore fast food. I knew we'd be meeting, so I just made enough for the two of us."

He could smell the divine mixture of tomato blended with savory spices. His stomach giving a happy rumble, reminding him that he hadn't eaten a decent meal since they'd stopped seeing each other. "Italian?" he asked.

"Yeah, it's my favorite, that and Southern comfort food. It's what I grew up on."

"I noticed a few lines of Italian passing between you and your father. Do you actually speak it?"

She nodded as she plated up a hefty serving for him. "It's my first language. I speak it, read it, and write it. I actually think it."

"What does that mean?"

"Most people who speak more than one language sort of translate in their heads. So when I want to say something in English, I think about the words in Italian, and then translate it in my head to English."

He watched her carefully. He'd noticed that she was never one to answer quickly when questioned. He'd always assumed it was because she was thinking over the question, deciding how best to answer, doing the lawyering thing in her head. He'd never known she was translating languages; he'd never actually known English wasn't her first language. Just one of the many mysteries she'd kept to herself during the course of their involvement.

"Were you born there?"

"In Italy?" she asked. When he nodded his head in reply she answered, "No, I wasn't born in Italy."

"So why isn't English your first language then?"

"Because both my parents spoke Italian to me," she replied. "It was my father's native tongue, and they'd always assumed that we'd be returning to my father's ancestral home. They never anticipated staying abroad for so long. I didn't begin speaking English until I began my formal education here."

She finished serving their food and sat across from him. They spent the first few moments in silence, focusing heavily on the food and the process of chewing and swallowing, everything other than each other.

He almost laughed at how juvenile their attempt to play nicely was. They were each trying so hard to be adults about their failed involvement that they both were stumbling over themselves to avoid the major topic in the room.

Might as well fill the awkward silence. He put down his fork long enough to pick his table up from the table. "I've been going over departmental line budgets with the individual department heads. There's something I wanted to run by you that's been puzzling me."

He tapped in the appropriate places on the tablet screen and handed her the tablet across the table. Her slender fingers lightly grazed his. The soft touch of her digits radiated warmth up his hands and spread throughout the rest of his body, especially the heavy dick threatening to break his damn zipper.

"I found this line in expenditures that no one could really explain to me. Do you know what it is?"

She looked quickly at the tablet and then nodded. "Yes, that's the quarterly budget for *Steal Away*."

"What's that?"

There was a distant look in her eyes, one he couldn't quite place. He could see her battling with herself about something. Knowing her it was another secret. They seemed to cling to her like the stink of a skunk.

"Remember that colorful young lady Carla that dropped in during our conversation in the parking lot behind Mac's Place? Well, I told you then I do pro bono work for a local women's shelter. *Steal Away* is the name of the shelter."

"You fund it with company money?"

She shook her head. "No, I built it with my own money, and Tenetti Enterprises donates a substantial amount of money annually to keep the doors open."

He turned the tablet back in his direction and read over the illuminated screen. "Even with the amount of tax deductions we must be getting for that type of donation, that's still a great deal of money, A.J."

"It is, but it's worth it. Many of those women are escaping violent relationships. They have children to protect, and nowhere to go, no skills to put forth in the real world. *Steal Away* helps them with all of that. We provide legal assistance, job training, bridge to college programs, as well as a safe and inviting place to raise their children while they rebuild their lives. We help them rebuild themselves so they can stand on their own.

It didn't surprise him that she was involved with something like this. Everything he'd learned about her in their time together was that she took care of everyone around her. But like always, something as significant as the help she provided for these women, she couldn't even find it within herself to share that with him.

"How have you been?" she asked changing the subject. It almost felt like there was a silent, *without me*, drifting in the atmosphere.

He looked up from the tablet and saw kind eyes filled with concern watching him. Moments like this, when she let down the wall that protected her from the rest of the world, he could see the real person inside. The one who cared about him, the one whose loyalty was unshakeable, that was the person he'd wanted in his life. That person was the one he was desperately in need of.

"Do you really want to know?"

"Of course I do. I wasn't the one that walked out, Alan, you were."

"I didn't simply walk out, A.J., you pushed me. Your secrets made it impossible for me to stay."

"It's been three months, Alan. Even Kenneth and Heart have found a way to forgive me. For God's sake, they made me godmother to their only child. Do you think they would have let me anywhere near Amare if they thought I was trying to get Kenneth killed? If they can forgive me and move beyond this, why can't the man who *claimed* to love me?"

There was something about the way she said the word "claimed," that grated on his nerves, as if he hadn't shown her over and over again just how much he loved her.

"I did love you, I do love you. My feelings for you are not the issue, A.J. My ability to trust you is. I can't be in a situation where I can't trust the people closest to me. I told you that before, I don't know why you find that so difficult to understand. Yeah, Kenneth and Heart may have found a way to forgive you. But if Heart is letting you anywhere near Kenneth and Amare after what happened to Kenneth, it's probably because she has all the facts. What I can't understand is why you don't think I deserve to know what's going on as well."

She sat there, quiet, still, unmoving. Her face not revealing any of what he suspected might be going on inside her head.

"Yeah, just like I thought...nothing. Thank you for being predictable and consistent."

He shoved his chair back and stood up. "Thanks for dinner; I'll email you all of my notes for the meeting we were supposed to have tonight. Suddenly I'm feeling a little ill."

A.J. watched Alan storm out of her office as she sat there trying to figure out what the fuck just happened. He was pissed, that much she was certain of, and she even understood why he was pissed. Being constantly lied to by the people you love had a way of making a person a little testy. But her hands were tied. There were too many lives at stake. Too many people that could die if she brought Alan into the world she really lived in.

She heard her cellphone ringing in the distance and moved to her desk to find it. "Hello," A.J. answered.

"Ms. Tenetti," A.J. locked in instantly into the shaky voice coming over the line.

"Carla? What's going on?"

"I kept asking for you, and they wouldn't let me talk to you. They told me they're putting me away," Carla hollered in one quick breath.

"Carla, what are you talking about? Who wants to put you away?"

"They're charging me with his murder!"

A.J. grabbed her briefcase, quickly placing documents she needed inside before slamming it closed with a loud click. By the time she was out of the door and standing at the elevator she had the vital information she needed. Carla was in police custody, either suspected of, or being charged with murder. Just when she thought the fight with Alan would send her night into the toilet, now she realized it had gone beyond the toilet and plummeted right into the depths of the filthy sewer.

"Counselor, you made it to the party? I was certain you weren't going to waste your time by coming down. This one is pretty open and shut, not much to do beyond putting it to bed."

A.J. barely gave the executive district attorney a passing glance as she headed for the inside of the courthouse. "Executive ADA, Samuel McKoy. I would think a case like this wouldn't be enough to get you out of bed this time of night. Don't you have underlings that take on the night work for you?"

"I like to take a hands-on approach where murder cases are involved."

A.J. rolled her eyes as she stepped inside of the courthouse. "Really, I couldn't really tell that by your conviction rate," she answered.

The middle-aged Caucasian man with a growing bald spot in the middle of his thinning head of hair, desperately attempting to conceal it with a pathetic comb-over tactic that just wasn't working in his favor, opened his mouth to speak, but she silenced him with a raised finger.

"I'm here to speak with my client, not volley with you. I'll let you know when I'm ready to talk to you." She left McKoy standing in the lobby and continued on her path.

She found Carla sitting behind the steel bars of a large cell. There were five other female prisoners there spread throughout the room. Carla sat huddled on a bench, her arms hugging her knees in the far corner of the room.

"Carla?"

The dark curls of the young woman's head shook as she snapped her head toward the bars. When she realized it was A.J., she ran to the bars, shoving her hands through to grab onto A.J.'s hands.

"Ms. Tenetti, you came," Carla cried as wide dark eyes swimming behind a veil of tears latched onto A.J.

"Why wouldn't I come, Carla?"

The young woman went to answer but A.J. stopped her. A.J. motioned for the court officer to open the cell. She stood aside while Carla was restrained in handcuffs and taken to a small interrogation room down the narrow corridor. When the court officer closed the door behind them and A.J. was certain they were alone, she prompted Carla to speak.

"Why would you think I wasn't coming?"

"Because that's what the cops told me. They said you weren't coming and that they had proof that I killed Nico."

"What exactly happened, Carla?"

"I was coming out of school. When I walked outside, he was there, just waiting for me. He called me over like he just expected me to come to him. I ran down the street. He followed me, pulled me into an alley, pushed me up against the wall, shoved a knife in my face and told me I was coming back to him or he was going to kill me. I was scared, and I knew he was going to hurt me, but I fought to get away. We fought, struggled for the knife. I got it away from him. He lunged at me, I held the knife out to keep him away, but he came anyway. Next thing I knew the knife was in his stomach. I ran away, made my way home. The cops arrived a few hours later."

"Were there any witnesses?" A.J. asked.

"It was late, my class ended at ten, there weren't very many people around."

"I need to know what streets you were running down. Write down everything you can remember, and don't worry, Carla. We're going to get this fixed."

"I'm so sorry, Ms. Tenetti. I know I screwed up, and now they're gonna put me away, aren't they?"

A.J. sat next to the petite young woman that looked so childlike sitting there in that small room.

"Nico told me he would take everything away from me if I didn't come back to him. He's dead, but he's still gonna keep his promise."

"Carla, the only time your enemies win is when you stop fighting. That son of a bitch sold your body, and brutalized you for years. You found the strength to walk away from him after he nearly killed you. The only way you lose after that is if you give up. He's dead, but he's still trying to take your life, don't let him. Fight Carla, take the fight to him."

Carla nodded her head and took the writing utensils A.J. offered. Carla wrote while A.J. made calls to find something to help pull Carla out of this mess. By the time Carla finished detailing the events of the night, including how the police deceived her into believing her lawyer wasn't coming; Carla's case number came up on the docket.

"Your honor," A.J. stated as she stood before the judge. "I move to have the charges against my client dismissed. Not only was she acting in self-defense against a man who had a documented history of terrorizing her, but my client wasn't properly Mirandized either, which led to an illegally obtained confession."

"Your honor," McKoy interrupted. "The police are allowed to use deceptive tactics when questioning a witness."

"Yes, but they aren't allowed to continue questioning when a suspect asks for a lawyer," A.J. continued. "And that's exactly what my client did. But instead of stopping the questioning process the officers told her that her lawyer refused to come to her aid, and that the only way she could help herself was by providing them with a detailed account of the events. They denied her right to counsel, making any confession obtained thereafter illegal and inadmissible."

The judge sat on his bench, writing down notes, not looking at either party in the courtroom. "Is that true, Mr. McKoy?"

"Your honor, the accused was made aware that she had a right to an attorney," McKoy said.

"Yes, and when my client invoked that right, the cops circumvented it."

"Your honor—"

"The police are allowed to lie to a suspect, but when that suspect explicitly asks for an attorney the police are not allowed to continue questioning the suspect and steamroll over Miranda. Charges dismissed. If your cops find something else to tie the defendant to the crime that isn't included in the tainted confession, feel free to resubmit charges against the defendant."

By the time the judge banged his gavel to end the proceedings, Carla had her arms locked around A.J.'s neck.

"Thank you, thank you!" Carla screamed.

A.J. wrapped her arms around Carla and basically held on while Carla hugged the life out of her. When Carla finally released her iron grip on A.J.'s neck, the fear that was clouding her eyes before was gone. Instead her eyes shone with gratitude and hope.

"Will the D.A. try to bring charges again?"

A.J. shook her head. "I don't think so, not the way I just spanked him in front of the judge. No worries, though, if he refiles, I'll be right here to help you."

Carla grabbed her neck again and gave her another hug. "They had me scared. I thought they were gonna lock me up. I thought all the work I'd done with *Steal Away* was for nothing, that Nico was still going to win."

A.J. smiled at the young woman. "I told you, Carla, the only way to win, is to take the fight to your enemy."

When they were done at the courthouse and Carla was on her way home, A.J. thought about the words she'd spoken to her client. She breathed a long sigh and realized it was time for her to take some of her own advice.

Alan wanted nothing to do with her because all he could see was her lies. She would only be able to stop lying when Reign was no longer a threat. All these years spent back and forth between Azuria and the States and there was still no end to this madness. She and her family still lived in the shadows and the maniac pursuing them was allowed to live his life in the bright light of day. As far as she was concerned, there was something very wrong with that scenario.

She pulled her phone from her pocket and connected the call she should have made a long time ago.

"Teague, I'm ready." The line was silent; she couldn't even hear his breathing coming through her phone. "Teague?"

"I'm here. Are you sure you want to do this? It's a solid plan, but even the most brilliant plans can go wrong. This could end badly for you, A.J. Capture, torture, death, they are all just as likely outcomes as you actually putting an end to Reign. Staying here, that's the best option for your safety that I can provide."

She laughed. Safety was a joke. Her family lived in hiding for so long, and Reign still managed to get close enough to lay hands on her twice in twelve years. She couldn't do this any longer. The lies, the secrets, they were going to kill her if Reign didn't do it first. And now she'd lost Alan, just another casualty in this war for the throne. Something had to be done.

She'd been held hostage by this man's actions since before she was born. Her fate was set the moment he'd marked her family for death. The only way to change things was to take the war to him. It was time for her to fight.

"I'm certain, Teague. Set the arrangements in place, we leave tonight."

CHAPTER 21

The buzzing sound coming from his doorbell pulled him out of his sleep. He rubbed his eyes with the heels of his palms attempting to clear the fog of sleep from his vision. He looked at the digital clock display on the nightstand and saw that it was midnight.

The buzzing became more insistent, followed by obnoxious banging now. Tired and annoyed, he didn't even bother putting on pants over his boxer-briefs, he just stomped his bare feet to the doorway and snatched open the door to find Heart Searlington standing on the other side.

"What the hell, Heart? Do you have any idea what time it is?"

She pushed past him and walked into the apartment, her lips turned up in a salacious grin. "I ought to come knocking more often at this time if that's how you're dressed."

"Aren't you supposed to be happily married to my best friend?"

"I am, but that doesn't mean I can't appreciate a pretty face… and…" she waved her hand in an up and down motion in the air spanning the length of his body. "I can see now why the lady lawyer is so sprung on you."

He didn't even answer her, just went back in his room to pull on his sweats. He came back out into the living room, and found Heart standing in the same spot he'd left her in.

"Why are you here, what's going on?"

She didn't hesitate, just jumped right in to her answer. "Kenneth got a call a little while ago from A.J.'s father asking if he'd seen A.J. Apparently no one has seen her since last night at the office. The family is not ready to file a missing person's report; they couldn't anyway considering it's been less than twenty-four hours since she was last seen. Her father asked if I could quietly take a look into it."

Heart looked the picture of calm; you'd think it was a regular occurrence for her to pop up unexpected on friends' doorsteps in the middle of the night.

"Heart, what the hell is going on? Don't talk to me like this is some routine visit. You're a cop; you wouldn't be here if you didn't think something was wrong. Has something happened to A.J.?"

"I don't know, Alan. That's why I'm here."

There was something strange about the way she was talking to him. "You know don't you?"

"That the two of you are seeing each other?"

"Were, past tense," he answered. "I ended it."

"Mind if I ask why?"

"She nearly killed Kenneth and she refuses to tell me what she was mixed up in that led to three attempts on his life. She just kept coming up with the same bullshit line that she can't tell me."

"What if it wasn't bullshit? What if she really couldn't tell you?"

"She told you, obviously."

Heart pointed to the badge resting on her belt. "She was compelled to inform Captain Searlington of a federal case that she was involved in. If I were just Heart Searlington, she wouldn't have been able to tell me either."

Alan processed what she said. Was A.J. really being as truthful with him as she could be? "Talk to me, Heart. Is she really in trouble?"

"All I can tell you, Alan, is that I'd be a lot happier if I knew where she was at this moment. Have you seen A.J.?"

"About three hours ago when I left work."

She attempted to step around him, heading in the direction of the door.

"Where are you going?"

"To try and find A.J., something is just off about this."

He stepped in front of her, preventing her from leaving. "Give me a sec to get dressed. I'm coming with you."

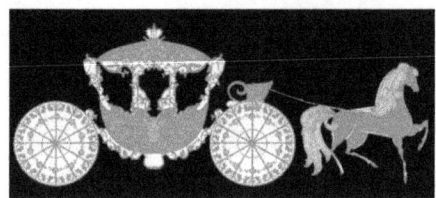

Alan stepped inside of the Tenetti residence behind Heart. They followed Jeovonni to the family room, where he sat next to Gracelyn. From the first moment he'd laid eyes on her, Gracelyn was always poised with a welcoming smile on her face.

Tonight, she sat on the couch, stooped over, elbows resting atop her thighs as she rung her hands repeatedly. Jeovonni sat next to his wife, pulled her hands into his in order to stop their frenzied motion.

"Heart, have you found her?" Jeovonni asked.

"No, I haven't. She's only been gone a few hours. I don't want the two of you getting yourself all worked up until we have more to go on."

"I hope it's all right that I followed Heart here. Once she told me you were looking for A.J., I knew I had to come."

Gracelyn reached for him. He went to her, kneeling in front of her, letting her wrap her arms around him.

"Thank you," she murmured softly.

"Why are the two of you so worried?"

"Because she always checks in, Alan," Gracelyn answered. "In twelve years, she has never missed a check in to let us know she's all right."

Alan's eyes flitted back and forth between Jeovonni and Gracelyn.

He somehow got the impression Gracelyn was referring to something more significant than a grown daughter saying, *I'm safe.*

He watched Gracelyn snatch her hands from her husband. Anger filled her somber face and burned in dark brown eyes.

"This is your fault," she spat at her husband. "If you'd just listened to her instead of—"

"Gracelyn!" Jeovonni's voice was sharp and filled with authority. The usual calm tone of his voice replaced with restrained fury.

Something wasn't right. This entire exchange felt so wrong.

"Gracelyn, Jeovonni, what's going on?"

Gracelyn stood up and walked out of the room. Her quick steps down the corridor were followed by the hard slam of a door. Alan's eyes left the now-empty corridor, then returned to Jeovonni. He saw conflict coloring the older man's face, as if he was warring with himself about something that only he and obviously his wife were privy to.

"Jeovonni?" Alan called to him.

The man battled himself for a few more moments before he finally spoke. "Not long ago my daughter came to me asking my permission to do something that I knew would put her in danger. She asked this impossible thing of me because she wanted to be completely honest with you about who she was, and the secrets she harbored. Out of fear for my daughter's safety, I refused. I guess I misjudged how much you actually mean to her. If I'm right, she went ahead and did what I told her not to anyway."

Alan tilted his head in puzzlement. All of these Tenetti people seemed to be able to talk in circles saying so much without saying much of anything at the same time.

"What are you talking about, Jeovonni? What's going on with A.J.?"

*J*eovonni Tenetti saw much more than concern in the young man's eyes. There was love there. He'd known from the moment he'd seen Alan storming out of A.J.'s office that day, that his daughter and Alan were attracted to each other. He'd been witness to many of their verbal altercations over the years, but that day there was a fire in Alan's eyes that Jeovonni had never witnessed before.

Wanting to make sure it was more than just boardroom bickering, he'd invited Alan to dinner, to see for himself if there was something present between the two. The moment he saw them together at the table he'd known then that Alan was the man that could bring his daughter out of the cold, desolate despair she cloaked herself in.

Children were under the impression that parents were stupid, unaware of what was happing in their lives. Jeovonni watched A.J.'s feelings grow for this man and delighted in knowing there might finally be someone willing to work through all her pain to get to the warm and loving person that resided inside of her.

He'd known they were headed in the right direction when A.J. informed him of her plan to rid them of his brother, Reign. When he'd told her no, he'd never believed she would defy him. She'd never done so in the past. She believed in and understood the hierarchy of the monarchy; she'd never willingly gone against the throne of Azuria. At least not before Alan, she didn't.

"Have you ever heard of a country called Azuria, Alan?" he asked carefully.

"I think so, it's somewhere in the Mediterranean, right? Other than that, I don't know much about it. Why?"

"Are you familiar with the story of Hannibal Barca?"

"No I am not," he said with a little more annoyance coloring his voice.

"Please, bear with me, I promise it will all make sense in the end. Hannibal was a Carthaginian military general during the Punic Wars. At the start of the second Punic war against Rome, he marched an army of one hundred thousand men and almost forty elephants across the Alps. The Romans thought it was impossible, and they thought Hannibal was suicidal, but in the end, they were fatally wrong.

"Not only did he successfully move his campaign across those mountains, but he defeated Rome and occupied Italy for approximately fifteen years. When Rome couldn't beat Hannibal on their own turf, they decided to take the war back to Carthage. Eventually Hannibal was forced to return to his homeland, where he was defeated, and Carthage was forced to agree to Rome's terms.

"Although he eventually lost to Rome, they respected him as a threat. They understood something after Hannibal that they never knew before, the great empire was vulnerable. Hannibal continued to serve several leaders after that as a military strategist, until he was betrayed. Or at least that's the version of the story the history books tell."

Alan's eyes narrowed as he continued to watch Jeovonni. "You speak as though you know differently."

"I do know differently. Hannibal was betrayed to the Roman Empire, this is true. But they never captured him, and he did not commit suicide. When he learned he was about to be betrayed, he fled from what is now modern day Turkey and he and a small amount of his supporters quietly slipped through the Mediterranean until they landed on a small, but beautiful and uninhabited island that he named Azuria.

"He became king, ruled for twenty years after his so-called death was reported, and died peacefully in his sleep with his queen and his children beside him. His legacy in Azuria was one of pride, wealth, and longevity. In fact, one of his great-great grandsons, give or take nearly seventeen hundred years, is still the reigning monarch of Azuria today."

He shook his head. "Jeovonni, this is all very interesting, but what does this have to do with A.J.'s disappearance?"

"My father was born there, Alan. And so was his father before him, and his father before him. We can trace our lineage back nearly seventeen hundred years, to the formation of the country."

"Wait, what? Are you saying…"

"Yes, Alan, I'm saying exactly that. I am a direct descendent of Hannibal Barca, I am Matteo Zinnah Casa di Barca, and the current sitting monarch to the throne of Azuria."

"And that would make A.J.?"

"Fellow countrywoman, because she was also born there, direct descendent to the line of King Hannibal Barca, and the crown princess Ilaria Noemi Casa di Barca of Azuria. One day in the future, she will be Queen of Azuria."

"Holy shit."

*H*e stood on the balcony, looking at the brightly lit bridge in the backdrop of the night. Alan nursed his second two fingers of scotch, still attempting to figure out if he could really believe the things he'd just heard. Tales of ancient monarchies, betrayal, crazy uncles who wanted to kill his brother and niece to be next in line for the throne, secret lives and identities, the American government coming to their ally's rescue, hiding them away in the U.S. until the coast was clear back home. It was like something out of a suspense movie, and if he dared to believe Jeovonni, he and his family spent nearly forty years living this madness.

He finished his drink and contemplated pouring another, but decided against it. He needed to be sober to process the rest of what

Jeovonni needed to say, and by the looks of him, what he'd told Alan was just the beginning.

"Are you all right?" Jeovonni asked while he cautiously took a step toward him.

"I'm all right, just a little unsure of what you're telling me. It all sounds so unbelievable."

"Why so unbelievable? You do know there are still monarchies in the world, right?"

He nodded his head.

"Some of which still maintain absolute power, such as Azuria, versus the political figureheads you see in constitutional monarchies such as the United Kingdom and Monaco."

He nodded his head again. Of course he was aware there were countries that still possessed monarchies. But he never imagined one of the members of an actual royal family would be standing next to him on a balcony in Brooklyn.

"This is all very fantastic, sir. Really it is. I mean it's not every day you find out you've been..." he stopped, realizing who he was talking to, and who he was talking about. "...*dating*," Alan finally spit out. "It's not every day you figure out you're dating the woman who will one day be the sovereign ruler of a country."

"But?" he interjected.

"But what does this have to do with her being missing? I'm assuming this has something to do with all the issues A.J. and I have been having regarding the situation with Kenneth. How is it all connected?"

Jeovonni moved closer to him. He stood next to Alan, seemingly staring at the bridge sitting in the center of the night view. "In a word, Reign," he huffed the name as if its weight was too heavy for his lungs to bear. "He's been plotting against me almost since the day I became King forty years ago. I've always managed to outsmart him, stay a few steps ahead of him, but this time, this time he's been able to get closer than he's ever been before."

He shook his head, he wasn't certain if it was the liquor he'd quickly consumed or Jeovonni's words that were confusing him, but things just didn't seem to add up in his mind.

"Jeovonni, I just don't get this. How has no one known these things about you and your family? You run and own a ridiculously lucrative business. How is it no one knows you're royalty, how has Reign not figured out who and where you are?"

"With the exception of people like Bill Gates, do you know what the heads of the top ten earning businesses of this country look like? No, you know why? The answer is simple really; most of us aren't out taking photo ops for the rag mags. When we need a public face, we send out a pretty PR person and they talk for us. The media doesn't care about us; we're boring, unless we're doing something for media coverage, which we normally try to avoid if we can."

Jeovonni was correct, even being raised in the corporate world; he still couldn't tell you who high-powered business executives were unless he were required to deal with them directly. Even when he was running his grandfather's company, he never really met with other business leaders unless it was absolutely necessary. Otherwise, he usually sent a representative from his executive pool. Apparently Tenetti Enterprises did the same thing.

"What about John? He lives in the media," Alan asked.

Jeovonni tilted his head just slightly then picked up his tablet from the lounge table. He motioned for Alan to join him as he tapped across the screen.

"Search for John T. and tell me what you find," he stated.

He took the tablet and did as Jeovonni asked. The articles he found were scarce, and even the tabloid coverage provided very little details about John other than his music and his suspected romantic liaisons. Considering how popular the man's music was there wasn't much there about his origin and his family, not even his wife and the girls.

"John very rarely plays up to the media. He doesn't talk about his personal life, when rumors abound, he ignores them. He owns his own record label; he doesn't have to bow down to any record execs that demand he present his image the way they want. But there's another reason the world has never connected him to the Azurian monarchy. They don't know that he exists."

He must have been able to read the get-the-fuck-out-of-here expression he was certain was etched on his face.

Jeovonni smiled, a small chuckle passing his lips as he continued his explanation. "When I say 'they' don't know he exists, I mean Azuria, and the world. There is no record of birth for a John Tenetti with the parents Jeovonni and Gracelyn Tenetti as parents. John Tenetti does not exist. I told you my brother has been trying to take the throne for nearly four decades. When I realized this, I knew any child we conceived would be placed in danger. When my wife discovered she was pregnant with John she told no one except me. We fled to the U.S., and my wife remained here under a newly assumed identity while she carried and then delivered our son."

"What happened to you?"

"I am the monarch, just as I do today, I only spend a certain amount of time here in this country before I travel back home. I cannot leave my people and throne unattended indefinitely.

"My wife delivered our son in secret, and John's birth was documented by a new name with parents other than us. He is thought to be the child of a childhood friend of my Gracelyn's who died in childbirth around the same time John was born. His origin story for the press is that he was an orphan taken in by friends of his dead mother. He didn't live with us, not as far as the public knew. Kenneth's father built this apartment building with a series of tunnels that connects certain entrances. Technically, John grew up two floors down with adoptive parents. Once he was inside the apartment, we were able to interact as a solidified family."

"So then how…" he let his sentence drift off into air.

"How is it Azuria knows about A.J? Why did we let them know she existed? It wasn't intentional. Or should I say, she wasn't intentional. My wife didn't realize she was pregnant with our daughter until she was nearly four months pregnant. She had some health concerns at the time that kind of threw off detection. Not to mention, one of Reign's men managed to get close enough to me on one of my return trips home to poison me. It took me many months to recover, and my wife left John here with a caretaker while she returned to Azuria to be by my bedside. It wasn't long before the entire country knew there was an heir on the way."

"So Kenneth didn't take well to finding all this out?" Alan questioned.

"I think he would've been fine with all of it if we hadn't kept it from him. I think even then, he still would have been fine if our secrecy hadn't placed him in danger. Because we couldn't tell Heart what was going on, she couldn't really protect him."

"You've known Kenneth for so long, how did he not know anything of this?"

"Kenneth's father, Kalvin, knew. As I said, he built this building for us. Some things came up hinky in the purchase of the property. Kalvin, doing his due diligence, came to the conclusion that we were frauds. He went to then Detective Porter, his friend, to investigate. It nearly triggered an international incident. The feds came in and smoothed everything over before things got out of control. Kalvin Searlington went to the grave with our secret."

Alan sat down on a nearby chair, burdened with the weight of Jeovonni's revelation.

"There it is," he breathed. "The long and short of it. I'm a king from a foreign land who has been fortunate enough to live in this country under political asylum. I've lived a great deal of my life behind carefully constructed lies. I have perpetuated those lies in defense of my family and my country. Those lies have poisoned almost every aspect of my life, including my family's friendship with Kenneth. I guess the only thing I'm waiting to find out now is just how it's affected this thing between you and my daughter."

Jeovonni was right. This was a very complicated situation, complicated even more by what Alan now knew was A.J.'s need to protect her homeland and family against her need to protect her friends.

He was pissed. Angered that she'd chosen to lie to him, to keep him out of the very small group of people that knew the truth of who she was. It hurt that she hadn't believed or considered the option of trusting him with her truth.

"Why wouldn't she trust me?" he asked, aching at the knowledge she'd been carrying such a burden.

That answer wrapped up in a question rubbed on something significant in his soul. Made him ache in a way he hadn't since his wife died. That space in the center of his chest that housed his guilt, the place that stored all of his self-blame for Beth's death. The ache he carried inside throbbed just enough for him to notice his guilt wasn't just about his deceased wife, but about this woman whose father now stood before him.

She'd accused him of taking Kenneth's side, in presuming her guilt. She hadn't been wrong. He'd known she was the cause of all this chaos; she was the mastermind of it, why wouldn't this time be her fault too?

If she felt that way, felt condemned by him, why would she trust him enough to share such delicate and powerful secrets about her life? If he was only going to see her flaws then why bother with exposing herself to him that way?

"Because the last person she trusted nearly caused our destruction twelve years ago."

"What do you mean destroyed, figuratively?" Alan asked almost frightened of the answer he would receive.

"Unfortunately it wasn't. My daughter fell in love for the first time in law school. She met a young man named David Upton."

Alan's body physically tightened at the mention of that name.

"You seem as if you've heard that name before," Jeovonni commented.

"I have. A.J. told me he was an ex-boyfriend that cheated on her."

Jeovonni nodded, but there was a sadness in his eyes that told Alan there was more to this story than just an indiscretion.

"He worked his way into her heart, and she was completely enamored with him. But something just never seemed right about him. Nothing particular, just the way he watched her, like she was an object, not someone he loved.

"One night, she went to his apartment unexpectedly and found him in bed with someone else. Turns out the woman wasn't just his sex partner, she was someone who worked for my brother. Apparently, Reign somehow managed to hack the FBI's files. He couldn't get much in the data breach, didn't know where we were, or what names we were living under. He was only able to piece together bits and pieces that led him to her law school.

"The plan was to take her to Reign for confirmation, but her finding him in bed with someone else blew the entire operation out of the water. So they beat her, nearly killed her, and attempted to kidnap her. The only thing that saved her life was an elephant charm I gave her. It was a tracker. She turned it on, and we found them before they could escape with her. The authorities dealt with them on the spot, my brother never learned where we were, or what happened to his operatives. Our identities were safe, and A.J. was returned to us. She's blamed herself for that incident for years. Trusting after something like that, it's almost impossible for her."

Alan's mind churned as all the missing pieces began to fall into place. "The *Steal Away* Project?" Alan asked.

"It's her way of helping other victims of abuse. It's how she conquers that particular demon in her life. Through advocacy for others, she's learned to fight for herself."

Fighting for others had always been her greatest strength, now he understood the drive, the need to represent those who had no say in this world.

Alan slumped in his chair as understanding moved quickly through him. All the things he'd believed about A.J., he'd never considered that perhaps her ability to fight for others was a way of working through her own demons. He of all people should have understood that. He should have recognized the signs of a person living in fear of her past. He saw that very same fear looking back at him in the mirror every morning.

Trusting someone else must have seemed impossible, it had for him. What must A.J. have experienced, especially when the man who claimed to love her accused her of lying? No, he hadn't had all of the facts, but he'd known her long enough that it should have been evident she hadn't purposely brought trouble to Kenneth.

And now she was in trouble again. Trying to right a wrong so she could appease him, give him the honesty that he demanded. Now her life was in the balance, and that all-important honesty didn't seem all that significant right now.

"Where is she, Jeovonni?"

"I don't know. But I will find out. And when I do, Alan, I need to know, are you going to be the type of man that my daughter deserves, the type of man that will stand by her? Or are you going to leave when things get murky and trouble is at her door? Decide which man you are, Alan, because as much as I like you, I'll be damned if I'll let you hurt her again."

CHAPTER 22

Alan sat in the dimly lit sports bar nursing his beer. He'd left the Tenettis' and refused the ride Heart offered him back home. It was late, and the streets were quiet, but he couldn't go home just yet. He hopped in a cab to downtown Brooklyn and found a local bar to duck into.

The woman he was seeing was royalty. She was an actual princess who would one day be a queen. As strange as that should sound, it all just seemed to make sense where A.J. was concerned. If there were anyone who was going to be a secret princess living in Brooklyn, it would be her.

Smart, funny, witty, and wise beyond her actual years, not to mention the confidence and power that blanketed her from head to toe kept him fascinated with the cinnamon-toned beauty.

He took another swig of his beer. Her father wanted him to think about his decision to be with her to make certain he was making the right decision. In the beginning, he'd done nothing but question his attraction for her, then his involvement with her. Now things somehow evolved into something he could never have imagined.

He loved her. He couldn't honestly say he'd have chosen to love her. He'd always known a woman like her possessed the power to ruin him. But he'd fallen for her, and now he needed to consider if that love was enough. The truth was he and A.J. were often times volatile together. Even now that they were separated, there was always this passionate undercurrent that made him feel like their relationship could implode at any moment.

"If you lousy sons of bitches would actually play some defense, we might have a chance at salvaging this fucking game."

Alan's attention was drawn from the beer in his hand to the man sitting a couple of stools over from him yelling at the widescreen television on the wall. It was quiet for a Thursday night. It was the only reason Alan could actually hear what the man was saying in the first place.

The man was slim, with penny brown skin, and a close cropped dark Cesar haircut. His lanky arms were jerking back and forth in an animated fashion, and he was going absolutely crazy as his team lost another point to their opponents.

"Hey man, I'm sorry if I'm being too loud. Just pisses me off how these suckers have been playing lately."

"Not a problem, I didn't know games ran this late," Alan replied.

The man leaned over the empty stool sitting between the two of them and extended his hand to Alan.

"Darius," he offered.

"Alan," he replied.

"They don't, the bartender records it on DVR for patrons like me that were working while it was playing. You watch?" Darius asked.

"When I have a moment free," Alan responded. "Between work and my lady..." Alan paused briefly. He knew he didn't have the right to call A.J. that. Not when he'd chosen to walk away from her. "Can't say there's been all that much time for watching games," he finished as he pasted a neutral smile on his face.

"Ohhh," Darius answered with little bit of a smile. "Sounds like you're happy and in love if you've got no time to watch a game or two."

Alan laughed. He let that be his only answer to the man. He didn't really want to think about the fact that he'd let bullshit get between he and his woman.

"You're lucky man, if she makes you smile like that, hold on to her. I didn't really play my cards right where my wife was concerned, and it left an opportunity for things to get bad between us."

"Sorry about that," Alan offered.

"Thanks, things got pretty bad for a time, but that's all behind us. We're working at it slowly."

"Wish you all the best with that, Darius," Alan added.

Alan glanced over at Darius, wondering if the bad things he mentioned could compare to any of the craziness Alan and A.J. were living right now. He doubted any other man was worried about the secret royal life of his girlfriend. But listening to Darius affirmed what Alan should have always known, he didn't want to lose A.J.

Alan finished his beer and settled his tab with the bartender.

"Running back to your lady?" Darius asked with a smile.

Alan returned the friendly smile. "Yeah, the beer and the company is good, but…"

"But spending time with your woman is better. No worries, man, I just wish I'd have been smart enough to go home to my woman when I should have."

Alan clapped a hand on Darius' shoulder. "Hindsight is twenty-twenty. The most important thing is you're trying to make it right. Good luck, man."

Alan stepped outside of the bar and headed for the train. He checked the new message beeping on his phone from Jeovonni.

Worse than I feared, she's headed to Azuria.

Alan flipped through a few screens until he found the contact he was looking for on his phone. "I need to borrow your plane," Alan stated.

"Any particular reason why?" the voice replied.
"Because I need to save the woman I love."

"How the hell did I not know this?"

Kenneth sat down across from him on the plush leather chair. He'd called his friend in a panic asking for his plane, and Kenneth being the friend that he was made it happen.

"You've had a lot on your plate. Recovering from a gunshot wound, the ups and downs you and Heart were having as a result of it; there was just too much going on at the time."

"I'm certain the fact that I wanted nothing to do with A.J. also didn't make you feel you could share this with me."

"You had a valid reason," Alan replied.

"There's never a good reason to not be there for the people you love," Kenneth responded.

The stone in Alan's gut felt heavier after that statement. There was no getting around the fact that he'd let the woman he loved down, again.

He looked up and passed a quick glance at the other passengers. A.J.'s parents and Heart, they were huddled together; probably talking tactical strategies or something of that nature if the intense expressions on each of their faces were any indication.

Everyone on this plane was there for one reason alone, A.J. was in danger. As he counted the hours until they landed in Azuria he could think of only one thing. He'd placed her there.

He looked out of the window, the endless darkness staring back at him. They'd left New York at nearly three in the morning. After eleven hours in the air and a six hour time difference waiting for them, it would be nearing eight in the evening when they arrived in Azuria. His body was tired, he hadn't slept save the hour or so he'd been in bed when Heart woke him up. But as painfully exhausted as he was, the only thought to cross his mind was A.J. needed him, and he'd failed her.

He'd done that before, failed the woman he loved. The results were catastrophic. He couldn't let that happen again.

"We'll get there in time." Kenneth's voice pulled him out of his head.

He blinked back the guilt that was attempting to swallow him whole. "We have to," was all he could utter. He was too afraid to even think about the consequences if they didn't.

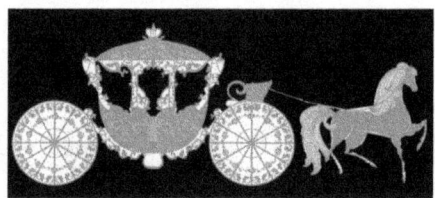

A.J. stepped out of the plane and onto the runway floor. She wanted to fall to the ground, let her fingers sift through the earth beneath her feet. She was home. She hadn't seen her birthplace in years, and never in the brightness of day.

She blinked back the tears that were threatening to overwhelm her in order to see the throng of people held behind the barricades.

My people.

She looked across the crowd; saw banners adorned with her coat of arms, the profile of a female monarch in the center of a heart-shaped heraldic symbol protected by two majestic elephants, displayed proudly across them as their bearers chanted her name in praise. This was how her father presented her to her countrymen on the day of her birth, and her people still held her symbol with such pride that it was almost too much for her fractured soul to bear.

Whenever her presence was called for in Azuria, she snuck in under the cover of night. Today, she stood proudly in front of her people, letting them see the princess they deserved, honored, confident, and strong.

A.J.'s eyes fell to the line of royal attendants standing at the waiting motorcade. A man of her father's age stepped forward. He was a tall man of African descent, with a slim build. He was dressed in a tailored black suit with the breast and shoulders of his suit jacket covered in the various insignias and badges indicating his extensive service to the royal house of Barca. He was the senior staff member to the royal family of Azuria, and he worked tirelessly to attend their needs and protect their persons. Marchio Mensah was his given name, but almost everyone called him by his titled designation, *Signore Cortigiano*.

He stepped in front of her, saluting her with the customary bow, granted to members of the royal house. "Your Highness, Azuria welcomes your safe return."

"You may rise, *Signore Cortigiano*. Thank you, I am just happy to stand foot on our land again."

The man rose to his full height and looked behind her as her travel companions exited the plane. "Are His and Her Majesty accompanying the princess Ilaria?"

"Not this time," she answered. The good thing about being the crown princess or any high-ranking member of the royal family is that people didn't often question your statements. They did not expect a monarch to explain, because the monarchy was absolute. If she'd explained she'd returned home without the permission of their king, her status would not have saved her.

"*Signore Cortigiano*, it's been a very long flight and I wish to retire quietly and quickly. Can you make that happen?"

He bowed again. "By your command, Your Highness."

He turned to face the crowd and raised his hand, silencing them. The sharp sounds of a blaring trumpet signaled the royal herald. "People of Azuria, I present to you, Her Royal Highness, Ilaria Noemi Casa di Barca, the crown princess, heir to the throne of Azuria."

A.J. heard the roar of her people. Felt the rush of their pride and praise thumping in the excited beat of her heart. She was home, and her people were happy she was home. No matter what happened beyond this moment, she would take their show of love and pride to her last breath.

She watched her companions surround her. They were dressed in Azurian Royal Guard uniforms, something to be expected in a monarch when returning home. Teague stood next to her, giving her a reassuring glance.

"Are you certain you still want to do this? I can just as easily put you back on that plane. No harm, no foul."

"This ends now, Teague. Whether I live or die, the monarchy will no longer live in fear of my uncle. Even if I don't survive this, my father will be able to return to his throne as was always intended. Azuria will survive my death, but not his, not now."

Teague nodded and fell in line with the rest of the guards surrounding her and they made their way to the royal motorcade. She slid inside the limousine and expected Teague to slide in beside her, instead, True Amare sat on one side of her, and her brother Law was positioned on the other.

"Does your cousin know you're here defending my life, True?"

"Heart only knows what I need her to know. But even though I didn't tell her, she'll find out soon enough."

A.J. grimaced. "What do you mean?"

"I received communication from our general, your parents and Heart are on a plane headed here as we speak. We've got about four hours before they get here. So we'd better get this shit done, or things are going to get more dangerous than they already are."

The forward motion of the vehicle jostled her slightly. True was right, the minute her parents stepped foot back in Azuria, things would become much more complicated than they already were.

"Do we know if Reign or his men are in country? I know we made it obvious that I was coming back for Festival Day, but do we know if he's taken the bait?"

"Yes," Law answered. He was gruff and quiet, and his monosyllabic answer fit his abrasive personality to a tee. But as intimidating as his exterior often appeared, knowing he was here to protect her gave her comfort. "According to our intel, he's mobilizing his supporters. We have eyes on him heading toward the palace."

She slid back into the cushions of her seat and closed her eyes. Regardless of the outcome, their plan was underway. No sense in worrying about how it would all unfold, there was no turning back now. She just prayed it would all be over one way or another before her parents arrived.

CHAPTER 23

She entered the throne room of the palace and stopped directly in front of the splendor that marked the seat of the Azurian monarchy.

There were three chairs on the dais. The center, the largest, covered in gold, the two armrests fashioned into the body of the fierce lion, the head, bold and proud at the end, its golden mane fanned out in a brilliant display, baring its teeth to any enemy that would dare approach. The chair on the left was smaller and slightly less ornate than the chair in the middle. It too bore the mark of the lion, but in female form, still mighty, still fierce. And then there was the chair set to the right of the center. It was smaller still than the left chair, but just as ornate at the center. Covered in gold like the center chair, but the armrests were carved elephants, their tusks and trunks lifted high in the air.

These were the seats of the three members of the royal family, created for each based on their hierarchal titles. Her father, the king, the most significant of the three, her mother his partner, but not born to the royal family, and the daughter, the next presumptive monarch.

When she was a child, whenever they'd visit Azuria, she would climb onto the throne and take the seat reserved for her father. Her father would smile at her small body being swallowed up by the massive piece of furniture and ask her, "Practicing to be a good Queen, Ilaria?"

Those tender and amusing moments were always far and few in between in their homeland. They were always on guard, always preparing for flight, always at the ready. She wanted her father to be able to have those moments. For her brother to be able to set foot on their father's ancestral home and assume his role as the prince.

She ran her hands over the lions on her father's seat and whispered, "Please forgive me, great lion. How I wish I could have made you understand that there was no other way."

"Aww, is the princess on the outs with her king?"

A.J. turned around to see the monster that haunted her dreams as far back as her childhood. Slightly shorter than her father, much more round in body stature, and his eyes were a muddy brown. That was where the differences between the two men ended. Reign shared the same rust-colored, wavy hair, the same olive-toned skin that was a perfect mix of their Italian and African ancestry, and the same ferociousness that sparkled in his father's eyes.

"Caino," she watched his eyes twitch at her use of his given name. She was sure he was equally irritated by her lack of use of any type of honorific before his name. She refused to call him by the moniker he used to run her family away from their home. As long as she lived, he would not reign over anything other than his own insanity. "Are you still lurking around my father's throne at night wishing it was yours? I figured you'd show up sooner or later. Surprised it took you this long to figure out I was in country."

"The Americans have spoiled you with their disrespect and distain for tradition. I am your elder, you will address me—"

"You are nothing to me," she howled. "I am the future queen of this nation and as such, you will remember your place when you stand in my presence!"

For a brief moment she saw the memorized response that most possessed who were raised in the royal court. You didn't just forget that deeply ingrained training because you decided to go off the bend.

"I am Reign, and you would do well to remember that, princess. I knew the moment you landed. Your father has always been skilled in keeping his plans secret from me, but you're not that clever, niece. Your mistake will be just the thing I need to move forward with my plans. Azuria will be mine."

"Azuria will never belong to any one man. And our people will never let a tyrant like you assume the throne. Who will protect you, Caino? The royal guard will turn from you; the army will fight against you. And the Americans will clasp a leash around your neck and parade you through the streets like the dog you truly are. Who will be the force behind you to keep you in place, Caino? You've spent the last forty years of your life trying to figure out how to kill my family, but you never thought beyond the moment of our deaths, did you?"

She could tell the truth of her statement resonated with him. Reign's power always resonated in fear. He possessed enough men to kill the monarchs yes, but would he ever be able to maintain the monarchy afterwards, no.

"You only saw the shiny crown, you didn't think about all it takes for my father to keep this country thriving. You have no clue what sacrifices my father has made in order to keep us safe, healthy, and successful. We are a tiny island nation amongst nations who are so much larger and who possess greater militaries than our own. Yet, none of them have ever threatened to breech our shores, or shown aggression toward us. That's because my father is a true king, and he does what is necessary to protect his people."

He stepped closer to her, an angry snarl pulling at his thin lips. "The Americans don't give a damn about us. They are raping this land of its natural resources in exchange for a flimsy promise that they will protect us from our enemies."

"So foolish," she uttered as she shook her head and wagged her finger in a scolding motion. "You have no clue what the Americans are willing to do for the Azurians. We share blood, and Americans will always back one of their own."

His laughter bubbled up from some place deep inside him. If the evil he carried inside him hadn't been so pervasive, she would almost fashion the smile that crept on his face as pleasant. "You think the American's care about a single woman from some backward ass hole in the Southeast? You're delusional, princess."

"There's much you don't know about my mother. You could only see her as a pretty accessory that my father adorned himself with. My mother is the daughter of a prominent senator in the United States. How do you think we've managed to elude your attempts all this time? Did you think it was solely because the Americans wanted to help us that they've protected us all this time? They weren't just protecting the Azurian monarchy; they were protecting one of their own."

"I think you're overstating things a bit, dear niece. She's the daughter of a junior senator from somewhere in the bush. That man has no authority or prowess in the American government."

She stepped away from him, walking until she stood in front of her father's seat. "Yes' my maternal grandfather was only a junior senator. But that doesn't mean he didn't have powerful friends. My grandfather served in the army with a man who would one day become a four-star general. A man who's sole job is to protect America and her people by any means necessary. He is a man who also happens to hold the ear of the current sitting President of the United States of America. So again, I ask you, are you really willing to risk what will become of your life if you massacre my family? And if you do, where will you run when America sets its sights on you?"

*A*lan stepped off the plane and into darkness. The empty landscape of nothingness surrounded them; there were no lights present to show them the way. Alan's heart rate hitched up in pace, unsure of what the actual hell they were walking into.

"Is this Azuria?" Alan asked.

"No, this is Sicily. We couldn't land Kenneth's plane in Azuria. I felt it was better to have military support going in," Jeovonni answered. Alan looked beyond Jeovonni to see lights turning on breaking through the darkness, revealing a mountainside he hadn't been able to decipher in the dark.

Soon they were surrounded by uniformed military personnel. Even with the newly applied light, it was still too dark for Alan to decipher exactly what branch of whose military, but the large guns carried by these soldiers were clue enough that these were not your everyday homeowners carrying guns for personal protection.

"Your Majesty, I'm Lieutenant Johnson of the United States Navy, welcome to Naval Air Station *Sigonella*."

Alan watched Jeovonni shake hands with the African American man. The lieutenant was probably somewhere near the same mid-thirties that Alan found himself in. He was fit, and he reeked of command. Alan didn't know dick about military ranks, but he could see how the other men in the assembling squad looked to this man for their direction.

"My men are going to be broken up into two teams to escort you and the Queen to Azuria. We've made contact with a small team of U.S. assets that are in country now. We're going in by helo."

"Wait a minute, what about Kenneth, Heart, and me?" Alan asked.

"Mr. Quillen—"

Alan faced the lieutenant, uncomfortable with the fact that the man knew his identity before Alan offered it.

"You and Mr. Searlington will not be allowed on the island until it can be deemed safe and all targets are in custody. Captain Searlington, your uncle, General Amare, assures me that you would be an asset to the operation, and I should bring you along if you desire to accompany us."

Heart's eyes sparked with a sliver of excitement, but then she met the concern on her husband's face and stepped back. "Thank you for the offer, but I just came for moral support of my husband and the king and queen."

Alan watched Kenneth release a relieved breath then pull his wife into his embrace. He'd come all this way to see A.J., protect her, and he couldn't, the ability taken completely out of his hand.

He felt Heart's hand touch his face in soft comforting strokes. He'd never seen her touch people much, usually reserving her affection for her husband. But in that moment that soft touch gave him the strength he needed to stay calm.

"Let them do their job, Alan," she whispered. "If there is a chance in hell A.J.'s going to walk out of this, these guys are going to be her saving grace. Not to mention, if my suspicions are correct, I think the princess is in trusted hands."

He'd have to believe her, for now anyway. The lieutenant directed the three of them to fall back a safe distance. Soon Alan heard the sound of the heavy metal blades of the helicopters slicing through the air. Lieutenant Johnson and his men quickly guiding the king and queen into their seats and within moments, the two helicopters were in the air, drifting into the darkened sky.

He kept looking into the night, long after the sight of the helicopters disappeared, long after the sound of their whooping blades became silent. "If they don't save her, she'll never know how proud I am of the sacrifices she's made. She'll never know how terrible I feel for all the miserable things I said to her. She'll die thinking I believed her to be a liar. She'll never know how much I loved her."

Kenneth flanked his other side and they both stood there, holding him, supporting him, reassuring him that this nightmare would be over soon. Neither of them, however, told him it would be all right. All three of them knew that would be an outright lie.

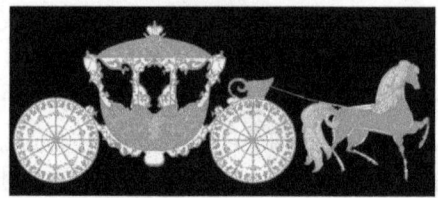

A.J. watched as several men entered the throne room, joining Reign's flanks. She slid a steady hand inside of her pocket and held tightly to the insurance policy True handed her before she'd walked onto this stage.

She kept her eyes fixed on Reign and his men as he smiled and they moved closer to her. Each of them was heavily armed with large weapons. She asserted the long practiced pose of command while she answered with a smile of her own.

She turned slightly, and sat on her father's throne. "You dare to defile my father's palace with your rabid pack of mangy dogs."

"Princess, you're really delusional if you think you alone can stop me from ascending to the throne."

A.J. heard the words she'd been waiting for whispered in her ear via the small earpiece placed by Teague earlier. "Everything on our end is completed. Let's wrap this up."

She held her back straight and kept the tremble dancing inside her body from reaching through to the outside. "I am the crown Princess Ilaria Noemi Casa di Barca, heir to the throne of Azuria. I bow before no one but God and my king. In the absence of my father, King Matteo Zinnah Casa di Barca, I am the regent and his sovereignty will be represented through my command. *Regnaba verbo et factis*, I rule by word and deed."

Her uncle and his men laughed loudly until they recognized the hand grenade clasped in her fingers. "Do you know the difference between a king and a tyrant, Caino?" she asked. "A king serves his people, even to death. A tyrant serves no one but himself, and will step on the backs of his people to save his own life. My father, and by extension me, has always been willing to die for our people. Are you?"

She laced her finger through the ring connected to the pin of the grenade. "Lay down your weapons and your lives will be spared," she announced. The men all looked cautiously at one another and then to her uncle. She could see from the brief glint of uncertainty in their eyes that they were concerned about her threat.

"You think you've won, you think you can stop me by flashing a grenade? I will have the throne, and I will destroy every member of your family in order to obtain what is mine. And I think I'm going to start with this one."

He pointed his hand toward the door and her world stopped. Her heart beat struck a chaotic rhythm, one she was certain wasn't intended to sustain life for long periods of time. The sound of it filled her ears as recognition made its way from her eyes to her brain.

His arm bound behind his back with a bright red gash marring his right cheek, her brother, John was dragged into the throne room. Reign turned his back briefly to reach for John. That was all the opening needed before the muted sound of bullets passing through silencers sifted through the air. Reign's men dropped almost simultaneously to the ground. As she realized what was happening, he grabbed John and positioned him in front of him.

"Let him go, Caino." Fear clutched at her throat. This was not part of her plan to use herself as bait to draw Reign out. She'd purposely placed herself in the line of fire so that her family would never have to stand there. How had he managed this without her knowing?

"What possible gain do you think placing this man in danger will leverage you?"

Reign laughed again. "So clever with your words, princess," he chuckled. "If I were a stupid man I'd question whether you actually knew him. But see, thanks to a conversation overheard on your secretary's phone, I learned the truth."

"No way in hell Carole is working for you," she snapped through clenched teeth.

"Oh, she's not," he laughed. "It took me years to get any information on you. When I breeched the FBI database twelve years ago, we literally obtained the tiniest pieces of information on my brother and his brood. For years I couldn't really make sense of it. The strongest lead I ever discovered was getting the name of your law school. Knowing how old you were, I was able to guess you'd be a student there."

Her throat tightened as she remembered that time. The memory of her first experience at love still shook her. Even after twelve years the flashes of her boyfriend and his lover beating her to a bloody pulp and trying to end her life still made her want to curl into the fetal position to protect herself.

"The plant I placed in the school was only able to get me a handful of names. After months of nothing, he finally set up a meet with me to give me a name, and then he miraculously disappeared before he could do so. It took me nearly ten more years to figure out a significant amount of money was being funneled into Azuria via a company named Tenetti Enterprises. And even once I figured that out, it was almost impossible for me to find a way in. I could never manage to get someone in that could get a listening device in the right place, and then one day one of my people bugged your secretary's phone. You never said anything, but one day this young man made a call from Carole's phone to your father."

Her insides clenched in fear, but she kept her gaze steady on her brother and his captor. "Imagine my surprise when I discovered I had a nephew I never knew about, and that he was so famous. I decided my new nephew and I needed to get to know each other. So I swapped his driver with a man of my own when he was leaving a venue on his tour so we'd have a chance to become acquainted." He smiled again making the fear settled in her heart churn into boiling anger.

"I will hunt you down like the dog you are if you don't walk away from him now," she growled between clenched teeth.

Reign raised a gun to John's head and eased his way toward the door. When he was gone, she screamed for Teague.

Teague and two of the Amare brothers raced from the hiding spaces within the walls and took off after him. When she moved to follow them, she felt a strong hand keep her planted in her seat.

"Let them handle it, Princess. Your presence will only complicate the situation," Justice said. He turned her around and removed the grenade from her hand before releasing her.

She was tempted to tell Justice to go to hell, but then she realized he was right. She possessed no military or combat training, how would she help by adding another body for them to protect? She heard yelling outside the palace window. She ran to see what was happening. There were two military helicopters landing with armed men jumping onto the ground, with their weapons drawn, screaming at Reign and his men to surrender.

Reign raised his weapon to John's head. A.J.'s shriek pierced the air, drawing Reign's attention back to the palace. The small distraction allowed True Amare to land a thrown blade into Reign's neck. He dropped his hold on John, and when he turned, a single bullet from True's gun met his skull in the dead center of his forehead.

Her breath left her chest and she fell to the cool marble floor. Just like that it was over, it worked, her family was free.

CHAPTER 24

A.J. stood on her balcony overlooking the crystal blue water of the Mediterranean Sea. The calming waves of the water swaying back and forth, lulled the island and its inhabitants, washing the anxiety of yesterday's events quietly away. A knock on the door drew her attention from the water.

"Your Highness, pardon my interruption, but there is someone here who is rather eager to see you."

She turned around with eyebrows drawn into a perfect point. "*Signore Cortigiano*, I've given my accounts of last night's events to all of the necessary authorities. If there are more, have them come back another time."

"I'm not here to take your report, A.J."

The sound of that voice pulled her away from the window. She walked toward it, not realizing how much she'd missed hearing it.

"Alan, how did you get here?"

He didn't respond, simply pulled her to him and crushed his mouth against hers. He didn't kiss her; he was drinking from her mouth, stealing her breath, and filling her with his desire all at once.

"If you ever do anything that crazy or dangerous ever again, I swear to God, I will throttle you myself. What the hell were you thinking dangling yourself as bait for that crazed maniac?"

"I was thinking that I couldn't risk living the way I was living any longer. The lies the secrets, it was just too much to bear anymore."

He caressed her hair; gently touching the curly strands as if he were making certain each one was present and accounted for.

"I didn't mean for you to do this, A.J. I would never have knowingly asked you to do this."

"You didn't know, Alan. You couldn't have. All the parties involved were sworn to secrecy by both the Azurian and American governments. There was nothing more that could be done."

"You didn't have to be the one to take it all on your shoulders, though."

She pressed a gentle kiss to his cheek and walked back to the window. "My father needed to focus on the country and the family. John couldn't be a part of it because we were trying to keep him hidden. The only person that could have accomplished this was me. That's the weight of leadership, the mantle of responsibility, knowing what your role is and being willing to sacrifice whatever you have to make certain your people are protected."

She laced her fingers through his and smiled up at him. "I want to show you my home, my people. You won't be able to understand why I did what I did, until you see my people and my kingdom, through my eyes."

Alan stepped outside onto the marble steps of the palace to see what looked to be a small caravan of horses and their riders.

All of the horses were draped in an ornate red cloth that sparkled in the bright sunlight and five of them whose saddles were empty. Of the five, four bore a coat of arms depicted on their drapes. The four images were all similar with minute differences between them. Two bore lions, one bore elephants, and the last possessed a set of unicorns. Alan turned to A.J. with questioning eyes as he pointed at the spectacle before them.

"Are we going horseback riding?" he asked.

"We have not been able to be with our people freely in years. This is the best way to see the parts of the country we're traveling to today. Can you ride?"

He nodded, and took her hand as she extended it to him. Soon they were joined by John, Jeovonni, and Gracelyn.

Once her parents joined them, the group of men attending the horses stood at attention and bowed their heads in the presence of their king. Alan watched the scene in awe; he'd never have imagined all of this pageantry existed.

He followed the Tenettis' to their waiting horses. When he attempted to help A.J., she smiled, took his hand, and allowed him to help her seat her steed. It was the first time he noticed her readily accept the help of another. She'd probably been riding right out of the womb, but she'd accepted his help with grace. The mantle of dark secrets no longer covered her and she seemed freer somehow.

They rode through certain parts of the country; crowds screaming in celebration as the royal caravan made its way through several small towns. A.J. and her family smiled and waved, and seemed equally as thrilled to be amongst their countrymen. It was all a little overwhelming witnessing this in person, being a part of it all.

But watching how these people celebrated the royal family, he now understood all of the sacrifices A.J. made. These people were her responsibility; they lived and died by her actions. The bright smiles, the beaming faces, would not exist if the royal family did not protect their shores, their land, their way of life.

He felt her eyes rest on him, her amber gaze speculative as it took him in. "You okay?" she asked. "I know this is all a little much for someone who isn't used to it."

"I don't think I've ever seen or felt anything like this in my life. The unity, the diversity all converging in one place, it's beautiful." He swept his hand across the throng of people celebrating in the streets. "Your people are just as ethnically diverse as America, and yet, there seems to be this common bond of brotherhood that I don't think I've ever really experienced back home."

"We don't really classify people in terms of race here. In America, I'm a black woman, in Azuria, I'm Azurian. It's not that we don't recognize that there are different classifications of ethnicities and races. We do. I am a black woman, I have always identified as such. Yes, if I straighten my hair or add the right lighting I could probably pass for something other than black, but that would be denying who I am. I'm proud of the African blood that runs through my veins, of the struggles my people have encountered, of the strength they've passed down to me through the ages. Having a white father and brother doesn't negate that. It also doesn't mean I can't love all of my family and people."

"It's a shame things aren't as clear cut in the States," he answered.

"I think the answer to that lies in the way my country was founded. This land was empty when King Hannibal and his people arrived. We've also historically been a country that welcomed those that were outcasts of the world here. When the first king arrived, he was fleeing capture by the Romans. That kind of set the national perspective on political persecution for us."

He was still having a hard time believing how extensive her family's lineage was. She knew all of these facts as if she'd lived them herself. He realized then that her power rested in that knowledge. It was the reason she always looked as if she wore greatness, because she knew it flowed in her blood.

"Our monarchs have always fought against tyranny and persecution," she continued, "some in actual battle, some in more intellectual ways. During the transatlantic slave trade the sitting monarch sent groups of our more European-looking citizens to Spain to purchase Africans who were enslaved and bring them back to Azuria. The rest of the world thought we were participating in chattel slavery right along with them. The moment those slaves reached our shores they were granted their freedom and allowed to either stay, or seek out their destinies elsewhere," she stated.

"What you call diversity, is just a result of our longstanding belief that we are all the same. Our culture is this beautiful kaleidoscope of people from all over the world. European, African, Latin, even as far as the Caribbean. The synthesis of traditions to create this one unique culture was the original goal of my ancestors. It's the reason Festival Day is the most important holiday in our culture."

"What is it exactly?" he asked.

"It's the day we celebrate everything that makes us, us. Every sect, every ethnicity, every subculture is celebrated. It's sort of like a carnival, there are parades, and food, and fun, and it's all a way for each of us to learn about our different points of origin while still embracing our fellowship. It's loud and spectacular, and this one will be the best I've ever experienced."

"Because Reign is dead?"

"Because my people and my family are free and because I get to spend it with you."

They made it to a small town that was strikingly different from the others. Where the previous communities were littered with modern style homes, paved roads, and many other amenities, one would expect to find in a city in the twenty-first century, this place sang of an ancient past.

The land was covered in dirt and sand. For miles out he saw no buildings made of modern brick, but stone and sand. Ancient buildings littered across the landscape and as the caravan moved further inland, the community's inhabitants began to gather around them. They were draped in robes, their heads covered in turbans, the exposed portions of the skin covered in what appeared to be intricate tribal markings of red, black, brown, and white paint.

The rest of the party dismounted, and Alan followed suit. As they stood there, an elder man, his headdress bigger and richer in color than any other Alan could see, stepped forward and began to speak in staccato words that Alan couldn't understand. Although there was force and bravado behind the deep tone of the man's voice, Alan felt no aggression from the man.

The tribal elder stepped forward and opened his arms wide. Jeovonni smiled and stepped into the man's embrace. Once the connection was made, the other members of the tribe began to chant and dance in some sort of celebration that Alan couldn't understand.

He looked to A.J. for an explanation, and met teary eyes and a smile. "What's happening?" he asked.

"These are the Tribù," she answered. "They are the aboriginal people of the island. They live like and keep the traditions of the ancient Carthaginians. They live here in this part of the country, keeping the old ways alive. They speak Phoenician, an ancient Mediterranean language that was spoken in places like Carthage, Israel, Egypt."

"Can you understand it?" he asked.

Her smile brightened. "Yes, I do. If I'm to serve all my people, then I must speak all their languages. He is the Tribù elder. He says the gods are celebrating the return of the great lion to our lands. That Azuria will receive bountiful blessings now that the rightful king has returned."

The elder looked in the direction of A.J. and called out something that sounded like, ill-ah-ree-ah. She stepped away from him and he gripped her arm with concern. She gave him a comforting glance and his hand dropped hesitantly from her.

The elder spoke several more words that Alan didn't understand, and embraced A.J. in much the same way as he had her father. Again the people began to chant and celebrate. When A.J. stepped out of his embrace, she walked back to where Alan stood amongst their group.

"What did he say to you?"

"That the gods smile because the king has returned so that he may make way for the new queen."

"What does that mean?"

She kissed him, and snuggled into his embrace. "I have no idea."

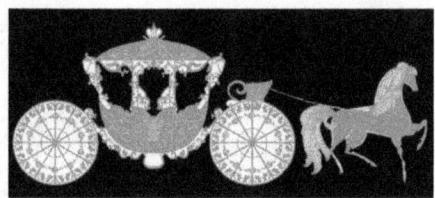

*A*lan stood in a great room that seemed to be some sort of library. Either that or a museum of some sort, he surmised. The four walls were each covered with the same coat of arms images he saw draped across the horses earlier.

He stepped closer to the wall with the elephants. This close, they appeared almost life like in size, grand and majestic, protecting the profiled cameo of the feminine likeness resting inside of a filigreed heart. If he thought about it hard enough, he could almost hear the great trumpeting sounds blasting from proud, upturned trunks.

"You like that one do you?"

Alan pulled his gaze from the tapestry and focused on a smiling Jeovonni.

"I saw you marveling at the design on the insignias worn by the royal caravan."

"Yes, Jeo…I mean…Your High…ahh, sir?" Alan shook his head a little, trying to find the right words in his head. So much happened in the last twenty-four hours, this man had gone from his employer, to a king in what seemed like the blink of an eye. *How do you address royalty?*

"You may call me Jeovonni; I'm rather taken with the name. Or you may use my birth name, Matteo. Whichever you prefer, no need to stand on ceremony, son."

"I've never met a king before," Alan stated.

"A king is no more than a man who's been chosen to serve his people, Alan. The pageantry that goes along with the title, well, that's just for fun. Don't worry about it. I'm still the same man you've always known."

Jeovonni pointed to the wall tapestry Alan was taken with, his face smoothing into a bright smile as he examined it.

"All coats of arms are created at the birth of the royal family members, or when someone marries into the royal family. This was created for my daughter."

Alan glanced at the tapestry and then returned his gaze to Jeovonni's face. He appeared content, filled with pride for a daughter he obviously treasured.

"Two things happen when a reigning monarch is born," Jeovonni began. "The first is a Tribù elder must bless the baby, the second is that same elder must reveal the life prophecy of the child. When I was born, the Tribù elder blessed me, then he told my father I would be the king who would be brave enough to keep Azuria safe during its darkest moment of tyranny. He said I would rule until Azuria was free, and usher in the age of wisdom.

"When my daughter was born the Tribù elder you met earlier gave her the customary blessing, then he turned to me and said, 'She bears the mantle of the great elephant. Her wisdom will outshine that of her ancestors and she will save us from the tyrant.'"

Jeovonni moved closer to the tapestry and caressed a section of it with careful fingers. It was obvious the intricately woven material was of great significance.

"I gave her elephants as her heraldic beast because they are a symbol of majesty, power, and wisdom. All the things I believe my daughter embodies. She will be a great queen, Alan, and if the prophecy is true, a lot sooner than she believed. As the absolute ruler of a nation, one has to be willing to sacrifice their needs, for the needs of the people."

Alan didn't doubt that. The fact that this family was so loved by the people of this nation was proof that they sacrificed for their people.

"Will she still be Queen now that Reign is dead, and John has been named prince? He's older; wouldn't he be the new heir?"

Jeovonni shook his head. "No, the Azurian monarchy is not chosen by order of birth. Yes, if John had been presented to the people as he should have, he might have been named the presumptive king. But his elevation to the title would have come only if I actually chose him as the new king. He also would have needed to accept my recommendation in order for his assumption to take place. I love my son, but being a king is not what he was born to do. John has always known his path, and dealing with a lifetime of politics is not what he wishes. My daughter will be the new queen."

Alan nodded, silently accepting Jeovonni's decree. It felt right. This place, this country, it was A.J.'s destiny. "It's obvious she loves Azuria, sir," Alan responded.

"She does, but she didn't nearly sacrifice herself solely for Azuria. She was ready to sacrifice her life to be the person that was worthy of your love, the person you needed her to be."

Alan felt a shift in the atmosphere. They weren't speaking of symbols and pageantry any longer. Jeovonni Tenetti faced Alan, his shoulders squared, his green eyes sharp and focused. "When I became king, my wife and I were married for several years before I took the throne. I knew that no matter what occurred, my lioness would fiercely walk by my side. A.J. doesn't have that. I thought she might until you walked out on her."

"Sir—" Alan attempted to interrupt.

"You walked away, Alan," he continued. "Or is my understanding of the events flawed? She was willing to sacrifice her life for you, be what you needed her to be. My question to you is what will you become to love her, what will you do?"

Alan swallowed the lump forming in his throat. A mixture of shame, and anger twisted inside of his stomach. Jeovonni was correct. Alan walked away. Grounded in his righteous indignation of being lied to, he refused to see through the veil and believe in the woman he loved.

A.J. was strong, she was opinionated, arrogant too, but when he thought about it, she was always at her best when she was fighting for someone else. Thinking back, she was at her most ferocious when she was protecting someone she cared for. How he could have missed it he wasn't certain, but the truth was he'd been so filled with the fear of feeling the pain of loss, he'd refused to see the trouble A.J. lived in.

"Jeovonni, this feels like you're asking me what my intentions are toward your daughter. If that's the case, let me attempt to put your mind at ease. I love her," he said proudly with his chin raised. "I didn't do the best job of displaying that love, but there is no question in my heart that I love her."

Jeovonni's emerald eyes softened. He nodded his head and stepped closer to the tapestry, absently stroking one of the hind legs of one of the elephants. "The secrets that my choices forced my daughter to keep painted a very difficult picture for you, Alan. I know that. I can only imagine how conflicting it was for you, falling in love with someone you didn't feel you could trust. I understand that, I do, but as her father, knowing what she's been through, knowing the changes that are about to take place in her life, I need to be certain of you."

Alan glanced up at the tapestry again. "I was foolish," he said as he returned his gaze to Jeovonni. "I let my past color my perception, and ultimately, I walked away from the person I most wanted because of my fear. After the Navy transported you to Azuria, I was ill with worry. I was so terrified she'd die before I had the chance to tell her how sorry I was for not trusting her. I thought I was afraid of being hurt by lies, but I found out the only thing that truly scared me was never being able to see her again. To answer your previous questions, what will I become, what will I do to be with her? The answer is simple, everything."

Jeovonni watched him warily, squinted eyes taking him in. He stepped closer to Alan, extended his hand and said, "Good, then you and I have some things to discuss."

A.J. walked into the East garden to find her brother and his wife sitting underneath the shaded patio. They were huddled together, Max touching and holding him, as if she was attempting to make sure he was still here, safe and still alive. A.J. stood still when she encountered them, the moment so precious and tender A.J. felt it was an intrusion for her to interrupt.

John's eyes caught sight of her first and waved her over to them. She kissed Max and hugged her. "Maxine, when did you get here? Are the girls with you?"

"This morning," she answered. "The authorities put me in touch with someone from the FBI. They sent someone from the Navy to escort us to Naval Air Station Sigonella where we were transported from there to here. The girls were exhausted by the time we landed. They're upstairs sleeping now."

A.J. hugged Maxine again, relieved her brother's wife and kids were safe.

"I'm going to check on them now." She smiled slightly as she waved a pointed finger between A.J. and John. "It'll give brother and sister some time alone to talk."

When Maxine left, A.J. turned around and fell into her brother's arms. She surrounded him as best she could, holding on as tightly as her arms would allow. She crushed herself to him, letting the fear that nearly killed her the night before bleed slowly out through her tears.

"I was so afraid. When I saw him, saw that he had you…"

"I'm fine, *sorellina*," he whispered as he kissed the top of her head.

She ran her fingers gently up and down his arms, hands, even his face, unconsciously marking the same places his wife's hands touched in much the same way only moments before.

"How did he get you?" she asked.

John scratched absently at a patch of the stubble on his chin. "Much like he said," he answered. "We were coming out of the airport. When we travel like that, with the entire crew around us, Max and the kids usually ride with me and the rest of the band and dancers ride in groups. We were walking out of the airport when one of the girls said she needed to use the restroom. Max took them both back inside to the restroom. The car pulled up, and as soon as I got inside, it pulled off. It was only dumb luck that Max and the girls didn't end up in that car with me."

Reign was dead, he and his men defeated, but A.J. could see just how painful the thought of Reign getting his hands on their kids was to her brother. He twisted his neck and shoulders attempting to free himself of the emotional vice that was visibly gripping him.

"Max didn't even realize what happened, thought I went ahead to the hotel and jumped on one of the tour buses with the band. It wasn't until hours later that all the pieces began to fit together. She called the authorities, but by the time they figured everything out, I was already here in Azuria."

She touched both hands to his face and held him in her gaze. "If I'd known he discovered you, I never would have put that plan into motion. I was trying to spare all of you, that's why I came here alone."

He shook his head and placed a finger across her lips. "It doesn't matter how it all played out, what matters is we're safe, and he's dead. We lived, so we win."

She gave him a shaky smile and hugged herself to him again. He was right, they did survive, her family was intact. There was no more important a victory than that.

"How long are the two of you staying?" she asked.

"Considering the fact that I was kidnapped by a maniac, the tour promoters are giving me eight weeks to get my shit together. I intend to spend that time in Azuria getting to know our people, spending time with our family."

John's eyes veered beyond the garden, on toward the beach. She followed his line of sight until she found Alan walking along the beach with their father.

"How is that working out for you?" John asked.

"Not really certain. We're at least speaking, but he hasn't really said anything. Even if he wants to try, it may be impossible."

"Why's that?"

She inhaled slowly, and released the large breath on a heavy sigh. "Because my place is here, John," she answered. "Azuria has lived too long without its monarchs in residence. They need us, I have to stay. I've always known I would have to leave America someday, Alan didn't really sign on for all of that."

John wrapped an arm around her shoulders, drawing her into his warmth. "A man will do just about anything to be with the woman he loves," he said. "If Alan loves you, he will find a way to make this work."

A tiny speck of hope lit in her heart as Alan stopped on the beach and waved at her, beckoning her to him. Perhaps her brother was correct; maybe they could work this out.

A.J. moved down to the beach where Alan stood by the shoreline. Her father stopped and held her to him, displaying yet again how relieved her entire family was that things hadn't worked out differently. He took one final look at her and kissed her gently on the cheek before heading back to the garden.

When she reached Alan, he held out a hand to her and they began a slow walk along the shore, fingers laced together, feet and ankles covered by the warm sea water.

"I'm sorry," she whispered.

"For what?"

"For keeping all of this from you," she answered.

They walked a little further before he spoke again. "You have nothing to be sorry for, you did what you needed to in order to protect your people."

They'd found themselves on a secluded section of the beach surrounded by the protective shield of mountainous cliffs that blocked the view of the palace from where they stood.

"Heart and Kenneth plan to leave first thing tomorrow morning. I suppose that means you'll be leaving with them?" she said, the words hesitantly slipping from her lips.

"That's the plan, A.J.," he sighed. "Or should I call you Ilaria?"

She smiled at the sound of her name on his lips. "Ilaria is more like an official title than my name at this point. I haven't been her in so long, at least not publicly anyway, I don't really know that I am her."

He nodded his head and pulled her into his arms. "You are her," he answered. "A.J. has always been too nondescript to accurately depict who you are. Ilaria sounds regal, larger than life, all the things I love about you."

A bittersweet smile crept on her lips as she looked up at him. "You love me, but not enough to stay?" She took in the sight of him, marking each line and angle of his face to memory. She closed her eyes, trying to imprint his image on her mind, hoping it would be enough to sustain her when he was gone. She stepped out of his embrace and continued along the sandy path.

"Is that an invitation?" he asked.

"Do you need one?" she replied fighting the well of emotion that threatened to spill over.

"Not really." He touched her hand, stopping her forward motion. "But I think you do."

She turned to him and found him on one knee. She wasn't exactly certain what he was doing there until he removed a small jewelry box from his pocket and opened it. A sparkling marquis-shaped diamond sat atop a slim gold band. It was simple, classic, breathtaking, and he was presenting it to her.

"I don't need an invitation to choose to stay, A.J.; I need to give you a reason to allow me to stay here. I want to share your life and your country with you. You're brave, and wise, and the loyalty you carry in your heart for the ones you love, the people you love, I just want to be here at your side to experience it all. Ilaria Noemi Casa di Barca, crown princess of Azuria, will you allow me to stand by your side as your husband? I'm not worthy, and the way I behaved, I certainly don't deserve it. But if you'll place your trust in me, I promise to never let you down again."

Her chest tightened. This was the most perfect moment in her life. The man she loved was asking to join his life with hers and the only thought she could wrap her mind around was, *I'm not worthy.*

"You have no idea how much I want this, Alan. But I've done too much, caused too much harm to those I love. I shouldn't be rewarded for that."

"You were in an impossible position," he responded. "I'm not happy about the lies, I'm not happy about you keeping me out of the loop. I hated it. But when I knew you were on your way to confront Reign, the only thing I could think of was none of that bullshit mattered. None of the things that were so important to me before mattered. The only thing that mattered was making sure you were safe, and getting you back in my arms. So please, can we both stop worrying about past wrongs, and whether either of us deserves each other? I don't care about anything other than this moment and the ones we create together afterward. Will you marry me?"

She was a wordsmith, someone who'd spent most of her adult years learning the art of rhetoric to convey her ideas. But standing here, during one of the most important moments of her life, the only thing her brain could muster up was a single word.

"Yes."

EPILOGUE

One year later...

"*How's it feel, man?*"

Alan looked over to his friend and best man, Kenneth who stood next to him with a wide grin. "Today has been one spectacular event after another. You're going to have to be a little more specific."

"Stop, you know exactly what I'm talking about," Kenneth responded.

Alan shrugged his shoulders and played along. "You mean the fact that I married the woman of my dreams earlier today?"

Kenneth shook his head.

"Oh, are you talking about the fact that her father made me a prince today after the wedding and made me CEO of the new Tenetti Enterprises headquarters here in Azuria?"

Kenneth still shook his head. "Can you stop bullshitting? This is so fucking huge; I can't believe you're not freaking out about this."

"Oh," Alan feigned prolonged thought as he looked up at nothing just long enough to piss Kenneth off a bit. "I suppose you mean the fact that my wife is going to be crowned Queen today."

"Stop saying that shit like it's an everyday occurrence," Kenneth answered. "Your wife is going to be the sovereign leader of a country."

Alan nodded his head as he thought about that. It was true, in a matter of moments his wife of all of about two hours would be crowned Queen of Azuria. When this journey began they'd barely been able to remain civil with one another in public. Now? Now he couldn't imagine living his life without her.

This last year was one of rebuilding. Alan flew back to the States the day after he'd proposed to A.J. and essentially packed his life up in New York and headed right back to Azuria. Wherever A.J. was, that's where he needed to be.

He'd spent his time in his new country helping his now father-in-law build the new headquarters for Tenetti Enterprises while his wife dedicated herself to reestablishing the monarchy's presence in front of the people.

They'd worked tirelessly to build their new life together here during the day, and spent their nights bound to each other. It was as if one appetite fueled the other. The harder they worked in their respective roles, the more intense their love making was.

"I know you are not standing in front of me thinking about smashing your wife, dude."

Kenneth's voice pulled him out of the memory of A.J. riding his cock until it was raw in the infinity pool the previous night. "We both know I spent five years in your office watching the goofy faces you made every time you were daydreaming about your wife. Cut me some slack."

They each bowled over in laughter. Kenneth's love for his wife was still evident. Alan could only hope that he and A.J.'s connection would remain as powerful.

"Prince Elliot."

Alan felt Kenneth's hand land on his shoulder trying to garner his attention. It was going to take some time to get used to this new official title. *"Signore Cortigiano?"*

Alan watched the palace's senior aid rush into the room. "Prince Elliot," the man took a moment to bow in front of Alan.

This shit is so trippy. Alan chuckled to himself.

"Your Highness, it is time for the royal procession in the Festival, you must take your place next to the King emeritus and the Queen mother," the man answered.

"Where's my wife?" Alan replied.

"It is customary for the incoming monarch to ride into the palace grounds to greet the people of Azuria. Once she has done so she will join you and the rest of the royal family on the balcony. Please, Your Highness, we must hurry."

Alan heard Kenneth snickering in the corner. "Yes, Your Highness," Kenneth mocked. "Your chariot waits."

Alan flipped his middle finger at Kenneth, causing a louder howl of laughter to escape his friend's mouth. They walked out onto the balcony facing the North gates of the palace. The balcony held two rows of four seats. A.J.'s parents sat in two of the seats in the first row and Heart sat alone in the second row.

Kenneth extended his hand to Alan before he took his place on the first row. "Congratulations, man. I don't think in all the years I've known you, I've ever seen you this happy, this at peace." He pulled Alan into a hug and slapped him affectionately on the back.

Alan felt the truth of their friendship wrapping around him. In his darkest hours Kenneth was there for him, and now that his life had taken a complete revolution, he was still here, supporting him, letting him know his friendship would always be a constant.

They took their seats, Alan looking out over the kingdom, his heart dancing along with the crowds of Azurians lining the streets.

The loud pounding of a drum filled the air. Tribal chanting tickled his ears. He looked closer to see John and Maxine mixed in with the Tribù. They were all dressed in white tribal loincloths accented with gold trim around the edges of their waists necks, biceps, wrists and calves. Their faces were painted in the same intricate pattern he'd witnessed before, their heads covered with grand headdresses adorned with white large feathers and flecks of gold.

The Tribù began to move and jump in sync with the quick boom-boom-tap rhythm of the drum. Soon the air was filled with musical rhythms that reminded him of what he'd erroneously called Calypso music in front of Heart once. He laughed at the memory when she'd told him, "Call it Calypso in Flatbush or on the Parkway during the parade and folks will instantly know how white you really are. It's called Soca."

Heart must have been remembering the same exchange because when he caught a glimpse of her outside the corner of her eye she was winking at him. He returned his eyes to the spectacle in front of him. Max and John were being blessed by the people, there was just no other way to describe it. As they marched toward the palace, the cheering people threw feathers and flowers at their feet while they danced to the music and chanted, *"Benvenuti nostro principe."* If his high school Italian were to be trusted, he believed that translated to, "Welcome our prince."

Once John and Maxine were seated next to Kenneth and Heart, loud rumblings in the crowd pulled Alan's attention to the spectacle before him. He looked at his in-laws for confirmation of the sight before him. A.J., his wife, the woman who would be crowned queen of this nation in merely a matter of moments, was riding on the back of an elephant.

A shard of panic pierced his heart and caused him to grip the banister of the balcony. But as he watched her, the confidence she always wore that told everyone in a room that she was the one in charge, shone through.

She was dressed in similar attire as the Tribù, her ancestral garb made more ornate by the addition of strands of jewels and gold strewn across her loincloth. From the wrong set of eyes this display would have been mistaken for a circus, something to be dismissed and belittled. But knowing how she loved her people, and knowing how this country adored her in return, he knew that the only reason she sat atop that great beast was because her people expected her to.

There was so much tradition involved in this exhibition, so much beauty to be embraced. His heart swelled with pride. This noble specimen of a woman was his now and forever.

The elephant bowed its large head at the foot of the palace steps. A.J. gave it a loving pat and climbed down. She stood on the steps of the palace and soaked in the love her people bestowed on her. When she'd waved from one side of the mall to the next, she held out her arms shoulders-wide and waited as her attendants draped a red cloak on her shoulders. She took the steps that led her up to the balcony where the rest of the royal family awaited her. She met Alan with a smile, and kiss, then turned to her parents.

Her father stood at the microphone and greeted the crowd. Once he was done, he called for the senior aid, and he arrived bearing a velvet-covered pillow with a crown resting on top of it.

"Azuria, it is my greatest honor to present to you our Queen, Ilaria Noemi born of the house of Barca. *Ea potestatem verbo et factis*," he announced, and waited for A.J. to bow her head slightly before him. "May she rule by word and deed." Her father affixed the crown to her head, and positioned her to face her nation.

They all joined in with the former king, chanting the litany over and over again, celebrating the woman who saved their nation by attempting to sacrifice herself.

She turned slightly, just enough to let him glimpse at those liquid amber eyes of hers. A teary smile danced across her lips and she beckoned him to join her at the podium. "This is your moment," he said. "You don't need me here."

She laced her fingers with his and pulled him closer, keeping him at her side. Her eyes fixed on him, filled with love, free of the shadows of secrets and lies that once wore on her so heavily. "I will always need you by my side, dear prince."

He nodded his agreement, "As you wish, my queen. Your pleasure is my privilege."

"It certainly will be," she whispered just loud enough for him to hear.

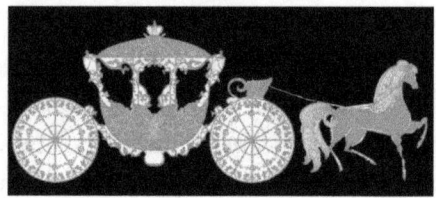

A.J. closed the door behind her and rested against the strong frame until her mind stopped swimming with the events of the day. She'd married Alan and become Queen to her people all in one day.

She stood before God and country and vowed to love him, and protect her people and their land. All weighty, but worthy commitments she'd go to the grave to honor. She dropped her clothes in a trail that led to the large en suite bathroom and quickly washed away the remnants of the multiple celebrations she'd attended today.

When she emerged, she found her husband waiting for her in the large four-poster bed. The golden skin of his chest bare, the rest of his body covered in layer of silk bedding covering what she knew to be an impressive cock.

She crawled up on the bed and straddled his hips and looked down into crisp blue eyes that sparkled in the moonlight. She could willingly drown in the sea-blue of those eyes that held so much love for her.

No words passed between them, no words were needed. He reached up, pulling her lips down to meet his and like always, fire erupted between them. He sat up, moving those fiery lips along the delicate line of her jaw, down the subtle curve of her neck, across her collar bones. Her breath caught in her chest as he buried his face in her cleavage line, tasting and biting the flesh there.

He flipped her over onto her back and spread her wide. He pressed one leg back and ran rough fingers over her cunt, split her, rubbing her until her nether lips were swollen with need, and her clit was matching the achy throb of her erratic heartbeat.

The burn of his flesh against hers made her shut her eyes. Lost in the pleasure he was offering her, the rough pads of his finger scraped just the right way against the blood-filled bud and she was coming apart under his touch.

She was still quivering when he entered her, stretching her, demanding her walls conform to the shape of his cock. From the first stroke, he rode her hard, his heavy balls making slick, slapping noises every time they smacked against the crack of her ass.

She could feel her body preparing for another shattering climax; he pressed the palm of his hand just at the hilt of her mound and applied the most delicious pressure. That coupled with the change in his angle, his cock massaging that sensitive spot inside of her with just the precise amount of pressure mixed with speed and she was screaming his name, her climax pouring out of her, soaking him in a deluge of her juices.

She just wanted to lay there limp in the cool puddle she'd just created. She could give a fuck about how nasty and uncomfortable that was. Her husband just fucked her stupid and she really wasn't all that concerned with moving at this moment for any reason.

"I know you don't think that's it?" His words were phrased like a question, but there was no mistaking the fact that he was expressing a declarative statement.

She cracked open an eye to watch him on his haunches, passing long slow strokes up and down the impressive length of his cock.

Fuck, just looking at it made the walls of her pussy clap involuntarily. She didn't even understand why she questioned how her body reacted to him. Her pussy was conditioned to be hungry and salivating every time she saw that stretched red cap pulled tight with arousal, just waiting for her to consume.

He flipped her over on her abdomen, pulled her ass up in the air, and planted himself within her walls with no finesse. It was hard, it was fast, and her cunt was so sloppy wet he was able to piston in and out of her so smoothly. He pressed down into her, pressed her down until she was pinned to the bed, splayed beneath him, grunting indecipherable sounds through gritted teeth.

"Fuck," crawled out his mouth cracking the air like thunder.

He slammed into her one last time. The first hot jet of his cum coating her walls triggered the beginning of her own climax. She shoved her hand beneath her, rubbing her clit and labia in a fast and circular motion until she felt herself fall over the cliff that Alan pushed her over.

He collapsed on top of her, his cock still pulsing, her cunt still spasming, their breathing still ragged. He leaned over, taking her mouth, mingling his tongue with hers until their passion ebbed and blood flow returned to the rational parts of their brains.

"Dammit, man," she huffed out. "It won't look good if the new queen can't address her people because her new husband fucked her into the mattress."

"There's an easy solution to that." He smiled as he placed gentle kisses on her shoulders, calming her. "You either remain in bed until you're all rested up, or I'll carry you wherever you need to go. Whichever you choose, I plan to be there right by your side."

She turned over, shaky hands tracing his lips. She looked up into those eyes again, the eyes that always held such sincerity and openness, and smiled. His promise wasn't in his words, but in his eyes, in the way he looked at her, in his touch, and the way he always made her feel delicate and precious.

"*Nos ergo diligamus verbo et factis*," she whispered.

He kissed her again and asked, "What's that mean?"

"It's Latin for, 'We love by word and deed.'"

He let his tongue slide inside of her mouth again and released a satisfied moan when her tongue met his. They lay that way for a while, kissing and nipping at each other's mouths, savoring the taste and feel of each other's bodies. He rolled onto his back and pulled her into his arms; head cradled against his chest and answered, "We certainly do, Queen Ilaria, we certainly do."

THE END

ABOUT THE AUTHOR

LaQuette is an erotic, multicultural romance author of M/F and M/M love stories. Her writing style brings intellect to the drama. She often crafts emotionally epic, fantastical tales that are deeply pigmented by reality's paintbrush. Her novels are filled with a unique mixture of savvy, sarcastic, brazen, and unapologetically sexy characters who are confident in their right to appear on the page.

This bestselling Erotic Romance Author is the 2016 Author of the Year Golden Apple Award Winner, 2016 Write Touch Award Winner for Best Contemporary Mid-length Novel, 2016 Swirl Awards 1st Place Winner in Romantic Suspense, and 2016 Aspen Gold Award Finalist in Erotic Romance. LaQuette—a native of Brooklyn, New York—spends her time catering to her three distinct personalities: Wife, Mother, and Educator.

Writing—her escape from everyday madness—has always been a friend and source of comfort. At the age of sixteen she read her first romance novel and realized the genre was missing something: people that looked and lived like her. As a result, her characters and settings are always designed to provide positive representations of people of color and various marginalized communities.

She loves hearing from readers and discussing the crazy characters that are running around in her head causing so much trouble. Contact her on:

Website: LaQuette.com
Email: LaQuette@LaQuette.com
Amazon: www.amazon.com/author/laquette
Facebook: www.facebook.com/LaQuetteTheAuthor
Twitter: twitter.com/LaQuetteWrites
Instagram: instagram.com/la_quette

OTHER TITLES

Wicked Wager: Texas vs. Brooklyn 1
Bedding The Enemy
Lies You Tell
Heart of the Matter: Queens of Kings: Book 1
Divided Heart: Queens of Kings: Book 2
Protected Heart: Queens of Kings Book 3
Power Privilege & Pleasure: Queens of Kings: Book 4
His True Strength: Queens of Kings: Book 5
My Beginning: Trinity Series: Book 1
Love's Changes

NEWSLETTER

Hello,

If you're interested in staying current with all the happenings with my writing, previews, and giveaways, sign up for my monthly newsletter at www.LaQuette.com.

Keep it sexy,
LaQuette

COMING SOON...

LOADED LONGSHOT

Texas vs. Brooklyn 2

Kandi Adkins, the executive manager of Sweet Sadie's Cosmetics, has her roots planted firmly in Brownsville, Brooklyn. Kandi knows what it's like to have nothing. Education and her friend's late mother, Sadie King, pulled her out of the mire of poverty and enabled her to grab hold to personal and professional security.

Life has taught Aaron Nakai to play his cards close to the vest. Reaching for more than you need only invites trouble into your life. That's what happened to his father, a man who died young attempting to make his mark on the world. He finds comfort and security living in his adoptive brother, Slade's, shadow. Aaron refuses to allow lofty dreams to rob him of the gains he made in life. Being Slade's lawyer and right-hand man suits him just fine.

When Slade needs Aaron to step out of the background and take care of an unexpected problem in New York, Aaron's quiet existence back in Texas is blown to bits by a quick-witted, sassy-mouthed fireball named Kandi. Their attraction is just as palpable as their distaste for one another, making the decision to wager their hearts and their careers a high-stakes game with potentially disastrous outcomes.

Will they fold? Or will they reach for a loaded longshot to win it all?

COMING SOON.

SEDUCTIVE STAKES

Texas vs. Brooklyn 3

Azure Carlisle is simply tired. She's tired of always struggling to do the right thing only to have life slap her down time and time again. She climbed her way out of the projects of Brooklyn by getting an education. Her Ph.D. in Chemistry was her ticket out of the 'hood, but the lingering student loans from both her undergraduate and graduate degrees crush any dreams of personal advancement.

When the financial juggling game she plays every month begins to topple, Azure stumbles upon a way out. With an offer to clear her debts in hand, Azure is nearly burden free. The only thing she must do to escape financial ruin is simple: betray the trust of the woman who offered her a job, and friendship.

Damien Mesías is the former CEO of Logan Industries. He's spent his life paying for the sin of his father's illegitimacy. When your dad is the result of a salacious affair between the respectably married tycoon and his maid, you're not as welcome to the family gatherings as your legitimate cousins.

Determined to prove his worth, and exact his revenge against the remaining Logan heir, his cousin, Slade Hamilton, Damien embarked on a dangerous path that nearly ruined him and the family business. Destroyed, divorced, and wallowing in a pit of despair, Damien aches for peace and forgiveness. But, with so much to atone for, those two things are elusive goals Damien isn't quite sure he can attain.

When an opportunity to get into Slade's good graces appears, Damien rushes to Brooklyn and finds his job is more complicated than he believed. One, the thief is a friend of the family, and two, she's the sexiest thing Damien has seen in a long time. Torn between his desire to do the right thing, and his need to have Azure, Damien is forced to make a decision that could destroy them all.

Will Damien ruin friendships, and Azure's life, by exposing her? Will Azure sell-out the people who have supported her to gain financial freedom? Or, will Damien's wild card play present seductive stakes that neither of them can walk away from?

CPSIA information can be obtained
at www.ICGtesting.com
Printed in the USA
LVHW031950030521
686351LV00004B/83